The Crossing Keeper's Daughter

by

C. Christopher

Published by

MELROSE
BOOKS

An Imprint of Melrose Press Limited
St Thomas Place, Ely
Cambridgeshire
CB7 4GG, UK
www.melrosebooks.co.uk

FIRST EDITION

ISBN 978-1-909757-49-3

Printed and bound in Great Britain by:
4edge Limited
7a Eldon Way, Eldon Way Industrial Estate
Hockley, Essex
SS5 4AD

FSC
www.fsc.org
MIX
Paper from
responsible sources
FSC® C020822

Chapter One

"Heaven's morning breaks and
Earth's vain shadows flee.
In life in death, Oh Lord,
Abide with me."

The last words of Lyte's funeral hymn faded from the lips of the congregation. Their very breath hung as a mist in the pews about them. Without, on that cold December afternoon, the light was already waning as sleet carried on an east wind blew against the stained glass windows. Within, the Reverend closed the service with the benediction, and with the slightest of nods beckoned the pall-bearers who, stepping forward, hoisted the coffin aloft and carried it slowly outside to its assigned resting place.

Standing over the unclosed grave, with his cassock billowing about him, the Reverend said the final words of comfort and prayer before tossing in the first sods of earth. Several mourners did the same until, eventually, the group dispersed leaving the deceased alone. For a few moments the inscription on the brass nameplate was still visible—Roberta Gherardini, born 4 Oct.1948, died 19 Dec.1968—before fading in the advancing gloom and disappearing forever under the exertions of Mr Smith the groundsman.

This tale really begins on New Year's Eve in 1947. On that

cold, dark Wednesday night many locomotive men running their trains through the last minutes of that year gave rousing fanfares on the engine whistles. It was not exactly wishing anyone Happy New Year, but more a sad farewell to the old four railway companies, that 'very poor bag of assets', the Southern, London & North Eastern, London Midland & Scottish and Great Western systems that on the following day would amalgamate, like a giant Hornby Dublo train set, to form Prime Minister Clement Attlee's new nationalised British Railways.

It was Attlee's Chancellor of the Exchequer that had described the railways so scathingly. "The permanent way is badly worn and the rolling stock in a state of great dilapidation", he had further added. But this was hardly surprising following virtual neglect during the long difficult years of the Second World War. How easily were the railways' vital contribution forgotten, and how denigrating it was to the railwaymen and women who had kept services running in the arduous conditions of black-out and air raid. Without the selfless efforts of these individuals victory may well have eluded us.

Also not appreciated were the efforts of prisoners of war, Italians in particular, who further contributed to our country's ultimate success. Involved in the construction of goods yards, additional loops and extended sidings, necessary for the war effort, were many gangs of these unfortunate men. Captured or shot down and lucky to survive, many of these men, disillusioned with both Mussolini and Hitler, were only too willing to escape the horrors of the conflict.

One such prisoner of war was Benito Gherardini, a carpenter from Brindisi on the Adriatic coast of Italy. A young patriotic soldier in the Italian Army, he saw active service in North Africa before British and Commonwealth troops captured

2

Tobruk in January 1941. Gherardini was one of thousands of Italians captured in the desert campaigns. For British soldiers following in the wake of the advance, long columns of Italians making their way back were a common sight. Gherardini found himself shipped to England with several hundred compatriots with building and construction skills, and sent to Oxford where just south of the city a new marshalling yard was being laid. Gherardini was responsible for the woodwork: steps, windows, roofs, floorboards for the two signal boxes and shunter's cabins being built to control this new yard in the meadows at Hinksey. He took pride in his work, but this could not be said for some of his fellow countrymen. Their brickwork in the North signal box at Hinksey bore the mistakes in bonding as a lasting legacy to unsupervised POWs. Hinksey North and South boxes were opened in the spring of 1942, and the yard became operational that summer. Following the completion of this work, Gherardini moved to Amersham in Buckinghamshire where the manufacture of luminous paint for aircraft and submarine dials required new laboratory buildings.

As the war progressed, and particularly after the D-Day landings of 1944, it slowly became clear that it was not a case of if Hitler would be overthrown, but when. As the need for construction diminished Gherardini was employed as a cowman, on a farm in Loudwater, and beneath this hilltop spread, through a tunnel, ran the London–Birmingham main line. Despite missing his native Italy those were happy days for him. His carpentry skills on the dilapidated farm buildings were very useful. Good timber was in short supply and his ability to fashion artefacts from whatever material was available was much appreciated. Such was his commitment that replacement barn door posts, for example, were made from an old railway sleeper sawn laboriously lengthways.

His expertise not only impressed the old farmer, but he took the fancy of the lonely Land Army girl who answered to the name of Babs. While her husband in the Royal Artillery resisted the Japs in the Burmese jungle, she offered no resistance at all in the meadows of Buckinghamshire. Within a month of meeting Gherardini she was carrying his child.

How the relationship would have progressed was never put to the test as tragedy struck in the August of 1944.

Early on a Saturday morning, the 12th, a stricken American Flying Fortress, having taken off from Bovingdon minutes before en route to a raid over Caen, turned across the Wooburn valley with one engine on fire in a heroic bid to return to base with its lethal load of bombs. Losing height as the flames increased, those on the farm watched in horror as the blazing plane skimmed over the rooftops before crashing into fields beyond. The aircraft, its load of bombs and ammunition exploded instantly. None of the crew survived. There was one fatality on the farm. The Land Army girl was caught in the blast, bringing a reluctant cow in for milking.

* * *

When hostilities eventually ended, Gherardini had little desire to return to Italy. His parents were both dead, and with no close family he chose to stay in Britain. Following the VJ celebrations of August 1945, he would leave the farm a free man determined to be successful. It was while he was exploring the footpaths that criss-crossed the farmland that he discovered the Paddington to Birmingham main line. He became fascinated by the sweep of double track that, from where he stood, stretched away northwards into a cutting and behind him disappeared into a tunnel. Gherardini visited the spot many times, the sound of the trains reminding him of the music of Verdi and Rossini. On several occasions he met a man, recently retired from the railway, who had become a professional photographer. Gherardini was soon as excited as he when a certain type of train, or a particular class of locomotive was expected, and related to his friend how he had helped in the construction of Hinksey Yards, and this brought about much discussion on trains, culminating in it being suggested that Gherardini apply for the vacancy of porter at Loudwater Station.

This caused Gherardini some amusement at first; after all, he had the more pressing problem of where he would live when he left the farm. But in the end, he reasoned, he would have greater chance of finding accommodation if he were already employed. So it was that Gherardini applied to become a porter on the Great Western Railway.

He suffered two interviews, the first at Paddington, which included a medical check-up, and the second which the station-master himself held in his office at Loudwater. Gherardini was successful on each occasion, and in the closing moments of the second meeting, after shaking the stationmaster's august hand, he tentatively enquired as to the availability of lodgings in the vicinity. August eyes narrowed at the request, but then reflected on the potential benefits of railway staff living near their place of work.

The stationmaster rummaged through drawers, and at length produced a slip of paper which he passed to Gherardini. "An elderly couple at that address might be willing to take you in," he said. "One of our signalmen lived with them once. They're Poles, but you should get on alright. Number four, Inglis Terrace, London Road."

"Should that be English Terrace?" Gherardini queried.

"No, no. Inglis. Named after the engineer who built the new

line. I'll call the people on the telephone and tell them to expect you."

The last job Gherardini did on the farm was to grub out the remains of a hedgerow devastated in the plane crash. It was on the completion of this that he unearthed an old leather purse. Subservient to the end, he handed the purse to the farmer, who shook its contents into the palm of his hand. Just two coins there were, a farthing and a penny. In disgust he gave them back to Gherardini. The only interesting thing about them it seemed was that they were of the same year, 1933.

Chapter Two

Loudwater was a typically rural GWR country station on the single track branch line from Maidenhead to High Wycombe. Opened in the summer of 1854, it was on the original Wycombe Railway that left the Great Western Paddington–Bristol main line at a junction at Maidenhead. The Wycombe Railway was extended to Oxford a decade later, making a connection with the GWR again as that system spread to Birmingham. The Wycombe Railway was originally laid to Brunel's 7ft 0¼in Broad Gauge but was soon a casualty of the Gauge War, and converted to 4ft 8½in as early as 1870.

Although Loudwater Station boasted a small goods yard it originally had only the one platform on its single line. A passing loop was laid in 1904, yet it was not provided with a platform until 1942.

Gherardini's first day as a railwayman was on Monday 8th October 1945. Not having voted for Mussolini since the invasion of Abyssinia in 1935, Gherardini was ashamed to share the same christian name as the Fascist leader, so on meeting his new colleagues on that chilly autumn morning all he said was, "Call me Ben."

While there were no services from Loudwater during the night, trains ran from early in the morning until late evening, and so on each shift (6 a.m.–2 p.m. and 2 p.m.–10 p.m.) were a signalman, booking office clerk and porter. The stationmaster graced the platforms with his august presence only between the hours of 8 a.m. and 6 p.m., during which time he also covered Wooburn Green, the next station along.

It came as no surprise to Gherardini to find his colleagues reticent and unwilling to include him in their conversation, and the porter on the opposite shift was particularly unhelpful, often leaving many tasks for Gherardini to do which he himself should have completed. Nevertheless they were happy days, if marred by prejudice, and Gherardini took care not to let unkind words or actions upset him, while his outward cheerfulness and helpful demeanour allowed him to learn much about railway work beyond the narrow confines of his rank. The work of the signalmen, who were both perfect gentlemen, was particularly fascinating to him, and on many Saturdays when there was no chance of the stationmaster putting in an appearance, they would allow him to operate the points and signals.

His favourite task was closing the crossing gates to traffic on the road immediately next to the signal box. This was effected by turning, by hand, through many degrees, a large wheel not unlike a ship's helm. So enthralled could Gherardini become with his power over the public that the signalman frequently had to remind him to reopen the gates once the train had passed. Another equally fascinating part of railway work was the giving and receiving of the token, that aspect of railway operation unique to the working of single lines. As this involved signalman and driver cooperation, Gherardini could only watch the exchange in awe. The whole Maidenhead–High Wycombe branch line was worked by the electric token system, which allowed for only one token to be available between two signal boxes at any one time. Thus a driver in possession of the token could be assured that his was the only train on that section of line. Down goods trains arriving in the sidings at Loudwater still had to relinquish their token to clear the single line, and with the signal box being at the opposite end of the station it meant a considerable walk for the signalman (or guard). Gherardini took great delight in performing this errand. He admired the steel key-like object on which, in a flattened area inlaid with brass, was the legend Wooburn Green–Loudwater. He would carry it back to the signalman, still within its hoop, like one would carry a trophy.

Some goods guards were more than willing to show Gherardini the art of shunting. Loudwater employed no shunter, so guards were obliged to perform the shunt themselves. He became proficient at coupling-up, and developed a respect for his own safety, realising how dangerous shunting, even a single wagon, could be. Gherardini also discovered that he was happiest in the signal box or in the yard, both of which were away from the public.

An event in the summer of 1946 brought a new wave of ill feeling when the Italian King and his family were forced to abdicate in favour of a republic. During one week of that August two incidents made Gherardini realise that his position of porter had become intolerable. In the first, a man snatched the cap from his head and threw it into the brake van of a goods train departing for High Wycombe. By the time Gherardini had retrieved it, it was travelling too fast for him to alight. The guard came out in alarm to stop him winding on the brake.

"You'll break a coupling!" he exclaimed, as a dozen wagons or so ahead the engine barked away furiously. "You'll have to go through to Wycombe now." Adding under his breath, "Bloody foreigners."

Gherardini was resigned for the long walk back, but when the driver heard the tale, with surprising compassion, he insisted on returning to Loudwater 'light engine'. But on Gherardini's return, not only did the stationmaster rebuke him and dock one hour's pay, he reported the driver for having an unauthorised person on his footplate.

The second incident involved four youths off a Friday evening train.

"Please, your tickets," said Gherardini, as they alighted. They refused, and another request followed before the ringleader collected them from his friends. But to Gherardini's astonishment crammed them into his mouth, chewing slowly with great bravado. The three young onlookers laughed; they knew what was coming next. Poor Gherardini did not, and was caught unawares as the fourth youth moved closer to him and spat the papier-mâché bolus into his face.

As Gherardini decided he could no longer work as porter, he recalled a conversation he had had with a relief signalman, Ted Davies, when one of the regular men at Loudwater had been on holiday.

Relief signalmen were qualified, and expected, to work any signal box within their district at short notice. This particular reliefman was a Class 1 man and, with the exception of the elite Special Class signal boxes, he could work any box classified as 1 or below. Davies made it clear to Gherardini that he took exception to having to man Spicer's Crossing which lay between Wooburn Green and Loudwater. Indeed, reliefmen were covering both turns on the gates at that time as there was no resident crossing keeper. Gherardini remembered Davies's words: "That would be a nice little job for you, Ben."

Almost a year to the day that Gherardini joined the railway he bid farewell to the staff at Loudwater Station, and also to Mr and Mrs Lubek at 4 Inglis Terrace, and moved into the substantial cottage that was provided for him as incumbent gatekeeper at Spicer's Crossing. For Gherardini's first week he was allowed the luxury of office hours, working from 8 a.m. to

4 p.m. He was also pleasantly surprised on his first day to find that the man who would explain his duties to him was none other than Ted Davies, who laughed when Gherardini told him he would be 'learning' for two weeks. "Two minutes more like. A chimpanzee would pick it up in five. If they think I'm sticking in this cubby hole with you for a fortnight they can think again. After I've seen a few trains with you, I'll be off down the 'Rose and Crown'. When the first train comes, I'll explain things then. It'll be easier to understand. In the meantime I'll make some tea."

Although Gherardini knew his colleague was older than he, he was surprised to learn that Davies was past retirement age and had only continued working to cover staff shortages during the war.

Spicer's Crossing was no signal box so was without token facilities, its purpose merely to allow traffic using Juniper Lane a safe passage over the railway. Motorists wishing to cross had to ask permission. The cabin possessed four levers and a block bell which rang all the codes sent between the signalmen on either side at Loudwater and Wooburn Green. By listening to the bell one would know whenever a train was in the offing. Two levers operated distant signals which when lowered indicated to the driver that he could expect to find the gates in his favour; the signals were left at 'caution' if the gates were across the line. Each distant signal was beneath the starting signal from the neighbouring box in the 'double arm' configuration. There was no stop signal protection at the gates themselves. If the gates were across the line responsibility rested solely with the train driver to approach cautiously and be prepared to stop.

Like the neighbouring signal boxes, the crossing was manned early and late turns only and overnight the gates were left open to the lane. The cabin at Spicer's was typically Great

Western in appearance and, built entirely of wood, resembled a small oblong garden shed. One narrow end—the upper half of which was partly glazed—faced the line, while the lower timbers were almost completely covered by a large nameplate bearing the legend 'Spicer's Crossing Ground Frame'.

As they enjoyed their tea the bell in the cabin rang one beat. "That'll be the Marlow–Aylesbury," Davies said. "Listen to this, Ben."

One beat rang again; then three pause one; and this code too was repeated. "That first bell was the 'Call Attention' from Wooburn, answered by his mate at Loudwater, then 'Is Line Clear?' for a local passenger, a 'three–one', which Loudwater accepted by ringing the code back and allowing Wooburn to release a token. The indicator under the bell shows 'Down Token Out' now, and over the whole railway 'Up' is to London and 'Down' is from."

The relief signalman paused to light a cigarette and then continued. "Always pull off when you hear the train accepted. If you wait for the 'on line', or 'Train Entering Section', two beats on the bell, the train would have already passed your distant 'on'. The driver will come round the bend expecting the gates across him and won't be best pleased to have eased right down for nothing. The gates are already closed," he added, "and locked—lever three does that—so you just need to pull number one."

Gherardini stepped forward and with considerable effort, and more than one attempt, pulled off the down main distant.

"The Branch boys have it easy. All their distant signals are 'Fixed At Caution'; you, Ben, have over half a mile of signal wire to pull. And, you have to work your gates by hand." The bell rang two beats. "Just off Wooburn. Pull number four now to lock the side gates—they save people getting run down and making a mess everywhere. But be sure no one is halfway over and gets locked in on railway property."

The approaching train was heard whistling furiously for the crossing, and Davies stepped outside and raised a hand to the driver, who popped the whistle again as he swept past on a 61 Class Prairie Tank hauling four coaches. As he rejoined Gherardini, he continued."You're not obliged to, but I always check each train as it passes, no doors open, or hot axle box, habit of a signalman I suppose." He paused and took what was the first of several glances out of the window looking up the lane as if expecting someone. "You can put back number one, Ben, and three and four, and I'll go and open the gates, but if anyone asks you're not meant to open the gates until you've heard 'Train Out of Section', two-one on the bell. With a freight you could have a breakaway, and if the guard didn't pull them up you'd have wagons running back through the gates." Moments after Davies returned to the cabin the bell rang two-one. "That's out, he said, "and the indicator now shows token back in." He broke off as a young woman cyclist came freewheeling down the lane and he went to the door to bid her good morning as she passed. She appeared not to hear but he gazed after wistfully nonetheless. "She comes by everything morning—busty wench—and if it's a windy day you'll see her suspenders! If I were twenty years younger—"

Although it was only his first day Gherardini knew he was going to be happy at Spicer's, and later his mentor rang the district inspector. "Yes, he's ready for you to pass him out." The inspector must have expressed doubts on the length of time Gherardini had spent at his new post, but Davies continued. "Oh yes, he's done his two weeks. Yes, time does fly, doesn't it?"

Replacing the receiver he turned to Gherardini. "He'll be down to see you on Thursday."

Chapter Three

As he predicted, Gherardini settled in well at Spicer's Crossing. The wages were meagre but, he concluded, money was not everything. He had a cottage that went with the job, a job that would never be as arduous as that of a porter, and the public were obliged to him for the service he cheerfully provided. He soon became well known to all the regulars that used Juniper Lane, and even the elusive young woman on the bicycle did not remain so for long. Gherardini made her acquaintance sooner than he expected. On a gloomy December morning either the train was a bit later than usual or she was; suffice to say that freewheeling down the hill as was her wont, she seemed unprepared for the gates being closed, and collided with the gate nearest to her.

Gherardini heard the crash and rushed from the cabin in alarm. But the girl was already back on her feet and, apart from being rather dishevelled, with ladders in her stockings and her hair in disarray, she seemed, except for embarrassment, none the worse for the accident. At that moment the expected train passed, and as soon as he could Gherardini opened the gates, retrieved her bicycle and offered his assistance. But she turned away to limp back up the lane. "I shall go home and change," she said somewhat coldly. When she returned a little later she had remembered her bicycle.

"You must not worry," Gherardini said. "I look after it for you." When she passed at her usual time later in the evening

Gherardini was off duty, but waiting for her. Having straight-ened the mudguards and front forks it was obvious, although he said nothing, that a new new front wheel had been fitted.

The next morning Gherardini looked out for her but instead of passing by she stopped at his cabin door. "I want to thank you for your kindness yesterday," she said. "I must have appeared very ungrateful. Please take these for your trouble". With that she gave him two half-crowns. As she turned to go she added, "I'm a school teacher. My name is Miss Hazlewood," and she offered her hand to Gherardini which he took and held for several seconds.

"Ben," he said. And the looks they exchanged spoke prob-ably more words than a Shakespeare play could have done.

"I might've known it wouldn't take you long," Relief Signalman Davies said coming up the lane to the crossing. "She's ignored me for eighteen months and you get to know her in about as many minutes. But what I've really come for is to invite you to Wooburn Green. I'm on lates there now so call in any day after you've finished here." Davies was keeping his word that would enable Gherardini to know both the signal boxes on either side of Spicer's Crossing.

* * *

Gherardini, already conversant with Loudwater, found the atmosphere of Wooburn Green quite bucolic. The signal box was situated on the one platform the station possessed and the gates were operated by hand. An interesting feature that Davies pointed out was that at a half mile distance towards Bourne End there was a ground frame to allow access into a paper mill. The key end of the token unlocked a set of points that allowed a train to enter the private sidings to put off or attach wagons as necessary.

Later, as Gherardini was returning home, he found himself walking up Juniper Lane with none other but the school teacher Miss Hazlewood. Passing over the railway, his cottage stood to their left but Gherardini offered to see her home. To his surprise and delight she accepted. "That would be lovely, Ben, thank you."

There was much he wanted to say to her but no words would come, and although he wheeled the bicycle for her, they walked in silence. It soon grew quite dark and the whispering trees on either side of the lane created a menacing atmosphere. All too soon the teacher pointed to an oil lamp glowing eerily ahead, and then they stood for a moment at her gate while she reclaimed her bicycle. "It was kind of you," she said, "to see me home. It's spooky up here."

"It was of no difficulty, Miss."

"Please call me Emma. I'm not in the classroom now. Goodnight."

"Buona notte."

Ben and Emma saw more and more of each other as time passed. Emma lived with her elderly mother only and she being of a kind and generous nature saw no reason to discourage her daughter from seeing an ex-POW as the friendship developed. Four months from her accident at his gates Gherardini proposed and Emma accepted. They were married in St. Peter's Church, Loudwater on August 16th 1947.

The wedding breakfast took place in the Happy Union pub opposite the church. The reception did not finish until late in the evening, and it was dark by the time the new bride and groom escorted by several guests made their way up to Loudwater Station to continue the party in the waiting room. The late turn porter (Ben's replacement) and the booking clerk also joined in. Never had that normally sparsely populated room seen such revelry, so much so that the stationmaster who lived in the adjoining house came out to investigate. On becoming acquainted with the situation, "Paddington won't like it," he remonstrated. Whether 'Paddington' (by which he meant GWR management) would have been concerned was never established. Nevertheless he gave the newlyweds his blessing and returned to his house.

When the wedding reception finally broke up it was agreed by all that everyone had enjoyed themselves enormously. With the last train having departed, all was dark save the lights from the signal lamps, and in the welcome silence the newlyweds walked the length of the platform and down onto the track towards Spicer's Crossing. Walking in the 'four foot' over ballast and sleepers was far from easy, and at Loudwater's advanced starter, with the distant arm for Spicer's underneath, they stopped to rest. Leaning against its new tubular steel post, but for someone exercising their dog on the links, the marriage might have been consummated there and then.

On they stumbled, finally reaching Spicer's Cabin, falling through the door, and collapsing into the old armchair on the stroke of twelve. They immediately tore at one another's clothes and within moments Ben was naked and Emma too left without a stitch save her stockings and garters.

"Ben," she exclaimed, "you remind me of my uncle's donkey. Please be gentle with me. I'm a virgin— OH!"

Over an hour was spent in the cabin before the happy couple took to their proper marital bed. They did not rise until noon. Later, on that first day of the rest of their lives together, they went on a picnic before ending up in the 'Rose and Crown' as recommended by Ted Davies. Then it was back to the cottage for an early night.

"After all," Ben said with a smile, "I'm on early turn tomorrow."

The happy couple were unable to afford a honeymoon, nor did Ben have any time off; but on the Monday morning, to their delight, many drivers gave an extra whistle and a wave as they passed. On the morning 'pick-up' goods the driver even stopped and dropped off the most enormous lump of coal anyone had ever seen. "It was too big for the firebox anyway," the fireman called down.

The first visitor to the cottage was Relief Signalman Ted Davies. After congratulating them both he announced that he really was now retiring from the railway and going back to his native Wales. The gift he left them was a pair of enormous brass candlesticks.

"Well," he admitted, "the wife never liked 'em and it'll save me packing them for Caerphilly. By the way, I'd like you to have this," and gave Ben a dog-eared note book. "I'd started to write a book on railways in this area, but never found the time. You were always asking lots of questions, Ben, so maybe you'll find what I've written of interest." He turned to go as they made their farewells and he winked at Emma as he went. "If I'd been twenty years younger. Arrivederci!" His departure left a certain sadness that was almost tangible; there was no doubt that Davies had been a very good friend to the Italian.

The months passed. Loudwater needed a signalman, but while Emma taught, Ben saw no reason to promote himself above his capabilities. Nevertheless he continued to develop his interest in Britain's railways and in particular their local history. What he learned from the writings of Ted Davies was quite fascinating. Not every railway through the Chilterns, Ben discovered, had been built by Isambard Kingdom Brunel.

Birmingham was on the GWR map for 1852 by way of Oxford and Leamington with a terminus at Snow Hill. Brunel, however, was not the first into the city. Robert Stephenson had completed his London to Birmingham Railway in 1838. Running through the Chiltern towns of Berkhamsted and Tring, to a terminus at Curzon Street, it was later extended under the streets of Birmingham into New Street Station.

* * *

Yet another railway company crossed the Chiltern Hills. On its way south from humble beginnings in Northern England, the Manchester, Sheffield and Lincolnshire became the Great Central Railway as it marched boldly south to become a joint line with the Metropolitan from Quainton into London Marylebone. However, the alliance was not a happy one and the GC sought further collaboration with the GWR to establish yet another joint line. The deal was of benefit to both companies. The GC gained a second line into the capital while the GWR was able to shorten its route to Birmingham by nearly twenty miles. This was achieved by rebuilding High Wycombe Station to main line status and extending south-eastwards to Northolt Junction and thence to Paddington.

From Princes Risborough on the old Wycombe Railway the GWR extended northwards through Ashendon to connect with the GC main line at Grendon Underwood. Building from Ashendon (now a junction) to Aynho, five miles south of Banbury, the 'new line' met the original system and this gave the GWR its direct route to Birmingham.

The Ashendon–Aynho link, 'the last main line' opened in 1910. Only four years later came the Great War and during this time all the railway companies were taken over by the state in the form of the Railway Executive Committee. Following the Armistice it was agreed that the railways should not return to a system where duplication of lines resulted in wasteful competition. The benefits of a co-ordinated system had become apparent. Stopping short of nationalisation, all the many companies (greater than 100) were grouped into just four: The Great Western, London Midland & Scottish, London and North Eastern and the Southern Railway companies were formed on 1st January 1923.

Stephenson's early line to Birmingham, already part of the London & North Western Railway, came under the aegis of the LMS, while the GC and the Metropolitan were taken in by the LNER. Only the GWR remained unchanged, although the company itself had absorbed a large number of minor lines, the old Wycombe Railway included.

Britain's railways of the late 1920s and early 30s saw much in the way of progress, but were often tainted by a struggle to produce any sort of profit in the face of general economic depression and growing competition from motor transport. The benefits of greater efficiency, high speed travel, and modernisation programmes such as diesel locomotive traction and electrification schemes scarcely became apparent before the country was again plunged into war.

Once more the railway companies were taken over by an executive, and once again it was the railways that played such a decisive role in the quest for victory. In the aftermath of the hostilities, with the four companies desperate for financial investment, nationalisation was inevitable and this came about on Thursday 1st January 1948. New Year's Eve 1947 saw the 8.15 p.m. Slough to Bescot goods running some three hours late following the complete failure of the booked 'Hall' 4-6-0 at Taplow with no substitute engine available. The regular service had long finished but Ben and his colleagues had to wait for the last train before they could go off duty. Emma had brought a wireless set with her while she waited with her husband, and they were both looking forward to hearing the chimes from Westminster to announce the New Year.

The 8.15p.m. Slough was belled at 11.45, and 'on line' was received at 11.58. Neither heard 'Big Ben' as Driver Garret on LMS 2-8-0 8477 took a long and passionate pull on the whistle lever. The bass Stanier rhapsody filled the air until dying away on the wind. It was replaced by the cacophony of sound as the signalmen at both Wooburn Green and Loudwater exchanged the 7-5-5 'closing signal box' bell code.

Emma had prepared a brandy toddy once her husband was off duty, and as neither was particularly anxious to return to a chilly cottage they each recited a toast in the warmth of the cabin.

"Happy New Year, Ben. Here's to the future."

"Buona fortuna!"

Emma, having swigged two toddies, made herself comfortable in the old armchair and invited her husband to join her. "Oh, Ben." Emma whispered. "Remember our wedding night?" Once again the old armchair rocked and squeaked until it threatened to burst through the timbers of the cabin.

Sown literally that night were the seeds for a railway prodigy of the future. 'Una bella figlia', a beautiful daughter, Roberta, was born on the 4th October 1948.

Chapter Four

The summer of 1959 was exceptional, and the last of day of term before the summer holiday at Loudwater School was particularly hot. Roberta Gherardini and the rest of her class were handing in their art work as the climax to their primary school days. By mid-afternoon, even with all the windows open, the air in the classroom was stifling. Mr Wilks the form teacher was keen to mark the artistic achievements and despatch the whole class off the premises as soon as possible. Roberta had, since very early childhood, been known as Bobbie, but for Mr Wilks etiquette was all important. "Next," he called, "Miss Gherardini."

Bobbie had been feeling increasingly uncomfortable that afternoon, not on account of the heat, but the expectation that her contribution for the theme 'Victorian England' was about to be ridiculed. Several girls before her had created almost life-size images of Queen Victoria, while the boys presented trains and smoky factories. Bobbie stepped to the front of the class in trepidation as Mr Wilks eyed her offering scornfully. "Well, well," he said. "Is this all it is?" He turned to the children. "What did I tell you to make, class?"

"A large eye-catching poster, Sir," they chorused.

"We have here," the teacher continued, "a postcard of a bicycle." Bobbie had stuck wire on to a small piece of card in the shape of a penny-farthing bicycle. The wheels were actual penny and farthing coins, hence the overall small size. "Two out of ten," Mr Wilks said, loud enough for all the class to hear. And, to add to their amusement, as he handed Bobbie back her work the penny coin fell off and rolled away over the bare floorboards. Mr Wilks retrieved it from under his desk, and added sarcastically, "You might've had an extra mark if the penny had been Victorian." He was about to pass the coin back to Bobbie when he paused and stared at the penny with mounting curiosity. Wilks then disappeared into the adjoining classroom leaving his own class, no longer grinning at Bobbie's misfortune, but wondering at the new development. He returned with Mrs Mills, the young arithmetic teacher, and together they studied Bobbie's coin.

"Where did you find this, dear?" Mrs Mills asked.

"My father found it on the farm where he worked during the war. It's my lucky penny."

The teachers then spoke so quietly that few children were able to hear their words. "Am I right?" Mr Wilks asked.

"Oh yes. Only about a dozen pennies were minted in 1933."

"Worth a bit, then?"

"Most definitely."

"A hundred?"

"Several, I should think," Mrs Mills agreed. "Maybe even—"

"You cannot be serious!"

"Oh I am; very much so, I'm afraid. And for goodness sake tell her to look after it."

The remainder of the afternoon dragged to its weary close and at last the time came for Mr Wilks to bid his class farewell. Alone at his desk he contemplated the extraordinary final lesson and how easily that rare penny could have rolled under the floorboards into oblivion. Mr Wilks never intended to be so harsh on his half-Italian pupil, but quite simply she bothered him, and it seemed the only way he could address her was with reproach. He had become quite distracted once when he had overdone the sarcasm and the dark eyes full of tears had turned on him so wistfully that he'd sent her out of the room. He had met her parents on a number of occasions and thought how voluptuous the mother was. The daughter had inherited similar characteristics, and was already looking like a younger Sophia Loren.

Bobbie had been quite well liked within the class. Many of the boys were interested in railways and wanted to be an engine driver, and occasionally Bobbie had secured, through her father and a friendly crew, a short trip for them on the footplate. Loudwater School was situated a good mile away from the village of the same name. But the branch line with which they were familiar ran nearby, and in the playground, although trees hid the trains from view, one could certainly hear them, barking up the rising gradient towards Wycombe. By comparison, across the valley, high upon an embankment, trains on the main line from Paddington to Birmingham could be clearly seen.

But Mr Wilks was also aware of another reason for her popularity. On the threshold of womanhood, Bobbie could be coerced by some boys that summer to lift her tee-shirt for sixpence. Indeed, Wilks imagined, she already had a bigger bust than Mrs Mills.

Secondary education for Bobbie in September was to be at the postwar, mixed but sex-segregated Hatters Lane School, and a number twenty bus took Bobbie from her home along the A40 to the bottom of this lane each school morning. No bus attempted the 1 in 7 climb, but for Bobbie the walk was worth the effort as about halfway up the lane it crossed by overbridge the familiar Paddington to Birmingham main line.

On occasions there was a reward for lingering and peering over the parapet. She once saw a Hughes/Fowler 2-6-0 No. 42870 mincing its way crab-like on a down freight. She observed, too, the motive power of the future when the second of the LMS/LMR diesels No. 10001 swept by beneath her on a northbound parcels train that autumn of 1959.

While Bobbie would not have readily admitted to watching trains it was soon apparent she did so. But this brought no condemnation, as many girls had brothers with visions of being the next generation of footplatemen. Indeed, Bobbie and a girl who she was particularly friends with, Donna Rice, and her two brothers, became a regular locospotting group who met on several Saturday mornings when the weather was clement.

Their favourite vantage point to view the trains on their line was a footpath crossing off the A40 road near Loudwater. By the double set of metals an old sign of GW & GC origin sternly informed them that a sum of forty shillings would be demanded should they trespass upon the railway. It was the same cast-iron notice that had warned Bobbie's father years before.

To their right the line curved left across an embankment before being swallowed up in the blackness of 342-yard White House Lane tunnel. Looking left from the crossing the line swept through a deep cutting, the chalk faces as white as Beachy Head, the spoil excavated no doubt providing the substance for the embankment. Midway through the cutting at its deepest point stood a two-aspect red/green colour light signal, allowing the long section between Beaconsfield and High Wycombe to be effectively halved, and permit greater line occupancy. A distant signal for the signal in the cutting was provided before the tunnel was entered. There was a similar arrangement for trains running in the opposite direction. The colour light signals were a replacement for Tyler's

Green signal box, closed in February 1953.

As valued as Bobbie was within the quartet she saw no point in taking engine numbers. To her, in particular the ex-GWR 4-6-0 classes, they all looked alike. Of course there were detail differences—stepped running plate or straight, inside or curved outside steam pipes, and the unique 'King' bogie—but illustrations in her Observer's Book of Railway Locomotives supported the view. Bobbie alone preferred ex-LMS engines which were only occasionally seen. While her friends extolled the virtues of God's Wonderful Railway, she praised Stanier's Black 5 and 8F 2-8-0 and with grace acknowledged the Churchward influence that Stanier had learned while at Swindon. Bobbie felt her LMS interest stemmed from her first visit to the line with her father early in 1956. Princess Royal Pacifics 46207 and 46210 deputised then for Kings which were being 'stopped' for bogie modifications.

The King 4-6-0s were designed by Churchward's successor, Collett. Introduced in 1927, the thirty locomotives of the class were named after Kings of England, although originally names for Cathedrals were considered. The Kings were a direct development of the highly successful Castle class. Together the Castles and Kings handled the majority of premier services on the Birmingham–Paddington main line. Express freight traffic was often in the hands of Hall class 4-6-0s or, less frequently, a Grange. Slower goods trains brought further variety of locomotive power. Austerity 2-8-0s, or those of the 28XX series, could be expected as well as brand new Standard 9Fs.

Trainspotting took on a new dimension in the Easter holidays of 1961. Some men were working on the up line, sleeper packing, between the crossing and tunnel. One man was designated the lookout, and it was his specific duty not to assist in the work, but solely advise his mates of the approach of trains. This man, who seemed little older than Bobbie or her friends, was very knowledgeable of railways. The boys, however, considered him stupid as he claimed not to know such fundamental details as which King class locomotive ran with a bell on its buffer beam. But the lookout man, whose name they discovered was Nigel, would always wink at Bobbie when denying such knowledge. His favourite comment was that the ten unique 9F 2-10-0s, nos. 92020–92029, had been built in Ireland by Frank O'Crostie.

Nigel the lookout man tried to widen the boys' interests. On freight he suggested they watch for the different colour of wagon. Grey, or what was originally grey beneath the rust, was for the antiquated un-braked wagon. Bauxite brown denoted piped or brake-fitted stock which could be run at speed on account of a greater ability to stop. "The position of the lamps on the front of the engine will tell you the class of train," Nigel had said. "One lamp above each buffer denotes an express passenger. A single lamp under the chimney is a stopper." But the boys would have none of it. All they were interested in was whether or not the engine was a 'cop'.

One day during the summer holiday of that year, rather than the morning only up at the crossing, they elected to spend the whole day. Bobbie was happy to see the return workings of engine, stock and crew as predicted by the lookout man, but the boys were disgusted seeing the same engines they had seen earlier. However, everyone was impressed by the fact that they'd witnessed the whole Pullman service (four round trips) worked by the same unit. The Blue Pullman sets introduced in September of 1960 were a taste of the modernisation that was rapidly to follow.

None of their young minds nor even those of the men working on the track envisaged just how drastic the changes would be. They all vaguely understood the Modernisation Plan of 1955 following which, experts confidently predicted, British Railways would be self-sufficient within just six years. Steam locomotives would be gradually superseded by diesels before mass electrification, and with major new marshalling yards and station reconstruction the loss of traffic to road transport would be arrested.

Yet, by that summer of 1961 there was little evidence of the £1,240 million investment. With the exception of some pre-grouping stalwarts that had gone to the great roundhouse in the sky, steam locomotive withdrawals were confined to those with a major defect or collision damage. After all, 92220 *Evening Star*, (the last steam locomotive to be built) had been turned out from Swindon barely a year before. However, as the months passed, the writing on the wall became more prominent, as no less than six of Bobbie's beloved 'Lizzie' Pacifics were withdrawn, and early in 1962 the first of the Kings followed. Incredibly, too, engines built after nationalisation were joining their condemned fellows on the scrap lines.

A significant impact of the Modernisation Plan was the introduction of diesel multiple units on all Marylebone local services. It was a sad farewell to the once ubiquitous Fairburn 2-6-4 tanks, as from 18th June 1962 all the suburban trains were formed of Derby-built 4-car sets. Nearer to home, Bobbie's 'Marlow Donkey' succumbed to just a single diesel unit of the 55000 class from Pressed Steel. Services of more importance were handled by 3-car sets from the same manufacturer.

It seemed inevitable that when the elder boy left school and set out on a career in accountancy that the spotting group would fold, and so it did. They met for one last time in the September of that year. Reminiscing over the two years all agreed that the prototype Co-Co diesel *Lion* on the 7.25 a.m. Wolverhampton, in bizarre white livery, was a particular highlight in addition to the numerous special trains run in connection with Football Association and Rugby League Cup Finals held at Wembley. They would never forget their shouts of delight on seeing Jubilees *Tasmania*, *Sandwich* and *Bechuanaland*, and V2 60827 *St. Peter's School York AD627* and Royal Scot 46160 *Queen Victoria's Rifleman*. However, at the close of the WR summer timetable for 1962 they learned of a great slaughter of former GWR 4-6-0s. Those withdrawn included 34 'Halls', 25 'Castles', 13 'Kings' and 3 'Counties'.

Although for most enthusiasts interest in railways declined as steam traction diminished, for Bobbie, and many others, in reality it was a fascinating period in locomotive history. The Paddington–Birmingham expresses became diesel-hauled by the D1000 Western class in all their experimental liveries. Sometimes D800 Warships substituted, or a service reverted to steam, but in a number of cases there was a steam and diesel combination, with the steam locomotive coupled 'inside' merely to provide adequate heating for the coaches, particularly during the severe winter weather that was to come.

Taken all round it was a momentous year as the British Transport Commission, the governing body of the railways since nationalisation, was abolished. The Minister of Transport, Ernest Marples, replaced the BTC with a more commercially-minded British Railways Board. The first chairman, a physicist on secondment from Imperial Chemical Industries (ICI), was Kent-born Dr Richard Beeching.

Chapter Five

The document 'The Reshaping of British Railways' more commonly known as the 'Beeching Report' was published on 25th March 1963. Following this, on Maundy Thursday, April 11th, it being the Easter holidays, Bobbie and her father were discussing its implications in the cabin at Spicer's Crossing. As well as describing the railway of the future, the report laid great emphasis on elimination of costs; not mere savings. Both Bobbie and her father were delighted that while many branch lines were listed for closure, theirs was not among them. However, an official visitor caught the end of their conversation.

"I can't see a future for it myself," District Inspector James Kendall said, as he squeezed himself into the cabin. "If the line stays this will all be gone," he prophesied, waving a hand around the cabin. "You'll have automatic barriers here worked from a power signal box from as far away as Aynho Junction."

Kendall was on one of his routine visits around his 'patch', and was a familiar figure to both Bobbie and her father. Bobbie always enjoyed meeting him, as he often had a tale to tell, and she knew of no-one more cynically realistic. He was against Government policy, whichever party was in power, and had never approved of nationalisation. Yet on Dr Beeching he seemed to hold an open mind.

When Bobbie first made Kendall's acquaintance he had regaled her on the subject of post-war locomotive development.

"I shall never understand," he had said, "why Rob Riddles designed so many new classes of steam engines. Apart from the 9Fs he only needed to build a few more Stanier 'Black Fives'. I met him once and he told me he was all for electrification but the Government wanted more steam as it wasn't so expensive."

On that Maundy Thursday Bobbie made the inspector a mug of tea and listened to an update of the railway scene. Kendall explained that electrification of the West Coast main line was progressing south of Bletchley, adding that, "they could have had the overhead wires up throughout the system, even on this little Hornby set by now, if they'd not wasted so much money before. I mean, think of the thousands of private owner wagons that were bought and then scrapped because they were non-standard!"

The conversation between the three soon drifted to a resumé of the worst winter weather since 1947, then, led by Bobbie, it turned to careers on the railway. An employment officer had recently visited her school and, for those like Bobbie who would be leaving that summer, given sound advice on the trials and tribulations of going out to work for a living. To Bobbie's amazement the woman showed no surprise that she was considering working on the railway. Her own father was an engine driver, recently 'dieselised' as the woman put it, to the extent that he was an instructor to other locomotive men making the transition to the new form of traction. She was clearly sold on the modern machines, as Bobbie explained to Kendall.

"She would be," he said. "But mark my words, a lot of the junk on the rails now will be scrapped long before steam is. In the past we've converted some engines to burn oil so why not do it again? No, I'm sure steam could carry on 'til we get the a.c. electrics. I don't think all these diesels are the answer."

Bobbie explained then what she had said to the employment

officer, about her secret wish to be a shunter. "But I know that I'd never lift the three-link couplings. Why can't the wagons couple themselves up like Triang or Hornby Dublo do?"

The inspector allowed himself a smile. "Actually," he said, "if you're serious about railway work I do need a lampman or should I say a lampwoman. I'm paying a fortune in overtime to keep my district illuminated. All you have to do is look after the signal lamps around High Wycombe. You keep the burners filled with paraffin, the wicks trimmed and, while you're up there, give the arms and spectacles a wipe over." He paused as it occurred to him that he might have oversimplified the role. "Mind you," he added, "drivers rely heavily on those lamps in the dark. So it's a very responsible job. But you won't need to worry about colour light signals, Wycombe will still be sema-phore for years yet." He finished his coercion with a query. "You're not by any chance acrophobic?" Both Gherardinis look puzzled. "I mean, you're not afraid of heights?"

"No, no," Bobbie replied.

"Good, well, think it over and I'll send for you to come and see me. During both wars, you know, many women did railway work while the men were away at the front."

Bobbie's interview with Inspector Kendall was arranged for one month hence, but fate cast an intervening hand during that short time. A relaying occupation north of Saunderton over the weekend of 18th/19th May necessitated single line working between High Wycombe North and Princes Risborough South signal boxes. Permanent way men had possession of the down line while all trains ran via the up. The down line was the origi-nal route of the Wycombe Railway, while the up line, only laid when the upgrading took place to main line standards in the early 1900s, took a slightly different route to avoid the worst of the gradient. However, the unique 'new line' deviation involved extensive earthworks as well as a tunnel.

In the early hours of the Sunday morning Jim Kendall met up with the ganger in charge of the relaying to see how the job was progressing, and intending to walk back to Risborough South box to advise the signalman there of the situation. However, the crew of the '38' class 2-8-0 attached to hopper wagons of new ballast decided that they were getting short of water, arranged to run 'light' to Risborough to top up the tender, and agreed to take the inspector along with them. Minutes later, when Kendall alighted at the station in the darkness he thought they were at the platform but the driver had stopped short of the ramp. The difference in height was considerable and as Kendall landed on *terra firma*, he injured his spine which forced him into early retirement.

So it was that when Bobbie presented herself at High Wycombe for interview she was introduced to Chief Inspector Rees-Black, a man familiar to her by name only. In his office Rees-Black waved a hand to a chair opposite his desk.

"Do sit down, Miss, er... er... "

"Gherardini."

"Yes, yes. Remind me why you're here."

"I—I—I've come about the job of signal lampman—I mean, woman."

Rees-Black's demeanour did nothing to allay Bobbie's nervousness. Dressed as he was for going out, in black overcoat and trilby hat, he did not sit down himself but perched on the edge of his desk frowning, and forbidding as a sparrowhawk.

"So what makes you think you're suited for railway work?" he asked.

Bobbie stammered about her father's job and that she too wanted to pursue a career on the railway.

"Yes, I've heard of Gherardini," Rees-Black said, "but the

real railway is no place for a young girl. You'll be tripping over signal wires, or not coming to work because you've had a row with your boyfriend. Have you ever been up a signal ladder?" Bobbie opened her mouth to admit that she had. But he cut her short.

"No, I suppose you haven't. And another thing," he added staring at her blouse, "you would never get through the safety hoop at the top. And I like my ladies to wear skirts and stockings. That would not be at all appropriate up a signal post."

Stung by indignation, and recalling Inspector Kendall's words, Bobbie spoke up. "Many women did railwaymen's work during the war."

Rees-Black glared at her, "Young lady, I'm well aware of that. No, you're quite unsuitable. Good day."

Bobbie left with tears of anger and frustration in her eyes. The chief inspector called out, "Try the booking office!" as his door slammed. "With tits as big as yours they'd never print tickets fast enough."

So ended Bobbie's tentative steps towards a railway career, but she left school that July, and after having some time off to herself she took a job as a waitress at a family-run bakery and tea shop in Wooburn Green situated near the railway station.

The baker's wife had recently been discharged from hospital following repair of a fractured femur and Bobbie's first few days were spent assisting with the woman's convalescence in particular with the use of crutches. Her first day in the bakery was actually Thursday 8th August. By noon of that day, however, everyone had learned of a daring robbery. More than two million pounds had been stolen from the Glasgow–Euston 'Up Postal', stopped by a faked red signal soon after 3 a.m. at Sear's Crossing just south of Leighton Buzzard. Driver Jack Mills and his secondman David Whitby on locomotive D326 were both overpowered and bullied into moving the locomotive and first coach only a further half mile to where many more robbers were waiting to unload the mailbags stuffed full of used notes.

The incident became known as the Great Train Robbery, notable both for the brilliant criminal skill in its execution and sheer incompetence afterwards. Bobbie felt sorry for the plight of the enginemen, and later learned that Mills had been courageous in trying to defend his cab, and that a retired driver had originally been recruited by the gang to perform the shunt. But this the hapless individual was unable to do as he found to his chagrin that he was not conversant with the controls of English Electric Type 4 diesels. Everyone within retail was asked to be vigilant in case anyone should produce a roll of banknotes for a purchase. Sadly for Bobbie, in the bakery at Wooburn Green, no-one did.

The following Thursday the railways were in the news once more. The signalman at Knowle and Dorridge accepted the 1 p.m. Birmingham Pullman from Bentley Heath Crossing (less than three quarters of a mile away) and allowed his colleague there to lower all his signals. Ignoring, or somehow forgetting the Pullman, the Knowle signalman permitted a pannier tank to propel carflats loaded with new Land Rovers down the up main straight into the path of the oncoming Pullman. That day, the 1 p.m. Birmingham was not the blue multiple unit but Western class diesel D1040, *Western Queen*, and nine Pullman coaches. Approaching Bentley Heath at 80mph, the Pullman's driver saw the adverse signals at Knowle and made a full emergency brake application, but disaster was inevitable, and the Pullman collided with the carflats at about 25mph.

The impact of the crash, which occurred beneath an archway of a bridge, broke the backs of the carflats, and in the restricted space the end of one wagon was deflected up into the cab of the Western. The Pullmans were always manned by two drivers and, because on that fateful day the service was loco-hauled stock, a secondman was also present. All three enginemen died in the collision. The crash emphasised what little protection there was in the cab of a diesel and how vulnerable footplatemen could be. Bobbie reasoned that had the locomotive been a 'King' the only harm would have been a bent buffer beam and a dented smokebox. But, moreover, Bobbie gave up contemplating a railway career completely. After all, if men with years of experience could make serious mistakes then there would never be a place on the railway for her.

Chapter Six

Bobbie settled down well in her chosen profession. She admitted that it was no career, but it gave her a wage and she found dealing with the public rather fascinating. The tea shop was attached to the bakery, and Bobbie and her colleague—known as the Mother Superior, a plump woman of forty—also sold fresh-baked bread and cream buns. Both women were meant to be able to wait at table, serve at counter and fetch bread in from the ovens, but in reality there was a distinct division of labour. The Mother Superior was developing arthritis in her knees while Bobbie was hopeless with the cash box.

Each day was predictable. In the morning busy mothers bought their daily bread, while a regular clientele of spinsters and widows called later for afternoon tea, and just occasionally train crew would drop by off the 'pick-up' goods at Wooburn Green if they wanted something a little more sophisticated than cold tea in the brake van.

One such driver, she discovered, had witnessed the horrific train crash at Harrow and Wealdstone in October 1952. He had been a 'passed fireman' then on the LMR, and he spoke of the ASLEF strike of June 1955. Driver and fireman, faces beaming as they happily steamed along, was an illusion, he said, found in train books only. He was not in ASLEF, but one of a number of drivers in the NUR.

"You soon found out who your friends were," was all he would say.

Soon after starting work Bobbie was measured for a uniform that became a waitress in a respectable establishment, a black skirt with white blouse and scarlet neckerchief with 'Hovis' embroidered on it in yellow. Previously Bobbie had sought to conceal the size of her bust beneath loose fitting jumpers so the Mother Superior approved of the new look but made some adjustments herself by unfastening the top buttons of Bobbie's blouse and standing back to admire the girl. "We ought to lower the tone of this place and turn it into a transport cafe," she said. "The place would be full of blokes staring at your cleavage and slapping my arse!"

Bobbie worked every day except Sundays, although both Wednesday and Saturday were 'half days' only. However, on Wednesdays it soon became customary for her to take the black labrador, owned by the baker's wife, for a walk. Bobbie was paid two hours' money for the task and woe betide her if she returned in under the allotted time. To avoid circumnavigating the village too often, Bobbie hit on the idea of returning to the old trainspotting haunt.

In the two years since she last visited the line there had been many changes. Transport Minister Ernest Marples had taken the railways by the scruff of the neck and dragged them into the twentieth century, yet for many railwaymen, the older man in particular, the period of transition was a bitter experience.

Nevertheless, there had been a number of exciting developments. Apart from the electrification of the west coast main line, the bulk transit of commodities such as fuels, the introduction of Freightliner, and the 'Merry-Go-Round' system for the movement of coal from pit to power station, were notable achievements of the modern railway. Elsewhere the system was contracting by thousands of miles with a number of line closures allegedly sanctioned from dubious statistics. Data taken during the quietest part of the day, without commuters or schoolchildren, inevitably skewed passenger surveys; while track renewal or station refurbishment boosted maintenance costs to an unrealistic high. Moreover, when journey times were quoted to promote an alternative bus service, the slowest train was compared with the quickest bus and omitting to acknowledge that the bus ran only on market day. Meanwhile, as the tonnage of merchandise freight fell, anger was expressed at the money invested in the construction of huge marshalling yards that would never realise their full potential and eventually become housing estates.

After two years Bobbie knew she could expect no passenger train to be steam-hauled within the London Division, and despite the Western Region having invested heavily with diesel hydraulics, BR policy was that future locomotives would possess electric transmission. During 1964 all the Western D1000s would be concentrated on the Bristol, South Wales and Plymouth routes, and services on the Paddington–Birmingham main line hauled by Brush 2750s. Since the regional boundary changes of 1962, when the WR lost the main line north of Bicester, the London Midland authorities had no wish to associate with anything bearing the GWR hallmark.

In addition to the motive power changes there were other differences Bobbie became aware of. What were once saplings were developing into young trees and, as a result of myxomatosis, grasses grew long and flowered in the absence of rabbits.

As 1965 dawned, the steam locomotives that survived presented an ever more depressing sight, and were only cleaned for special occasions. Not without some irony, it became customary for depots to brighten up the appearance of a locomotive by picking out front end details, such as smokebox door hinges with white paint, thereby at least making the locomotive visible, to a degree, to permanent way men and shed staff. Former LMS locomotives still visited the line, and some of these sported a yellow stripe across the cabside. Again, this was not for cosmetic purposes but served as a warning to the driver that his engine exceeded the 13ft. 1in. height limit and was banned from running on lines electrified with the overhead catenary. Jubilees, 0-6-0 4Fs and Royal Scots were examples so adorned.

One particular Saturday evening, Bobbie, with nothing else better to do, decided to call at the bakery and walk the dog as a favour. The mutt was there, barking in response to her knocking, but no one came to answer the door. Despite the lack of canine company Bobbie decided to go to the main line alone.

Although some two hours of daylight remained, somehow the scene appeared desolate. For some considerable time no train passed and nothing was signalled. A man and woman out walking passed over the crossing and looked at Bobbie curiously waiting there. But no words were exchanged, and Bobbie soon forgot them as at last the colour light signal in the cutting was showing green for a northbound train. Before long a whistle sounded from the tunnel and, enveloped in steam, a down fitted freight appeared. Judging by the design of the front bogie it was a Modified Hall, but there attempts at identification ended, for as the locomotive passed, it was devoid not only of smoke-box numberplate but of cabside plate as well, and where a nameplate would have been only three brackets like raised fingers remained. However, a chalked number below the cab window saved the day. The train was a long one, and after the last of the vanfits had jostled by Bobbie heard a voice calling to her from the other side of the line. "What was it, did you get the number?"

In the moment it took to respond the individual had crossed

the lines and Bobbie found herself confronted by Jon Rice, former member of the trainspotting group who had left school to become an accountant.

"Six nine sixty-seven, I think," she answered.

"You only think?" He had clearly lost none of his arrogance.

"Well", Bobbie said defending herself, "I know it was something 67. It definitely was a Modified Hall and as there were only thirty of the 79 series, it had to be 6967." For Bobbie it was a triumph of logic, but with bad grace the youth said nothing. A DMU passed at that moment on its way to Marylebone, but it was Rice that broke the silence that followed as he looked Bobbie up and down with obvious approval. "I remember you now," he said.

He invited Bobbie to join him in walking over the top of the cutting. "No," she said declining the offer. "It'll be dark soon. I'm going home."

"Yes, me too," Rice agreed and they left the lineside together. He crossed the stile first then waited for Bobbie, enjoying the flash of bare leg as she too stepped over. Once clear of the stile, as a gentleman might do, he took Bobbie's arm but it was only to steer her off the path into their old camp, a cave-like leafy haven that gave shelter from a shower of rain and a place to enjoy their Tizer and crisps. But, suddenly, Jon Rice seemed to lose his footing and in falling took Bobbie down with him. She immediately realised the tumble was no accident as in a moment he was kneeling astride her.

Bobbie screamed but he put a hand over her mouth to silence her. "Any more of that," hissed Rice, "and you'll get far worse." Taking no chances he kept her mouth covered but ran his free hand over her blouse, undoing the buttons as he did so. "That's a pretty bra. Now let's see how big you really are. Stand up—and keep quiet." And he put a fist to her face to make his point. Bobbie struggled to her feet and began to cry but reluctantly took off her blouse. She then paused hoping that her actions thus far were sufficient. She was mistaken.

"Get that bra off," Rice insisted, and watched eagerly while Bobbie again did as she was told. As he snatched away the offending item of lingerie, he exclaimed, "Jesus, what a pair!"

As Bobbie pleaded tearfully with him once more to leave her alone, neither heard footsteps on the path nearby. Bobbie became aware of someone else being present, but Rice was oblivious until someone smote the back of his head with a stub of a fallen branch. He roared with pain as he turned to face his assailant, but the visitor still held the billet to prevent reprisal; the jacket he had been carrying over his shoulder he threw to Bobbie who accepted it gratefully to cover her charms.

It had taken her a few moments to recognise her saviour. It was Nigel the lookout man, and in a few words she explained her own identity. Jon Rice stood rubbing his head and Nigel addressed him.

"You better push off, Rice, before I dump you in the 'four foot' in front of the next train."

"Ten to one I wouldn't have been the first to shag her," he snarled. "All the boys saw her tits at school. Eyetie bitch!"

Nigel took a threatening step closer, but Rice was striding away. Dismissing the youth, Nigel turned his attention again to Bobbie. "Get yourself dressed and I'll meet you up at the stile." Bobbie did as he suggested and soon joined her Good Samaritan who insisted she keep his jacket to ward off the chill of the approaching night. Nigel explained that the reason for his nocturnal visit was for photographing trains after dark. "But I can't let you walk home alone," he said, "he might still be about. I can always get my night shots another time, but the Rugby parcels will be coming down shortly. There's usually a B1 on it."

Apart from a V2 on a Wembley Cup Final special, Bobbie had seen nothing of the LNER since the L1 2-6-4 tanks had worked the local trains to Marylebone. So she agreed to wait with Nigel and use the time to recover from her ordeal.

There was a faint hum of traffic from the A40 road, but otherwise all was silent and it was certainly a new experience to be up at the line at that time of night. The elements of excitement increased as the signal in the cutting eventually switched to green. Presently the rails began to sing, then a whistle shrieked from the direction of the tunnel, the mouth indefinable in the darkness.

A cloud of steam tinted crimson with the glow from the firebox shot skywards as the train emerged from the tunnel and sped towards them. To Bobbie the sounds should have been familiar but they were strangely unreal.

"It's not a B1. It's a three-cylinder job," she heard Nigel shout above the noise as the train bore down on them. "It's an A3!"

The cacophony of sound from the locomotive subsided to be replaced by the lesser notes of the bogie vans dum-dumming over the rail-joints until those sounds too diminished and finally disappeared. A combination of a grubby engine and the darkness meant neither got the engine number, but they both realised they had witnessed something rather special together like seeing a shooting star, and a respectful silence followed.

Eventually Nigel said, "Well, we must be going, your parents will be so worried. I live in those terraced cottages along the main road, and Juniper Lane won't be much out of my way."

Little conversation passed between them as they walked along. Nigel pointed out his home, and when they arrived at Spicer's Crossing Bobbie found that her parents had not returned from their night out so she faced no awkward questions. She hugged Nigel appreciatively.

"Thank you for saving me. How can I ever repay you?"

"Think nothing of it. I was in the right place at the right time for once."

"But," Bobbie asked, "just one question. How did you know who that boy was? It's been years since we were trainspotting together?"

"I know him well," Nigel replied. "He never became an accountant. He works with me in the permanent way gang."

Chapter Seven

At the end of May 1965 Dr Beeching relinquished the chairmanship of BR. For the previous eight months, under a Labour Government, Tom Fraser had been the Transport Minister. Without Marples, Dr Beeching found his position untenable and he returned to ICI.

The summer of 1965 was also notable for the running of the last regularly steam-hauled train from Paddington. On 11th June, *Clun Castle*, on the 4.15 p.m. from Paddington, sped past Bobbie and Nigel at their vantage point of the crossing on its way to Banbury. No.7029 was specially clean for the service and sported a GWR style number on the buffer beam even though, as Nigel explained, 7029 was not built until after nationalisation.

* * *

Two months had passed since Nigel had rescued Bobbie from Jon Rice, and during that time Nigel had become a regular customer at the Bakery Tea Shop. To see the final steam working was, effectively, their first date.

They watched *Clun Castle* on that warm Friday afternoon disappear into the history books, then turned somewhat sadly away. Nigel, at twenty-four years, still lived with his mother and this, together with the fact that he played with a model railway, tended to discourage most young ladies he met. His mother, a churchgoer, would often arrange introductions with nubile daughters of other church members, but to date none of the relationships had developed. Only one was sustained for any length of time. A deaconess, an extraordinarily passionate female for one supposedly devoted to Jesus, would reward Nigel for helping set out the hymn books. Her favourite position was in the pulpit leaning over the lectern while Nigel ministered to her from behind. Sadly, the young lady turned her attentions to the older men in the choir.

Inevitably, Nigel fell madly in love with the crossing keeper's daughter. But there was deep respect with the attraction, as a brother might love a sister. Hence, on the walk home from the lineside, he invited her to see his '00' gauge layout, with no sexual inclination whatever.

"I've redecorated my room", he explained as they reached the front door of his terraced cottage. "My ceiling rafters are exposed beams again with words engraved on them. Mum wonders if it's Italian and whether you could translate it."

"Hello, dear. I'm Mrs Frost," Nigel's mother said as she welcomed the pair in. "Bobbie for Roberta, yes? I liked Edith Nesbitt books too." Mrs Frost didn't see the puzzled glance Bobbie threw at Nigel as he disappeared into the kitchen. However, in the few minutes it took for him to make some tea, Mrs Frost extracted from her young visitor all the personal details she could possibly wish to know. Conversation flowed easily and Mrs Frost soon remarked that Bobbie should call her Kath. That discreet lady remained downstairs while Bobbie agreed to see the model railway.

Disregarding the unprototypical three-rail track, the layout certainly was impressive. 7032 *Denbigh Castle* with four brown and cream corridor coaches formed the Red Dragon and a 2-8-0 waited in the goods yard with a train of mineral wagons. In the engine shed lurked a diesel shunter with DP2 for company. However, on a shelf above the railway, still in its box, was the AL1 class Bo-Bo electric E3002. Nigel followed Bobbie's gaze. "My Mum bought it for me," he said, "but I can't run it until I've converted it for 3-rail operation. She thinks I'm waiting until I get coaches for it. Trouble is, they've stopped making Hornby Dublo now and it's difficult to buy."

Mrs Frost had come up the stairs and, as her son's door was open, stepped into his room to enquire about the carvings on the beams. When the handiwork was pointed out Bobbie jumped in amazement. "Santa Maria!" she exclaimed, and then turning to the Frosts said in almost a whisper, "It was done by my father."

It was the turn of Nigel and his mother to look surprised.

"Yes, but what does it say, dear?" asked Mrs Frost.

"It says 'bella casa—bella gente'," Bobbie replied. "Lovely house, lovely people. Then comes my father's name and the date—MCMXLVI."

The three could scarcely contain their astonishment and they discussed it at length downstairs to the effect that Bobbie found herself staying for dinner. She did not leave the Frosts until late in the evening, but when she arrived home she was unable to tell her father; he had more important things to worry about as earlier that day a train had run through the crossing gates.

Casting her mind back to the Frost's house, Bobbie remembered that a number of years after Mr Gherardini had left 4 Inglis Terrace, the elderly owners had sold the property and returned to Poland, and the next inhabitants were the family from whom Mrs Frost had bought the house in 1960. Mrs Frost had been widowed soon after her son was conceived in 1940, a German sniper in France robbing Nigel of the father he never knew.

The weeks passed and it was August when Bobbie gave her friend an unusual proposition. She wanted him to walk her through White House Lane Tunnel. Nigel's reply was to the effect that not only was it dangerous but they would be deliberately trespassing. Such advice failed to dampen Bobbie's enthusiasm, and Nigel reluctantly agreed. However, he did insist that the adventure could only take place on a Sunday, and when he had consulted the working timetable which gave not only passenger services but freight and engine movements as well. A suggestion that she try Saunderton Tunnel, which at eighty-eight yards was little more than a bridge, was ignored, and Nigel realised that the attraction was the fact that her father had worked on the land above. Nigel had of course walked through the tunnel on several occasions including the one at Ardley, very much longer at 1147 yards. In the event, they met at the crossing in the evening of August Bank Holiday Monday which had, since 1964, been moved to the end of the month rather than the beginning.

Halfway between the crossing and the tunnel stood a permanent way man's cabin on the up side of the line, and it was here where they waited for the local service to subside. Indeed, the two DMUs must have passed each other actually in the tunnel. Nigel then knew that there was almost a whole hour available to them. With Bobbie convincingly dressed in overalls to partner Nigel they made their way up the line. The tunnel mouth loomed cavernously above them, and to Bobbie it was awesome, as Nigel led the way in the cess of the down main. Her footsteps on the ballast sounded extraordinarily loud in the eerie silence while a strange draught fanned her face. She only faltered when, having gone some distance, they reached the point where retreat was possible but going further meant going all the way. She thought of the 1902 roof fall and admitted to Nigel that she was scared.

"I'd be surprised if you weren't," he said. "I think it will be better if you lead; that way you'll be able to see the light at the far mouth. Don't worry I'll still hold your hand—come on."

They restarted, plodding on steadily, and finally emerged out at the other end. They sat together in the long grass beside the line while Bobbie reflected on the most unusual walk of her life. "We have to go back through," Nigel said. "There's no way I know of over the fields."

Bobbie was keen to relive the experience. On Nigel's insistence that railwaymen always faced the direction of traffic they crossed over the tracks and now walked down the up main line. This time the Staffordshire Blue lair held no terrors. But at about the halfway point Nigel stopped and listened. Sure enough the rails were 'singing'. He knew what that meant.

"A train's coming!" he exclaimed."Get into a recess quick; it may be on this track." Bobbie seemed rooted to the spot. "Come on!" he shouted. They ran stumbling in the darkness to the nearest refuge. A whistle screamed as they pressed their bodies into the niche.

"It's on the up," Nigel shouted in Bobbie's ear. Further words were lost as a crescendo of sound filled the tunnel carried on the vortex of displaced air. Bobbie was trembling but she had to steal a look. She saw in the enveloping fog of smoke and steam the twin lamps of an express passenger as it sped past in a draught that threatened to tear the clothes off their backs. She saw, too, people in the coaches oblivious to her on their subterranean journey. As silence returned and the sulphurous gases thinned the pair hurried out to fresh air and daylight.

"That must've been a returning excursion," Nigel said. "I'm a fool not to have looked on the special notices." There was an edge to his voice that Bobbie had not heard before.

They continued their walk back to the crossing but neither spoke until they had regained the safety and familiarity of the crossing and stile. "I shouldn't have taken you in there," Nigel continued to remonstrate.

"Don't be cross with me," Bobbie pleaded.

"I'm not, I'm just angry with myself and, well, I suppose it's because I care about you."

"Oh, Nigel," said Bobbie, "come here and let me show you something." She moved to the boundary fence and pointed out a particular post. Carved into the wood the writing was still legible: 'R. loves M.P.' (Mike Pender of The Searchers) but beneath in much larger letters was the inscription 'R. loves N'.

"And I still do."

Nigel laughed away his embarrassment. "Oh, you should find someone nearer your own age, someone with a sports car, a good career, and who doesn't still live with his Mum."

"But I don't want to," replied Bobbie. "If I meet a boy, he's nothing more than a *bambino*. Like my father you are a real man."

With the aid of Bobbie's pocket mirror they realised how dirty both of them were. Hands and faces were streaked and blackened. "Come back to number four with me and clean up," Nigel suggested, "and I'll have the trainset running too."

Bobbie did not refuse the offer, and hand in hand they made their way to Nigel's house. Mrs Frost was not at home. A note to the effect lay on the kitchen table. Nigel gave Bobbie directions to the bathroom and, having sent her upstairs, busied himself making tea. He took the tray of refreshments up to his room then set the Dublo 8F to chase its brake van with a long line of mineral wagons loaded with real coal. It was then Bobbie came out of the bathroom with only a towel around her. She was carrying her clothes and had clearly done more than simply freshen up.

"Oh," she said," I thought you were still downstairs."

She must not have heard the creaking of the stairs nor the sound of the railway running, but Nigel took his leave and left her to dress. Yet on his return she was still admiring the layout, clad in only the towel. At a loss for words, Nigel indicated to her that the tea was growing cold, so they sat together on his bed and enjoyed the tea and biscuits. Nigel was aware of how near, yet also how far, Bobbie was from him. How easily he could snatch away the towel. But, no, his respect for her was greater than the naughty ideas in his head. She would have to make the first move.

While *Denbigh Castle* fictitiously sped on towards sunny Carmarthen, Bobbie murmured her thanks for a lovely afternoon and added that she would not be asking him to take her through any more tunnels. She kissed his cheek and again lustful images crossed Nigel's mind, but any thoughts of action were dismissed when he heard his mother return. He wasn't sure if he was relieved or not to hear her voice. Yet she merely called up that to say that she was visiting a neighbour and would make supper later. But Bobbie decided she ought to leave so Nigel stood up and, being a gentleman, turned his back so she might dress discreetly, but actually, from his vantage point, Nigel could see her clearly in his wardrobe door mirror. He watched her discard the towel, and ogled at her breasts and the dark curls below her navel. He longed to touch her, but staring at her surreptitiously brought pangs of guilt so he averted his gaze, and when he looked again she was fully clothed. Before Bobbie left Nigel, he arranged for her to accompany him again on a session of late-night photography, one that he hoped would be more successful than the last.

On Saturday evening the colour light signal in the cutting once again shone brilliant green, proving their greater efficiency over the old oil-lit semaphores. Nigel explained about the train they'd met in the tunnel. "It wasn't a special, but the 11.40 Birkenhead running an hour late. The Brush diesel had failed at Leamington, and Tyseley Loco sent out 6831 *Bearley Grange* to assist. It did very well, apparently, even making up some time with 12 on and 100 tons of D1690."

The train signalled earlier, a 4-car DMU, passed on its way, according to the destination blind, to Aylesbury, and the signal reverted to red. Yet only a few minutes later the bass Stanier hooter was heard from the direction of the tunnel and Class 5 45218 passed with steam shut off and the van wheels squealing in protest as the brakes took effect. "One of your hero's best machines," Nigel commented. "Wait here, it will make a fantastic shot."

He scurried away through the cutting alongside the stationary train. The firebox doors were open as the 4-6-0 stood waiting patiently at the signal, illuminating the driver leaning over the cabside and the chalk face of the cutting for the ultimate study in night photography. The driver appeared not to notice the flash that split the gloom as at the same moment the safety valves lifted and the signal changed to green. The driver drained the cylinder cocks, opened the regulator and got his train on the move.

Nigel enthused about how he would send the photograph off to railway magazines and hopefully see his work published, then spoke at length about shutter speeds and exposures, but all Bobbie wanted was to go home now that the night had turned cold. She suggested they bought fish and chips on the way and Nigel readily concurred. As they approached Spicer's Crossing the late turn man cycled down the lane on his way to a pint at the 'Rose and Crown'; his departure so prompt that as the pair reached the cabin door the 7-5-5 'Closing Signal Box' bell code was still being rung by the signalmen at both Loudwater and Wooburn Green.

Bobbie retrieved the key to the cabin from beneath an old sleeper and within a few minutes had relit the oil lamp, and both she and Nigel were enjoying their meal whilst listening to Radio Luxembourg. Bobbie knew that no one was going to disturb them as her parents had gone to Wales for the weekend to visit Ted Davies. She and Nigel had the whole place to themselves and could do just what they liked.

Chapter Eight

"Now, Ben," said Ted Davies as he and the Gherardinis sat digesting their lunch in his parlour, "tell me about the train that crashed through your gates. I told you it would happen one day." Mr Gherardini was drawing on a large cigar at that moment so it was Mrs Gherardini who took up the tale.

"It was on a Friday in June. A young man comes up and introduces himself as deputy assistant to the Assistant, or whatever, one of the new breed of officers that has a degree in railway management but doesn't know one end of a Hornby engine from the other. Anyway, after a few minutes he remarks to Ben that the lamps aren't lit on the gates and he should set about relighting them. Me, I'm trimming the hedge in our garden, so I see and hear everything."

"Yes," her husband broke in, "he said to me didn't I understand that the big red targets on the gates are my stop signals and the lamps above them must be lit during hours of darkness."

"But, in June," Ted said, "no trains run when it's dark."

"Exactly," replied Mrs Gherardini, as she continued the tale, "so he adds pompously 'and in fog and falling snow.' By now it's getting quite amusing and there's a train signalled from Loudwater, but Ben still goes up the line to the oil shed, hearing the 'train on line' signal ring as he went. Ben fills his can, turns to walk back and sees that matey has only opened the gates and let a car go across! Ben drops the can and runs down the line shouting 'Treno!, Treno!' (Italian for train) then dives for cover into the allotments."

"Lucky I did," Ben said. "It was a just single diesel unit but it took both gates off. It was running brake-end leading so the driver was able to jump into the arms of the guard and escape the wreck of his cab. It was good fortune no one at all was hurt."

For afternoon entertainment Ted planned to show Ben an area of Barry Docks. So leaving the ladies shopping in Cardiff, Ben drove his Fiat Multipla to Woodham's Brothers scrapyard where sidings filled with condemned steam locomotives rusted in the hostile air off the Bristol Channel. WR types predominated, but other regions were represented even to include BR 9Fs 92207 and 92245, both less than seven years old. Several indigenous 0-6-2 and 2-8-0 tank engines (rarely seen in the Home Counties) were there, details of which Mr Gherardini scribbled down for the benefit of his daughter. Of express passenger engines, two 'Kings' were noted, 6023/24, five 'Castles', four 'West Countries', four 'Merchant Navies', 35006/9/18/25 and a 'Jubilee', 45699. Also of particular interest were 2-8-0s 53808/9 off the Somerset and Dorset. Some locomotives were in various stages of scrapping but the majority stood in forlorn rows awaiting the cutting torch. It was quite a moving experience.

It was not the case of a late drive back home for the Gherardinis as they were staying over until the following day. That evening Mr and Mrs Davies treated their guests to a buffet supper and a choice of wines and the time was spent most convivially.

Over 100 miles away in Buckinghamshire, the atmosphere in Spicer's Crossing cabin was equally convivial as Bobbie

Gherardini had raided her father's wine cellar, insisting that a glass (or two) of claret should accompany their meal and entertainment from Radio Luxembourg. Later, appetites satiated, Bobbie turned off her radio, and Nigel took this to be a cue for him to take his leave so he stood and thanked his hostess for a very pleasant evening.

Despite the late hour Bobbie seemed reluctant to let the evening end. "You don't have to go," she said, "there's still some wine left. Why not come up to the house? My Mum and Dad are away."

Nigel too was enjoying Bobbie's company very much so he readily agreed to her suggestion. He watched while she secured the cabin then followed her up to Spicer's Crossing house, he carrying the wine and glasses, she the radio.

In the kitchen Bobbie served the remainder of the claret then tuned her transistor radio in again to 208. Cher was singing solo, without husband Sonny, 'All I Really Want To Do' but the quality of the music fluctuated so Bobbie made a suggestion. "Let's take our drinks and listen to it in my bedroom. You get better reception upstairs."

Somewhere within the house a clock chimed 12 midnight, and once in her private retreat Bobbie let Nigel nervously admire her wallpaper for a moment before she beckoned him to sit beside her on her double bed (it once belonged to her parents) and quaff the last of the wine.

Later, that same clock was heard to chime 12.30 and Nigel once again hinted that perhaps it was time for him to leave but Bobbie caught his sleeve. "Stay a bit longer—just while I freshen up. I have some old photographs for you to look at".

Nigel, still in no hurry to go, agreed to stay whilst Bobbie visited the bathroom. In her absence he studied the snapshots she'd given him. Of particular interest was an

Edwardian-looking scene, judging by the dress of the onlookers, of an outside-framed 4-4-0 having crashed through the gates with an excursion train. On the back was a note from Ted Davies: 'It happens to every crossing keeper at least once in their career!'

Also of interest was a photograph of a younger Bobbie Gherardini in the front vestibule of the auto-coach on the push/pull 'Marlow Donkey'. Nigel flipped the view over but no details were written on the back. Bobbie rejoined him at that moment and read his thoughts. "It was taken at Bourne End, when I was ten," she said, "but I've changed a bit since then!"

Bobbie was clad in a dressing gown and it did not take Nigel long to wonder if that was all she was wearing. She certainly wasn't wearing a bra, for as often as she pulled the garment around her, it fell open. She smiled when she caught him staring at her cleavage.

"Is that a gun in your pocket, Nigel! Or are you pleased to see me?"

"I didn't know you could quote Mae West," the young man said in reply.

"There's probably a lot you don't know about me," Bobbie continued as she sidled up to Nigel and took his hands, "like I don't want to be alone in this old house tonight."

Nigel was taken aback by the implications of her words and mumbled something about permanent way men on night jobs would get their heads down in guards vans, on station seats, or wherever an opportunity presented itself. He offered to sleep in a chair but, no, Bobbie wanted him to share her bed.

Nigel had long dreamed of sleeping with the girl but, having so much respect for her, had shied away from taking any initiative. Yet here she was making the first move. It was great encouragement, and of course simplicity itself, to divest

Bobbie of her dressing gown and to discover that, no, she was not wearing anything else at all.

With such a wealth of feminine charms available to him, Nigel was like a child in a sweet shop. He was still fully dressed until Bobbie decided she should even the score. How she nearly swooned when something sprang out to greet her, defying the laws of gravity and reminding her of the cobra she'd seen on a nature programme. No sooner was Bobbie stretched out on her bed than Nigel was upon her; however, he did manage to pause and relish the moment he'd long dreamed of until he could delay his intentions no longer, or ignore the want in the girl's eyes.

To date, Bobbie's sex education had been purely theoretical; that learned from a tattered copy of *Fanny Hill* passed around the school playground and the Mother Superior's shameless tales of her astrological journeys she'd had with her husband the night before. So when Mars entered her Venus, Bobbie realised with a gasp the truth of the good lady's words and for the next few minutes, had Mr and Mrs Gherardini been at home they would have heard their daughter enjoying herself enormously.

Yet, as wonderful as the experience was, Bobbie felt that something somehow had eluded her. Pulling the bedclothes around her she reached for her cigarettes and concealed her frustration by lighting up. After inhaling deeply she offered it to Nigel who, although a non-smoker, accepted a drag before passing it back. With no parental eye to disapprove and one shot of nicotine seemingly insufficient, Bobbie lit another cigarette but wisely opened her bedroom window in case her parents detected a smell of tobacco smoke when they returned.

It was as Bobbie and Nigel shared the second cigarette that, with words unspoken, they agreed there just had to be an encore performance. "I've heard it's better the other way round," Bobbie murmured, heeding again the Mother Superior's words of wisdom. "Me on top of you!"

Nigel needed little persuasion and, back on the bed, Bobbie was quickly astride, and impaled upon, her lover. She began to move her body rhythmically up and down above him, her breasts bouncing around in a most erotic manner as she gained momentum. But such intense passion could only be finite, and when Bobbie's big moment came at last, she shared it with Nigel, and the sounds of her ecstasy carried far on the night air through her open window, making the neighbourhood dogs start barking.

Thoroughly spent, the lovers slipped beneath the bedclothes and slept until the dawn chorus woke them at 5 a.m. Nigel declined Bobbie's offer of breakfast as, although he did not admit to it, he was anxious to be home before his mother discovered his absence.

After Nigel had left, Bobbie worried that when her parents came home they would know what she had done. But only a sparkle in her eyes gave any clue that she had crossed the threshold into womanhood.

As it happened, Nigel called round to see Bobbie again later that same day. He had, he said, an important message for her. But whilst there he took advantage of the absence of the old Fiat Multipla, and bedded the crossing keeper's daughter for a third time. The fact that Mr and Mrs Gherardini might've put in an appearance at any moment added an exciting element of urgency to the sex. It was as Nigel was leaving that he remembered the message he was meant to deliver. It was regarding a vacancy at the bookstall on High Wycombe Station and would Bobbie be interested? The prospect was not immediately appealing as it was not railway work, but after some consideration she decided to contact the manager, a Mr Peter Vere, after all.

In due course Bobbie was invited to attend an interview and short trial for the job on the bookstall. She was keen to tell Nigel her news, and as she had not seen him for several days decided to call at his home. Bobbie had heard, too, of a fatality on the line among the men in his gang so she was also curious to know the circumstances surrounding the tragedy. But when Bobbie approached Inglis Terrace she sensed something was wrong as even though it was still daylight all curtains were tightly closed. In answer to her knocking, the door eventually opened a little and the face of Mrs Frost peered out. Her drawn features and red eyes made her appear almost a stranger.

"Is—is Nigel in?" Bobbie stammered, filled with terrible misgivings.

Mrs Frost wiped her eyes on her apron before she answered.

"You won't have heard then," she said. "My son, he's—he's dead. He was run down by a train. It was his funeral only yesterday, and—" But no further words were audible as Mrs Frost hid her face in her hands and wept for the loss of her son.

It was some moments before Mrs Frost regained her composure. "I'm packing up his railway set," she sniffed. "It's going to his nephew. I hope he takes care of it, but he's a right little tearaway. Come on up and choose something. It's what Nigel would have wished."

Bobbie surveyed the part-dismantled layout and brushed away her own tears. She chose a water crane for her bedroom mantelpiece. "Is that all, dear, wouldn't you like something else?" Then Bobbie noticed the AL1 electric locomotive E3002. "It's never been played with," Mrs Frost said, her tone indicating that not necessarily all items were on the disposal list.

"No," Bobbie said, "nor shall it ever." The two women's eyes met and both imagined the young new owner running everything to destruction. Mrs Frost decided that the locomotive did indeed deserve a better fate.

Before Bobbie left she learned the details of Nigel's death. "It was like this," Mrs Frost said. "They were busy near the tunnel—so close he came home for his dinner. In the afternoon, when they'd just about done for the day, he whistles to his mates to stand clear for the up 'Cambrian' but he steps back into the 'four-foot' on the down into the path of one of them little parcel diesel things coming out of the tunnel quietly like so as to stop at the red light in the cutting, and well, he wasn't struck bad, more pushed like, but by the time they'd run to the 'Mother Redcap' to telephone for an ambulance it was too late. My son," she finished, her voice faltering, "looked out for everyone, but when it mattered no one looked out for him."

Chapter Nine

"I remember you from last time," the elderly ticket inspector said to Bobbie Gherardini as she explained her situation. "I hope you have better luck today. The bookstall is on this platform, number two, and Mr Vere is expecting you."

The crossing keeper's daughter smiled her thanks, and within a few moments was facing the laden counter of the establishment she was hoping to work for. The bookstall was quiet that morning of September 20th, but someone knew she was there.

"Won't keep you a moment," a voice called, and in a minute the face to which the voice belonged rose from below the counter. "What can I get you, love?"

"Well, nothing, Mr Vere, thank you," Bobbie replied. "I'm Miss Roberta Gherardini and I have come to work here, perhaps."

Mr Vere stared at Bobbie almost in disbelief for several seconds."Gosh! I mean, sorry! Have you really?" he said, and extended a hand across the counter to squeeze Bobbie's hand politely. "I'm Pete Vere. Come on round."

Bobbie did as he requested and joined him on the business side of the establishment, and within the next ten minutes, while he served a number of customers, gave him a resumé of herself while he in turn described the services of the bookstall.

An express ran in on the up platform line and a breathless

gentleman came, demanding a newspaper before he missed his train.

"Don't worry, you have several minutes yet," Bobbie reassured him. The passenger calmed noticeably and smiled at Bobbie as he left. "It's the 7.10 Shrewsbury," she said to Vere, "last stop Leamington. They must've had a good run up as now they'll be waiting 'time'."

The words were hardly out of her mouth when they heard the shriek of a guard's whistle, the answering hoot from the diesel, and the train opposite them begin to move out. Bobbie was mortified as it dawned on her that the new winter timetable was in force. Not surprisingly a disgruntled passenger returned to buy a magazine, and to ask if giving incorrect information was a ploy to generate sales as he now faced a lengthy wait for the next fast train to Paddington or caught the imminent, but slow, stopping train to Marylebone. Vere apologised profusely and as a gesture of goodwill refused payment for the magazine.

Bobbie agreed to deal with the next customer herself, but as a tall figure approached wearing a black overcoat and hat her enthusiasm turned to dismay. It was Chief Inspector Rees-Black. He recognised her at once but spoke only to Vere.

"Is my 'usual' in yet?"

"No, Sir. Try again tomorrow."

Rees-Black nodded then chose some items he wanted that morning. Vere did the totting up. "That comes to six shillings and eightpence." Bobbie took the pound note that Rees-Black offered, but under his penetrating eyes her mental arithmetic deserted her completely.

"Er, wh—what's six and eight from a pound?"

"Thirteen and fourpence," growled the chief inspector.

As Rees-Black took his change and left, a disappointed Peter Vere remonstrated with Bobbie.

"You must do better than that. I'll have no customers after a week!"

Poor Bobbie said nothing, but the tears welled up in her eyes. Vere, realising that he'd been too quick to admonish her, made a gesture of comfort—and to his surprise the girl, a stranger an hour before, fell in to his arms and cried bitterly, the stress of an interview, Rees-Black, and the loss of Nigel Frost all coming to the fore in her tears. Vere gave Bobbie his handkerchief and as she dried her eyes he said, "Look, I'm sorry. Forget about the Chief; you'll soon pick it up, that is, if you want to. Go away and think about it and let me know."

Bobbie left him to yet more customers and walked the length of the platform and continued down the subway and up to platform three on the London-bound side. She met Rees-Black again as he left his office. He sarcastically presumed she possessed a platform ticket before he went on his way, leaving Bobbie to retrace her steps back to tell Mr Vere that she couldn't possibly take the job under any circumstances.

As she returned to the bookstall Vere looked at her enquiringly. "I'll start as soon as you want me," she said.

Bobbie's last day at the bakery was a sad occasion as the Mother Superior had decided that she no longer wanted to work without her young friend and she was leaving too. A party was arranged for them on the Friday evening of October 1st.

It was a small affair but with plenty of stale buns and cakes to eat. The baker's wife joined them and Bobbie realised she would not miss that querulous soul, nor the uncouth delivery boy, but she was going to miss the dog, and she made a fuss of him whenever an opportunity arose. Someone else would have to do the walking now. As if reading her thoughts the mutt whined to be let out and Bobbie obliged. In the back yard the Morris 'J' delivery van stood silent, but Bobbie's attention was directed to the flour store above. There was a light on up there which puzzled her and sounds of what she took to be people fighting. Ascending the steps to the store she peeped in and was amazed to see the Mother Superior, naked from the waist down, and the baker spanking her huge posterior. The punishment was clearly foreplay as after a few more hearty slaps she rolled onto the sacks of flour and spread her plump thighs to accommodate her tormentor.

Bobbie blinked back a tear remembering her own night of passion with Nigel, but watched in awe as the pair had sex in front of her. The activity was brief and urgent and the Mother Superior came to a climax very quickly, muting her cries as best she could. Bobbie stole away at this point, to collect the dog and rejoin the party. Moments later the lovers returned too, both taking pains to ignore each other completely. Bobbie looked at the baker's wife and wondered if she knew what was going on. She recalled previous occasions when the Mother Superior had appeared red-faced and dusty with flour following an urgent request for stocktaking. As the baker's wife could no longer manage stairs the flour store was an ideal love eyrie.

Before too long the party wound down—there being a finite number of times one could appreciate 'If you gotta go, go now' by Manfred Mann. But tearful farewells would be held back until the morrow, their last working day. Nevertheless, it was the time for gifts. The baker's gift to the Mother Superior for services rendered (which were what exactly, Bobbie wondered) was a conventional handbag. But for Bobbie there was a heavy item wrapped up in a Daily Sketch; it was a cast-iron shed-code plate (84F), something normally found on the smokebox of a steam locomotive.

"I found it here as I was closing up one evening, some years ago," the baker explained. "Someone said it might've been nicked off a loco in Wooburn yard as a souvenir or was left on the footplate when the engine was transferred to these parts. Either way it must be ever so old. I used it as a paperweight."

Bobbie expressed her thanks for the unusual present. She knew that London Division sheds were numbered '81' and the '84' series hailed originally from the Wolverhampton area before those former Great Western sheds were transferred to the LMR. 84F had once been Stourbridge Junction.

Bobbie's first day on the station bookstall was Monday 4th October, her seventeenth birthday, and when she made the tea for their elevenses she realised how tired she felt. The bakery would never see such custom in all its existence.

The colloquial name for the bookstall was the 'Toad', a somewhat unwholesome term for an establishment that in addition to magazines, paperbacks and newspapers, sold sweets and cigarettes. But 'Toad' was appropriate as the structure strongly resembled a GWR type brake van. The enclosed section provided a store area while the open 'verandah' end encompassed the serving counter. The crossing keeper's daughter and Mr Vere got on well together, and while mental arithmetic was a cause for concern, Bobbie would smile and giggle at her own ineptitude which only served to enhance her popularity. Their environment was similar to working in the corridor of an express train but without the swaying. In such a confined space bodily contact was inevitable and although initially accompanied with apologies, touch became commonplace and later intentional. Bobbie felt sure her new career in the 'Toad' was going to be a very happy one.

Although she knew from what Nigel Frost had said to her that Jon Rice worked in the permanent way gang, thankfully the awful youth had yet to be a customer. However, she understood he was working in Reading where she hoped his temporary posting would last until, at least, he retired.

* * *

Chief inspector Rees-Black was still very much as irksome as ever. Bobbie did not serve him often but when she did she bore the brunt of his sarcasm. One morning he stood beside a woman Bobbie was serving and implored the passenger to tender the correct money as she would never get the right change, and on another occasion he claimed it would be to everyone's benefit if items were priced in lire. One morning he presented himself at the bookstall while Vere was away at a wholesalers. "Tell Vere I want my usual," he demanded.

"He's not here," Bobbie replied. She never called him 'Sir' like others did. She knew this antagonised him.

"You'll have to give it to me then," he said. "It'll be under the counter in a large envelope with my name on. And be quick about it."

Bobbie found the envelope which Rees-Black simply snatched from her grasp and hurried off. "It's already paid for!" he shouted back.

Mr Vere returned at this point and Bobbie asked him what exactly Rees-Black's 'usual' was. Vere's reply was somewhat evasive. "A fishing magazine, I expect. A lot of people have things put by."

Some three weeks later as they were closing on the Monday evening, a delivery of 'specials' came in. Bobbie noticed one addressed to Mr Rees-Black. It was agreed that they would sort them out next day, so as Bobbie locked up she slipped the awful man's order into her bag. It was merely a question of safe keeping, she reasoned. Later that evening in the privacy of her bedroom, she prised open the envelope and was shocked by what she saw. In two magazines of American origin were photographs of naked or semi-naked women.

It was the next morning that Rees-Black stood glowering before her. "Your 'usual' came in," Bobbie said, "but I gave them to your wife. She wanted something to read on the train to London. She's on platform three now."

"You did what?" the gentleman gasped in horror. Young lady, you must get those magazines back at once." He snatched up a copy of 'Woman's Realm' while looking anxiously back down the line to see if the expected train was coming. "Give her this," he said, and thrust the magazine along with a ten shilling note into Bobbie's hands. "You can run faster than me."

"I won't be long," Bobbie said to a puzzled Vere, who had just come through from the storeroom and with that she hurried away to all intents and purposes on her errand, having not given Mrs Rees-Black anything at all and once out of sight gave the 'Woman's Realm' to the the first lady she met.

Returning to the 'Toad', Bobbie sneaked in through the store to get to the counter and present a visibly relieved Rees-Black with his 'usual'. "Kindly do not encumber my wife again with my magazines," he said. He turned to go, but stopped, cleared his throat and added quietly, "I'm obliged to you, Miss. Keep the change."

Bobbie maintained her interest in the trains that passed. Few of the express trains from Paddington to Birmingham and beyond called at High Wycombe. Those that did call provided a higher level of activity not only involving the station staff but also those on the bookstall as well. There was an air of urgency whenever a fast train was due, none more so than when the Pullman diesel called at 10.38 a.m. as the 10.10 a.m. Paddington to Birmingham. Originating from Wolverhampton earlier in the day it would pass majestically through on the up main at 9 a.m. but condescend to grace the platform at High Wycombe on its return north, and so much anxiety surrounded its arrival and departure that what should have been an exciting event was quite spoiled. Woe betide any railwayman (or passenger) who delayed that premier service. Bobbie learned that several local dignitaries used the Pullman. Peter Vere explained how he had once met a Miss Mary O'Brian. But devoid of make-up and wearing an overcoat it was only later (after Rees-Black had pointed her out) that he realised he had served the singer Dusty Springfield.

Again from the spotting days Bobbie recalled The Cambrian Coast Express, 9.45 Aberystwyth and 11.10 Paddington, but neither called at High Wycombe, and while the titles still appeared in timetables no train carried the once familiar name-board. In any case the smokebox- shaped feature simply did not look right on a diesel.

Although Bobbie Gherardini and Peter Vere were not employed by BR they were both a part of the railway fraternity, and as the weeks passed Bobbie got to know many railwaymen.

As several trains terminated at High Wycombe the drivers became familiar too as they passed their time before starting back. Former Neasden men (now based at Marylebone since the closure of the shed) were responsible for the main line suburban services, while the Maidenhead branch was worked by Slough men. One particularly young driver, when being served, would incline his head towards Bobbie and ask Vere out of the corner of his mouth, "Have you nobbed it yet? You know, have you dipped your wick?" Pete Vere always pretended not to understand and wondered if the driver was the same individual who had scratched out three letters on the enamel sign by the ticket barrier, to read ALL TITS MUST BE

SHEWN HERE.

In the evenings when going home, Bobbie caught the 5.24 departure through to Wooburn Green. She often travelled with the guard in the brake compartment behind the cab of the single unit diesel. However, one evening in late November its nice driver invited her through to join him. He cared little now about regulations and spoke scathingly of railway management. Moreover, he insisted on stopping at Spicer's Crossing to allow Bobbie to alight there.

"I should be on the 'Thousands' to Bristol," he said bitterly. "But they reckoned I'd misread the signals. The guard was alongside me and agreed that we had all the 'boards' off at Loudwater but they refused to call him as a witness."

Bobbie realised that he was the driver who had run through the gates at Spicer's Crossing back in the summer.

Chapter Ten

Thursday December 1st saw Bobbie Gherardini opening the first window on her Advent calendar, and by the time she and Mr Vere were having their morning coffee she had persuaded him to agree to putting up Christmas decorations later over the 'Toad'.

Since starting work on the station Bobbie realised that, although the passenger service remained similar to when she first experienced it, the freight traffic had fallen off dramatically. Nevertheless, despite the absence of clanking WD 2-8-0s, once so familiar, some interesting freight did still appear. Of note were the trains of new stock for the London Underground. From the manufacturer in Birmingham the new coaches were transferred from BR to the LTE at West Ruislip. These trains were often hauled by English Electric Type 4 diesels, more usually seen on the West Coast main line. But early that December a special freight drew to a stand on the down main, making a particularly sorry sight.

Hauled by a Western class diesel, the load consisted of two withdrawn Merchant Navy 4-6-2s. With much of the motion removed the Bulleid 'box pok' wheels were clearly visible. The guard came to the 'Toad' to stock up on tobacco, and the cortege was, he explained, bound for Tyseley where another engine (a Hall, he thought) was to be added for the final journey to Barry. However, the engines seemed reluctant to make that final journey as both had developed hot axle boxes, and for the time being were going no further than Wycombe North yard. The C-C diesel returned 'light' to Old Oak Common.

However, steam did return briefly in reality the following week when the locomotive off the morning Banbury– Wycombe North yard freight required to run round its train before the return trip could be made. Normally this warranted a short run up to the Middle box to use the crossover there. But this particular day news travelled fast that the train was steam-hauled and the Wycombe Middle signalman decided he was unable to complete the manoeuvre and sent the LMR 8F on to the South box instead, thereby ensuring a greater audience for the 2-8-0 and its enthusiastic crew. The safety valves lifted as the engine moved over the points and charged tender-first back through the station with the regulator wide open; the fireman waving and the driver pipping the hooter to acknowledge those looking on. However, few envied them their journey back to Banbury, as despite the bulk of the tender there would be scant protection from the elements.

On the morning of Monday, December 13th, Bobbie arrived for work laden with Christmas decorations, and early that same afternoon the 'Toad' took on a festive appearance, and even Rees-Black approved. On the days leading up to Christmas record takings were realised.

December 24th was a Friday in 1965 and the news was that MP for Blackburn, Mrs Barbara Castle, had been elected the new Minister of Transport. That day too a glass of punch was available for a shilling, served by Bobbie appropriately dressed in an inappropriate Santa suit. The seasonal wear had been supplied from Mrs Gherardini's primary school drama group and intended for girls of no more than eleven years; consequently it showed Bobbie's figure to advantage, and was so short in length it barely covered the tops of her stockings.

Attired as she was, Pete Vere found his young assistant made him feel incredibly horny, and every chance he got he followed her into the stockroom, knowing full well he would have a splendid view when she bent over. Naïve Bobbie Gherardini suspected nothing!

The punch was non-alcoholic (more or less!), but passengers alighting from trains who took more than one glass were observed to stumble on the way to the station car park. Mrs Castle's breathalyser was still eighteen months away.

It had been agreed that because it was Christmas Eve they would stay open later than usual and close following the departure of the Fridays-only 6.05 p.m. Paddington–Birmingham, calling specially at High Wycombe. Few people were going up to London but large numbers were still coming away.

Pete Vere was making a start on cashing up as the train drew in, the secondman already standing in the cab doorway looking back for his driver, both impatient for the 'right away'. But such was the volume of passengers alighting that platform time cost them some four minutes' delay and probably as many as seven overall. But as D1682 accelerated away with '12 on', the platform very quickly became deserted, and as Bobbie wound down the shutters on the 'Toad' she and Vere surveyed the denuded shelves and the drained punch bowl and smiled wearily.

The silence was tangible. "Right," Mr Vere said, "I must be off home. I've got to check my boy's Scalex—". He stopped abruptly. He'd never let on that he was married or that he had a son. "I have some things to sort out for tomorrow."

But Bobbie was not going to let him get away quite so easily.

"First," she said. "First, I have to change—my mother got me into this and you'll have to help me take it off!" She grabbed his tie, and putting it over her shoulder, used it to tow him not unwillingly into the store area.

In the privacy of the stockroom she turned her back on her colleague and made him unzip the Santa suit so that she could divest herself of it, a task Vere gladly performed. It was not his intention to undo her bra as well, but observing that only the middle hook of three was serving any purpose he felt that some adjustment was necessary. But under his fumbling fingers the straps sprang apart completely and defied recovery.

"Oh, that's naughty," Bobbie said, and turned to admonish her boss while attempting to hide her breasts, but the more she tried the less she succeeded, and she gave up and removed her bra completely,dropping her hands and spreading them by way of apology.

"Look at me," she said, giving Vere an open invitation to stare at her, "I'm a freak! All the girls at school said so."

"They must have been jealous." Vere replied. "I should be the one apologising, but don't catch cold, come here."

Bobbie stepped towards him and he hugged her close then moved to kiss her on the cheek, but to his surprise and delight she turned her mouth to meet his and they had their first real kiss. Although reluctant to let go, Vere did push her away slightly as he simply couldn't let the opportunity of touching her breasts pass, something he had dreamed of doing ever since they'd first met. He expected a rebuke, but none came. Bobbie could have disengaged herself at any time, but she did not.

Just where the situation might have led is uncertain as there came a rapping on the door and a reminder from Rees-Black. "It's Christmas Eve! Haven't you got homes to go to?"

"Goodness! It's seven thirty!" Vere exclaimed. But how much he'd wanted time to stand still.

He left Bobbie to dress, and a little later at the station

entrance they exchanged presents before finally going their separate ways. It was a happy Christmas, and over the holiday both secretly anticipated how their friendship might progress.

As it happened it developed just a week later before the old year was out. One of the evening DMU services from Marylebone would set down its passengers, then shunt and wait a considerable length of time in the bay siding before returning as empty stock. It was in this 8-car set, Bobbie had insisted on a first class compartment, that Pete Vere finally 'dipped his wick', and it was not to be the only occasion.

A.D.1966 brought no surprises regarding the future of the railways. Harold Wilson's Labour Government had pledged to reconsider many aspects of the Beeching Plan, but nevertheless whole routes were to close, notably the Somerset and Dorset, much of the Great Central, and the Waverley route in the Border Counties. Nearer to home the new image gained momentum as locomotives were outshopped in blue, reminiscent of the early, short-lived British Railways livery, and coaches received a blue and pearl grey scheme. The station signs in brown with cream text were discarded for replacements with black letters on a white background.

It was against this changing scene that Bobbie remembered the huge success of the seasonally bedecked bookstall, and had the brainwave to celebrate the sixtieth anniversary of the first trains to run on the new line to London. Passenger services from the rebuilt station had begun from 2nd April 1906 and to commemorate the event it was decided to hold a small exhibition with a transport theme.

The display began with Bobbie's collage of the penny-farthing which had not seen the light of day since that hot afternoon at Loudwater School in 1959. She would have liked her Art teacher to have seen it again, and wondered how many other contributions still existed.

Many railwaymen possessed a train set, but acquiring donations for the exhibition proved far from straightforward as few models were available commercially that were representative of the motive power used on the line. There were no Austerity 2-8-0s, for example; no L1 or Fairburn Tanks, and the response was far greater than expected. Many men took offence when their prized locomotive was not chosen.

The booking office clerk had a beautiful Midland 'Spinner' 4-2-2 by Bing but, in Gauge 2, it would have completely overshadowed all other models. The gauge chosen was 00, and on Triang 'Series 3" track the locomotives that finally made the display were the Kitmaster 'Rocket' (made by Vere), Triang's Dean 'Single', Hornby Dublo's Castle, 7032, and the Trix D1000 Class diesel. An appropriate addition would have been the Triang 'Blue Pullman' but nothing was offered. To conclude, as an indication of the future of railways in general, Bobbie's E3002 electric was added at the last minute.

The sixtieth anniversary exhibition of the opening of the new line proved popular and Bobbie's penny-farthing created much interest. Back in 1959 Bobbie had not taken seriously her teacher's words that the penny was of significant value. Nor had she said anything to her parents; consequently it had been put away and forgotten. But now a railwayman took an exceptional interest in the exhibition and in the penny-farthing particularly. Over the few days that the exhibition ran he discovered that the 1933 penny had been found on land his family now owned.

Bobbie's lusty appetite for sex, and her boss's willingness to please, ultimately led to their fall. One Friday evening, having closed early, they were oblivious to the fact that the bookstall's owner, a lady of German extract, was in High Wycombe intent on visiting her local establishment before returning to London.

An elderly lady, a potential customer, was nearby. "I think there's a religious meeting going on," she said. "I'm sure I heard a girl call out 'Jesus, I'm coming'."

So with the 'Toad' shut but lights on within, the owner decided to investigate using her own key. She was appalled at what she saw. Both employees were naked, the girl spread-eagled upon the floor, while the manager was giving her enormous pleasure using only his fingers.

"Stop that at once!" the owner demanded indignantly.

To the lovers the sound of the formidable woman's voice was like the receipt of an electric shock. They sprang apart, and scrambled to get into some clothes in order to appear reasonably decent.

"What do you think you're doing, Vere? You should still be open!"

"We weren't doing any harm," Bobbie pleaded for them both.

"I wasn't talking to you, girl," the owner retorted. "But I'll tell you what you are doing Vere—you're leaving. Sacked! And you too, girl!"

The couple had no choice but to comply with the owner's demands. At the station entrance Bobbie burst into tears. "Oh, Pete," she wept. "I'm so sorry."

"I'm as much to blame. Look, don't worry too much. If Germany had won the World Cup she would have said nothing at all. She'll ask us back next week, you'll see." But the uncompromising Frau did not.

Chapter Eleven

"**M**iss Gherardini, it is Tuesday and the second time this week you have been late. It's not going to happen again, is it?"

"No, Mrs Denny."

How Bobbie wished that the shoe shop manageress was her friend the Mother Superior from the bakery days. But really it was the bus company that was at fault for not providing a reliable service; for an earlier bus Bobbie just could not rise from her bed, such was the enthusiasm she had for her work at the High Wycombe branch of Thames Valley Shoes.

By Thursday the bus was in trouble again with the engine stalling at every stop and traffic light. With a mile still to go it expired completely. "Have to wait for the next one I'm afraid, love" the bus conductress apologised, "in half hour's time."

Bobbie, however, refused to wait and decided to walk instead. Fearful of being late again and having seen a freight train struggling along the branch line a few moments earlier, she decided to use the railway as a short cut. Exhaust fumes from the NBL Bo-Bo diesel still lingered in the air as Bobbie scrambled up the embankment to the track. Yet she had barely walked ten yards when, to her amazement, she saw the same train coming back towards her. It only took a moment to realise that it was a breakaway, and that several wagons with the brake van leading were running back towards Loudwater.

As the raft of wagons approached, Bobbie saw that the

guard was winding on the handbrake in an effort to bring his half of the train to a stand. But he appeared not to be managing at all well. She never paused to consider the foolhardiness of jumping aboard a moving train, but she bravely did so, and inched her way along the continuous step to join the guard in his van. He was, she saw, deathly pale and sweating profusely.

"Help me, help me," he said, in a voice little more than a whisper. As Bobbie took his place and succeeded in applying more turns on the brake, the guard sat down weakly and clutched his chest to try and alleviate the worst of the pain. He was having a heart attack. Despite the falling gradient and the number of jostling wagons, Bobbie managed to bring the errant portion of train finally to a stand. Looking as though it was to be his last day on the planet, the guard explained that she must protect the train with detonators as, whilst the signalling regulations should prevent it, they were in danger of being run into by another train.

Taking the detonators the guard handed her, Bobbie got down onto the track and began running in the direction the breakaway had been heading. A poor judge of distance Bobbie put down three 'shots' at what she estimated to be a half-mile from the obstruction and then turned to run forward to repeat the procedure. As she passed the marooned wagons she saw that the guard had regained some colour to his face before she became aware of Wycombe's 350hp diesel shunter bearing down upon them, whistling furiously.

Bobbie ran ahead to warn the crew but it became obvious that the shunter had been sent out in search of the missing 'flock'. Bobbie joined the crew in the cab and they moved slowly off, stopping just short of the offending wagon with the broken link. It was difficult to talk above the noise of the engine, but Bobbie expressed her fears for the guard. But the driver was more concerned that the brakes were pinned down on the wagons before him.

"One nudge," he said, "and the buggers will be on their way again."

Using a coil of signal wire the secondman hooked his locomotive to the wagons, and leaving Bobbie alone in the cab, the driver went to the brake van. In a moment he was hurrying back.

"He's unconscious. We have to get him to hospital right away!." Addressing his mate, he said, "Once you've taken the brakes off you ride in the van." He then turned to Bobbie. "Think you can watch the improvised coupling for me?" Bobbie nodded in agreement. The driver smiled. "Good girl. Right—let's get moving!"

As fast as he dared allow it, the slack in the couplings was taken up and D3753 growled away up the bank towards High Wycombe. On arrival the priority was to summon an ambulance for the guard, and once he was safely despatched the wagon with the broken link was shunted out and the remaining wagons reunited with their train.

Back in Loudwater traffic began to move again. The signalman there, on receiving the alarming 'Train Running Away' signal from Wycombe South, had no option but to close his crossing gates to the road for the duration of the emergency to avoid a possible collision.

Mr Gherardini at Spicer's Crossing was also aware of the situation. His daughter meanwhile, her deeds of heroism over, belatedly continued on her way to Thames Valley Shoes. Bobbie had hardly got in the door before Mrs Denny pounced on her.

"Don't bother taking your coat off," she said, "you're not stopping."

"But you don't understand," Bobbie protested.

"I'll not hear a single word of excuses. Good morning!"

Alone on the pavement outside the shop Bobbie held back the tears as she considered what she should do. She dared not go home and announce to her parents that she had again been dismissed. She walked the streets, before finally ending up in the 'Castle Café'. The establishment was frequented mainly by lorry drivers, but Bobbie remained impervious to the stares and muttered comments.

Following her prolonged lunch she decided, for no particular reason, to visit the railway station. There she learned that the guard taken ill that morning was now a patient in Amersham Hospital. On impulse Bobbie decided to visit the gentleman and boarded a bus for the old market town. There, she discovered, those with heart conditions were nursed on Ward F. The ward sister on duty was initially quite reluctant to allow Bobbie to visit but eventually relented.

"He's a sick man and needs complete rest," she explained. "There's a member of his family here already but you may have five minutes."

The sister led Bobbie to the patient, and although he was asleep she spoke as if he could hear her.

"Mr Hawes, you have another visitor." She then turned to the man already seated at the bedside. "I said she may have five minutes. See that it is no more." With that she left the three alone. Bobbie smiled a greeting to the first visitor and then stared at him in amazement. It was Rees-Black!

"Oh!" she exclaimed, "I'm so sorry. I'll—I'll come back another time."

"Please don't go on my account," the inspector begged." My uncle and I owe you a big thank you."

"Your uncle?"

"Yes. Did you not know?"

Bobbie shook her head. "Is he going to be alright?" she asked.

"Apparently, yes. But from what the doctor has said, any more effort on that handbrake wheel would have been fatal. Uncle George and I are both convinced that you saved his life."

Bobbie was embarrassed by the praise and wished that poor Uncle George would wake up, but he slept peacefully on. The main evidence of life was the monitor he was connected up to, showing how his heart was functioning by a trace continuously flickering across the screen. Nourishment for him came in the form of intravenous fluids dripping slowly into his left arm.

For Bobbie it felt strange to be in such close company with the chief inspector; at one time there was no one she hated more. Yet without the long black coat and trilby hat there was nothing of the Gestapo about him; he was an anxious nephew, human and vulnerable. Bobbie appreciated his efforts at making light conversation.

"It seems that his train was stopped by signals on the approaches to High Wycombe," Rees-Black said. "Quite steep when coming off the branch. They get the road and pull away, probably too sharply if the truth were known, and a coupling hook gets metal fatigue."

"Every freight should be vacuum fitted," Bobbie said.

"What? Er, oh, yes," Rees-Black replied. "Yes of course. You might still have a severed link but never a runaway."

There was a silence then, broken only by a gentle snoring from Uncle George. Bobbie glanced at the ward clock, almost with relief. "I have had my five minutes now," Bobbie said. "Please give him my love when he wakes up."

"Of course, but I must be going too," Rees-Black said." I don't feel as if I'm achieving anything here. I'll return when he's less sedated. Look, why don't I give you a lift home? I live in Marlow and I can easily go the Wooburn Green way."

Bobbie refused at first but the inspector would not take no for an answer. Also Bobbie realised that she could be home within twenty minutes instead of two hours, so graciously accepted his offer.

Bobbie gently touched the guard's hand and softly said goodbye, and discreetly left Rees-Black for a moment of privacy with his uncle. The two visitors walked in silence down the steep corridor from Ward F and out to where Rees-Black had parked his car. He drove an impressive red Volkswagen Karmann-Ghia. He did not speak as he drove but Bobbie felt that on a number of occasions he seemed on the point of saying something profound only to close his mouth and concentrate on driving along the rural lanes.

Passing the Squirrel pub in Penn Street, Rees-Black braked sharply, put the car into reverse, and turned in to the car park.

"I need a drink," he said. "And maybe you would care for one too?" Bobbie accepted the offer and, seated at a window table, where they could watch the last of the daylight disappear, Rees-Black gave voice to what had been troubling him.

"You not only deserve a big thank you for helping my uncle," he said," I owe you an even bigger apology for being so unkind to you." Bobbie stared at him in surprise. "I treated you abominably," he continued. "And, well, I just want you to forgive me. Friends?"

"Friends."

At Bobbie's request he dropped her later at the foot of Juniper Lane. "Thank you for the lift—and the drink," she said.

"Not at all. I'm going to visit him again on Saturday. Er— would you care to join me? I know my uncle would like to see you." Without considering what she was agreeing to, Bobbie found herself accepting the invitation.

"Excellent. I'll pick you up here at 1.45, Saturday afternoon."

Bobbie stood lost in thought as she watched him drive away. It had been a roller coaster of a day. Strangely she found herself actually looking forward to seeing the awesome Mr Rees-Black again.

Chapter Twelve

The closure of the Great Central main line was effective from the 3rd September 1966. That Saturday, 4-6-0 No.44984 on the 5.15 p.m. from Nottingham, was the last through service to Marylebone. The smoke-box of the 'Black 5' was suitably adorned with a wreath, but many of the stations passed en route were already closed and derelict. Great Central expresses had been observed by Mr Gherardini during his time spent on the farm during the war. But no GC express had used the Wycombe route since November 1960. Mr Gherardini had never been back to the farm, but that autumn his wife expressed the wish not only to appreciate the changing colours of the leaves, but also to see where her husband served his time. It had been over twenty years since Mr Gherardini last stood in the old farm entrance. The five-bar gate that he had leant on in 1944 no longer existed, and several cars were parked where once there had been pig sties. The barn which he had helped renovate with railway sleepers still stood, his carpentry handiwork looking better than the remaining masonry. The old farmhouse was how he remembered it too, but all was silent save the scratching of a few hens. Ben felt quite emotional as he remembered the Land Army girl and the hospitality shown by the then farm owners during those difficult years. The farm had changed hands since then, and later owners had found that farm work demanded more hours of their time than they were prepared to give. Crops did not just appear at harvest festivals or cows look after themselves.

As the Gherardinis turned to walk back to Juniper Lane, sounds of a door slamming and loud voices made them both stop and look back. Two young men were seen getting into a Land Rover and driving off as if they were at Silverstone. It was odd that both had got in on the passenger side.

Mr and Mrs Gherardini's return home coincided with that of their daughter. During tea Bobbie related how Guard Hawes had made such remarkable progress that he was threatening to discharge himself from hospital.

"And when we go and see George again," she told them, "Mr Rees-Black has invited me to dinner at the Crown Hotel as a way of saying thank you."

"I thought you hated the man," her mother remarked.

"Well, yes," Bobbie admitted," I did—but I know him better now."

"I'm not sure that I approve of you seeing him."

"I would not worry," her father broke in. "I hear he has big new job in Reading. He will never get away from his office to trouble anyone."

Bobbie was surprised that Rees-Black had not mentioned it already, and it was she who raised the subject when they next met. They had left Mr Hawes tucked up in bed, all thoughts of discharging himself forgotten as he began to enjoy nurses pampering him, and it was his wish that his nephew should have an enjoyable evening.

"I hear you're about to leave us," Bobbie said, once they had given their order and were waiting for the first course to arrive.

"Yes. Sadly," Mr Rees-Black replied. "I might not see you again. That is why this evening is so special."

He explained his new role within railway management in

Reading while they ate. He enlightened Bobbie further with the fact that High Wycombe was defunct as an individual 'patch' since it now came under the aegis of the Slough District. Halfway through their sirloin steaks Bobbie was on her fourth glass of Bordeaux, and had she observed her host more closely, she may have noticed that although he topped up his own glass as frequently as he did hers, he actually drank very little. So by the time they were enjoying an erotically named chocolate dessert, Bobbie, on her fifth glass, was a very happy and tactile young woman.

"Two coffees to finish with, waiter," Rees-Black said, and addressing Bobbie added ,"l have a room here. I'll take you home afterwards—I mean later—of course, but we'll be more comfortable upstairs." Bobbie agreed, repeating the order, giggling with slurred speech. "Cameriere! Two coffees up to the gen'leman's room at once!" Rees-Black decided it was time to take the girl up before she became an embarrassment.

In the privacy of the room Rees-Black suggested that he and Bobbie sat together on the bed rather than in the less comfortable looking armchairs. However, before inviting Bobbie to sit, he took a blanket from his suitcase and laid it on top of the bedclothes; his explanation being that he never felt warm enough in hotels.

After an interval of some minutes the waiter came up with the coffees for Mr Rees-Black. He paused outside the door and knocked as was his custom. There was no reply but strange noises could be heard coming from within. The waiter tried the handle but the door was locked, so using his pass key he gently opened the door and peeped inside. He had waited on the gentleman and his voluptuous young guest throughout the evening and considered her the most attractive female he had ever served. Now he was astonished by what he saw. The girl lay on the bed, still clothed, but her dress was lifted up way above her stockings and her panties were discarded on the floor. But what astonished the voyeuristic waiter most was that the gentleman's face was buried between the girl's widely parted legs. Exactly what he was doing the waiter could only guess, but the girl was obviously getting enormous pleasure from it as her body writhed in ecstasy and she murmured her appreciation, beginning sotto voce at first then rising crescendo before the point where she let out a cry and lay still. The waiter gathered the show was over and softly closed the door. It took him some moments to regain his composure but he stayed at the door and was about to relock it when he heard the unmistakable sounds of renewed activity. Opening the door slightly once again he caught his breath at the scene before him.

Completely naked now save her nylons and suspenders, the girl, in a new position, on the bed on all fours, was being vigorously taken from behind by the gentleman of whom only his hands were visible as he tightly clasped her buttocks. Her big breasts swayed with the action and so engrossed were the couple that the waiter felt he might have gone in and poured the coffee without either noticing.

The coffee had turned cold but the waiter, although worried about his absence from the restaurant, simply could not tear himself away from watching a girl on the brink of another orgasm. He did not have to wait long, however. As the man's thrusts increased to a final frenzy so his lover cried out so noisily that surely all of Amersham could hear. Weak at the knees, the waiter left them and returned to the restaurant, the coffee quite forgotten.

A little later he observed the girl walking alone out through the main entrance. Then after a gap of a couple of minutes the gentleman appeared, carrying his suitcase, and stopped at the reception desk to speak to the manager.

"I don't know what happened to the coffee but I have decided not to stay after all. I have been called away on urgent business. I want my bill for the meal only please." For the manager this was no new experience.

"Yes, Sir. Of course, Sir."

As Rees-Black drove Bobbie home he reflected upon the passion of the evening. He had seen a side of female sexuality he never thought existed. In that thirty minutes, in the Crown Hotel, Bobbie had been more responsive than Mrs Rees-Black had in all their married life.

Later, as he drove on to Marlow, having seen Bobbie safely home, he reflected, as Pete Vere had done, on the extraordinary naïvety of the girl. She asked no awkward questions—just opened her legs!

Guard George Hawes was to be discharged home within the next few days and Bobbie and Rees-Black only went to Amersham once more. Returning Bobbie home after this last visit Rees-Black approached Spicer's crossing from Flackwell Heath, and in so doing, drove his car down Juniper Lane. A quietly cautious descent of that rural byway was essential, and therefore they approached the gates unnoticed and able to witness a scene quite extraordinary.

The gates were open to them but Rees-Black stopped his car and it took a moment or two to comprehend what was happening. Two youths were present both wearing hideous Guy Fawkes masks.

One was holding Mr Gherardini by the lapels of his jacket while the other made menacing swings with a cricket bat. They were demanding something from Mr Gherardini that he clearly did not have, and his bewilderment and inability to produce it only made them more angry. The individual armed with the bat took out his frustration on a gate lamp but the tough ground glass did not smash.

"It'll be your greasy head next," the youth threatened.

It was at this moment they became aware of the red car. Bobbie leapt out of it first but running to her father's side she allowed herself to be caught by the bat swinging thug who also warned off Mr Rees-Black.

"One more step, Guv, and both of 'em cop it."

His companion seemed delighted with this new turn of events.

"Yeah! Give her a whack and then a good shagging. Eyetie bitch!"

To Bobbie's amazement she had heard such an epithet before. "It's Jon Rice!" she exclaimed incredulously. The youth started, and Mr Gherardini took the opportunity to tear off the disguise. It *was* Jon Rice, and the wind went completely out of his sails. His companion, no longer swinging the bat, hung his head too. Mr Rees-Black stepped forward and took his mask away. "I thought there was something familiar in the voice," Rees-Black said, and turning to address everyone present he continued, "This is my Lampman. Or rather, I should say, was! And the boy Rice is—was!—in the permanent way gang."

He might have continued the introductions had not another car come down the lane. Rees-Black had to move his to allow it to pass, and while this move was going on the youths took themselves off—both, Bobbie noticed, getting in through the passenger side of their Land Rover as the driver's door was taped shut. Her father noticed this too, and remembered where he had seen the same Land Rover before.

Rees-Black joined Bobbie and her father in the cabin.

"They were after an old coin," Mr Gherardini explained. "They kept on saying it was valuable and it belonged to them.

I don't know what would've happened if you had not come along. I remember finding coins many years ago but I don't know where they are now." Bobbie said nothing. The coins were in her purse that very moment!

"Should I inform the railway police?" Rees-Black asked.

"No," Mr Gherardini replied, "they are gone and dismissed. It is over."

His daughter did not share his optimism and she was about to voice her fears when the bell rang its familiar 3 pause 1 code indicating a train was due; then Mrs Gherardini, coming home with the shopping, arrived on the scene. The cabin would not accommodate four so Mr Gherardini went out to move the gates.

Bobbie politely introduced Mrs Gherardini to the chief inspector but her mother regarded him so coldly he fleetingly wondered if the lady could detect he had bedded her daughter. Unabashed he announced that henceforth there was a vacancy for a lamp-person (Rees-Black chose his words carefully) and would Miss Gherardini like to apply?

Chapter Thirteen

It had been Bobbie's birthday the day she started on the bookstall, and ironically it was her birthday again the first day she became the lampwoman for High Wycombe.

While she waited outside the station for her mentor, from her satchel she withdrew some papers she had been sent which mapped out her designated area of responsibility with a list of signal boxes attached. There were three in High Wycombe alone: South, Middle and North. Saunderton was included, as were the immediate signals for trains going over the branch line. The mention of West Wycombe (closed April 1966) was scribbled out.

Her guide turned up eventually, profusely apologising by explaining that he was the lampman for Princes Risborough as well as providing relief cover for Wycombe. He had, as Bobbie soon learned, worked in several different places and in as many roles.

"Porter, crossing keeper, ticket collector, you name it I've done it! But lamping is the best one of them all, even if it does mean the only friends you'll have are the signals. You are your own boss, especially when you're out in the countryside. Doesn't suit everyone, of course.

"My name's Joe, by the way. Don't worry about my surname; no one can pronounce it properly, not even me! Too many Zeds. We have a busy day—but first it's a cup of tea in the South box." Briskly he led the way through the station.

"They're off up the main," he observed. "that'll be the Pullman. The chap at the Middle box had a signal wire break once and got me to go up and hold down the arm just so's the Pullman wouldn't get a clobbering!" he added, making conversation.

They threaded their way past people on the platform, and Bobbie felt very superior as they walked off the ramp at the end and continued up the line to the South box. A few moments later, as expected, the Birmingham Pullman swept majestically by on its way to London.

"Believe it or not," Bobbie's guide continued, "when it comes back, it actually stops here. I'm sure you know your ups and downs, but up is going to London while down is coming away, but within the station limits they might shunt back up the down main, for instance, so always look both ways when you cross any line."

A DMU was approaching them, signalled into the down platform, and the driver gave two long brays on the hooter. Bobbie watched Joe raise an arm in acknowledgement.

"Always do that," he said. "Obviously he's seen you, so let the driver know that you've seen him."

They were walking alongside the line that the train was approaching on, but stepped over to another line as the DMU from Marylebone came past them. "And another thing," Joe added, shouting now to make himself heard. "Never step out of the way of one train into the path of another. One chap in the P-way gang a while back did just that. Nasty business."

Bobbie looked away. She knew to whom he was referring.

Bobbie had visited the signal box at Loudwater, but High Wycombe South was her first main line establishment, and was like entering another world. A frame of over ninety levers stretched away before her, the polished steel handles gleaming in the rays of sunlight shining through the equally clean windows. The red linoleum floor shone so much that Bobbie was reluctant to step on it, but the signalman bade them welcome and introduced himself for Bobbie's benefit.

"Come on in! I'm Bob Gillespie, 'Big Bob', and this here," pointing at a young man seated at a desk, "is 'Little Bob', Bob Hawkins." Joe took the opportunity to make some comic introductions. "Bob, this is Bob! Bob, meet Bob! Bob—Bob!" Everyone laughed and shook hands, and Bobbie felt quite at home.

Wycombe South Box was unusual in that in addition to the signalman a telegraphist (booking boy) was employed. Primarily his role was to maintain the Train Register book, thus alleviating a busy signalman from the task. But at the South the boy's role was twofold: in addition to clerical duties he was also responsible for collecting and delivering the token for the branch line. Officially he played no part in the actual signalling of trains but frequently did.

"All good signalmen were once booking boys," Mr Gillespie said as he accepted a mug of tea the boy had made.

Bells rang, levers were pulled or thrown back, all it seemed to Bobbie for no particular reason, but a 4-car DMU departed for Marylebone and single unit W55022, seen arriving earlier, was already preparing for a return journey to Maidenhead.

Apart from giving up his seat the booking boy was a shy youth, but seemed more than competent at working the box without apparently consulting the signalman at all. The lad was his most impressive when he signalled the Maidenhead train.

Having extracted a token for its authority to proceed over the single line, he clipped it deftly into a hooped carrier then hurried down the box steps to hand it up to the driver of the approaching railcar. The driver lent from his cab, and with a cheery word hooked in the token and accelerated away along the branch.

The boy returned to the box and put the signals back to danger in the wake of the disappearing unit. The signalman joined in the fun again and invited Bobbie to press the Loudwater bell plunger twice. She did so and almost immediately it rang two beats back as a reply.

"What you sent was 'train entering section'," the signalman explained. "If you wait about six more minutes you'll hear 'train out'."

"But we've got lamps to attend to," protested Joe.

"Well, you'd better get cracking then," laughed the signalman. "You stay as long as you like, love. You'll always be welcome when I'm on duty—even if you did short-change me once!" Bobbie could not recall serving the signalman but the comment got more laughs, and sure enough a few minutes later, faintly heard above the noise of a passing express from Wolverhampton, the Loudwater bell rang 2-1.

Bobbie and Joe thanked their hosts for their kind hospitality and went about their business. The signal lampman's hut was the third and the smallest of structures opposite the South signal box. In the hut Joe poured paraffin into a can with a narrow spout, picked up a cloth that must have been someone's shirt years before, collected a box of matches and told Bobbie to follow him up the line.

"Like I was saying," Joe said," you are your own boss. As long as all the signals get done it doesn't matter how you do it. As I've a full can I'm not going to carry it all the way out to the branch distant signal; it's well over a ¼ mile away. We'll do that one when the can is nearly empty. My way is as good a way as any, and that means beginning at the London end."

They were both walking in the 'four foot' of the down main

and they could see that a down express was signalled. In a few moments the melodious warning horn of a Brush Type 4 sounded and, as they stepped aside, the 9.10 Paddington hurried past them on its way in to the platform for its first stop en route to Birkenhead. To increase line capacity the down line had both a inner home and an outer home signal, and the latter was the first to receive attention from Joe and Bobbie.

"I'll do the first couple and talk you through what I'm doing," Joe said. He mounted the steel ladder and deftly climbed up the post carrying his paraffin can. He called down to Bobbie from the small platform near the top of the signal.

"Always be careful up here, it can be slippery even in the height of summer and I don't recommend the shortcut down. Now, I've opened up the lamp casing and unscrewed the cap to the tank; make sure you don't lose it. Refill tank—sorry! Taking care not to slop it on your colleague's head! Then just give the arm and spectacle plate a wipe over and ... job done. Both the flame and wick are fine."

As he rejoined Bobbie he explained his awareness that the signal arm may have moved at any time.

Similarly the second, inner home, signal was dealt with by Joe then, together, they moved on to the up main advanced starter where Bobbie did the work herself. She remembered all she had learned and Joe seemed satisfied with her performance, his only comment being that it was a pity she wasn't wearing a skirt! Dealing next with the starters for both the up main and up platform line extension brought them close to their hut, and as the Pullman diesel went by on its way back to Birmingham, Joe announced that it was time for their official tea break.

Their own hut was for lamp maintenance and paraffin storage only, so Joe explained that they had full use of the facilities in the signal lineman's cabin next door and it was to this building they went.

"The two blokes keep this place nice and clean," he said, "unlike the pigsty where the P-way men hang out. Don't you go in there." Bobbie assured him that it was the last place she would want to go.

The lineman's cabin was quite homely. There was an abundance of pot plants, and several framed photographs adorned the walls. One of a signal gantry caught Bobbie's attention in particular. "That used to be just outside Rugby on the West Coast main line," Joe explained. "Forty-four signals on that gantry, the largest in the country. It's not as complicated as it looks, though. Its signals are for just three diverging routes, and originally there were only twenty-two, but when the GC was built the new girder bridge tended to obscure the sighting, so duplicate signals were added above the originals."

"Must have been a lot of hard work," Bobbie commented.

"I don't think it was, you know," Joe considered. "It was probably only a day or so's work, but all in one place. Less of the walking up and down that we have to do."

As they left the cabin and resumed their duties, a delayed 7.45 a.m. Wellington was signalled up, and the driver of D1663 diligently made the pair aware of his approach. The diesel was named pleasantly enough *Sir Daniel Gooch*, but somehow it did not have the same impact it once had when on Castle class No. 5070.

"I love that sound, "Joe said, as the driver blew the horn again as he roared past.

"E flat and G flat," Bobbie enlightened him.

"Is it, by God? Well, I never would've known that. Are you musical?"

"Not really. My father is—not that he plays anything, though."

Joe's advice that they finished the London end of their patch first entailed a walk along the single line to the distant signal for incoming branch line trains. This was an example, as the majority were on that single line, of one permanently 'fixed at caution', and Joe advised that they took with them a spare inner lamp.

"It's a long walk back if you should need to replace it. Kids might've been throwing stones at it, and once somebody had even nicked it!"

Bobbie only had the pleasure of Joe's company for that single day. He told her he had every faith in her and that any signalman would be only too pleased to help or give advice. "Good luck to you," he said as their day ended. "Remember, I'll be up on the next train if ever you need me."

It was later in the month when Bobbie was walking out to the branch distant signal that she became aware of someone else on the track behind her. Bobbie was walking, not in the 'four foot', but in the left hand 'cess' and the individual, originally on the right of the track, then crossed over the rails to be on the same path as herself. There was something in the person's gait that made her uneasy. She slowed her pace so as to be on Bowerdean Road overbridge where below her several people were passing. Had she quickened her pace she would have been out in the country and away from civilisation. Looking back at the approaching figure her fears were confirmed. It was Jon Rice.

"I need to speak to you," he called, when he was but a few yards off.

"Look, just leave me alone, will you?" Bobbie answered. "I'm sorry you were sacked but it was all your own fault."

Rice laughed. "I was OK, I was reinstated. My mate wasn't, though." He paused to watch an express pass on the nearby main line. "Your Dad," he continued, "has a valuable coin that he found on the land my mate's family owns. That means it belongs to them. And right now the farm needs money."

"Yes, my father did find the coin," Bobbie asserted, "but he handed it to the farmer, who gave it back to him to keep. No one knew it was worth anything."

"That's all irrelevant. It's their land, their coin, and they want it back."

"But it wasn't their land then," Bobbie reasoned.

"Look, I'm not arguing with you," Rice continued. "I'm just telling you they want the penny, alright?" He stopped speaking but only to look Bobbie up and down and add, "Of course we could always come to an arrangement. I could say that it's all a mistake and get them to leave you alone, but you would have to be very nice to me. Very nice indeed, if you get my meaning. I should think it over."

Chapter Fourteen

The worst of being threatened was that one never knew when, or if at all, the perpetrators might strike. The victim would be unable to foresee, and therefore live in a constant state of anxiety. Not that Bobbie allowed this to happen. A cigarette enjoyed when out in the country helped considerably. She kept no regular pattern of working, varying her routine frequently. At home, too, she became security conscious and her rosary became a permanent feature around her neck. Fortunately, of Jon Rice she had seen nothing since he had accosted her, but that was not surprising since he was working in Reading. He and many of his colleagues had been at High Wycombe dismantling the goods yard which was destined to become a car park. The large shed, and the original station building, survived to be taken over by private industry.

Stations down the branch line did not escape rationalisation either. Wooburn Green with its very simple layout was scarcely affected, but Loudwater became a shadow of its former self.

On the 21st October, though, Bobbie's own personal worries, and those of all sentient people in the country, became insignificant in the wake of a tragedy that occurred in South Wales. The pupils at Pantglas Junior School in Aberfan were looking forward to the half-term holiday that fateful Friday when a veritable mountain of colliery waste finally gave way and engulfed the classrooms with an avalanche of spoil. 116 children died, in addition to five teachers.

The Duke of Edinburgh alone visited the scene of the disaster. It was alleged that the Queen and other female members of the Royal Family would have found the visit too distressing.

However, a week or so later, on a much happier occasion, the Queen Mother travelled back from her Warwickshire engagements to London by rail. Bobbie was up in the South box that Thursday evening of 3rd November as the Royal Train (4.15 p.m. from Leamington Spa) swept majestically by. Signalman, booking boy and lampwoman all went to the window to see Her Majesty safely on her way, but sadly no occupant could be seen, not even a lady-in-waiting. But it was interesting to hear the 4-4-4 bell code used and see an immaculate Brush Type 4 with the unique 1X01 reporting number.

Before Bobbie left, her two colleagues made comments for her benefit about Royal Train safety had another signalman been on duty.

"He'd've sent her over the branch," the younger Bob said, before adding in a high pitched wail, "I thought she was going to Windsor!"

Recruiting into the signalling grades was as difficult as attracting men onto the footplate. At one time a railway career was seen as a very prestigious occupation, but those days had gone and it was with some embarrassment that one admitted to working on the railway at all. In the need to fill vacancies, many men were promoted simply because they were keen enough to apply, yet lacking the years of experience normally associated with the role. Thus there were Class 1 (only Special Class was higher) signalmen who had barely 'come of age' and steam locomotive firemen who needed prompting by their driver to do the most basic of tasks like putting coal in the firebox and water in the boiler.

This did not concern Mr Gherardini and his daughter too

much. Mr Gherardini was happy being a mere crossing keeper. It well suited his woodcarving business he ran in the quiet periods between trains. The Somerset and Dorset route over the Mendips had closed several months before, and now, with the recent loss of the Great Central, the Gherardinis realised that they were working for what remained of the 'old' railway and that they should enjoy their careers while they could.

And enjoy her work Bobbie did. She ensured the signals—her signals, as she called them—were immaculate, and was disappointed that the mechanics of them were not included in her duties. So high were her standards of maintenance that she was dismayed early one afternoon to be advised by the signalman at the South box that the driver of the Birmingham Pullman had reported lights out on all signals on the unique five-arm gantry that controlled the leads from the up main and platform lines.

Bobbie set off to investigate, worrying all the time how the situation could have occurred. Had she missed the gantry completely on her last round, or had some freak gale blown out all the lamps?

The Pullmans were always manned by Stafford Road drivers who wore long white coats and were men to be revered. This particular driver, Bobbie considered, must have been exceptionally observant.

She was halfway up the signal ladder when she realised that no one, not even a Pullman driver speeding below in daylight, could possibly see that a tiny flame was missing from a lamp, let alone all five, and moreover, how exactly had the driver informed the signalman? The train certainly hadn't stopped; she had seen it go by herself. But while she was there she considered it in her best interests to check that all was well and sure enough all lamps were burning correctly.

She returned to the signal box to be greeted by gales of laughter from not only both Bobs, booking boy and signalman, but the two signal and telegraph men who were also present. "Oh, you were so anxious as you went off," the signalman chuckled. "We could hear the lire drop from here!" Then, with a wink to his mates, he turned the conversation to not going to work on an empty stomach.

"Yes," Bobbie agreed. "I always feel better with something inside me." An innocent comment that brought with it even more hilarity.

The S&T men eventually took their leave, but Bobbie stayed behind to observe a session of box work. The 9.45 a.m. Aberystwyth (the old Cambrian Coast Express) followed the Pullman up, meeting the 3.10 Paddington–Shrewsbury opposite the box, and a little later a railcar arrived from Bourne End. The boy went to the door but paused.

"Would you like to collect the token for me?" he suggested. "You'll find it hanging on the 'cow horn' post at the bottom of the box steps." These were the first real words that the youth had spoken to her and Bobbie was delighted to oblige. On her return with the coveted item, the signalman-to-be extracted the token from the hoop carrier, and guided Bobbie through the procedure of returning the token to the magazine, and she herself rang the 2–1 (train out of section) bell code to Loudwater.

"We'll make a signalwoman of you yet," young Bob declared.

Bobbie was thrilled with the praise and accepted an invitation to be involved in more railway work on the Saturday afternoon. She envied the excellent working relationship that the two Roberts had; it reminded her of the bakery and the Mother Superior. However, the pair were not always rostered together as, while the signal box was manned continuously, there was no night shift on the book so a given partnership coincided only periodically.

Bobbie visited Wycombe South box on the Saturday afternoon of 5th November. She stayed over four hours, and by the end of the session was able to signal a train herself. Moreover, signalling procedures that had once been mysterious were understood with greater clarity. For example, Bobbie always marvelled at how of all the bells present, the signalman or boy knew which of the four had rung. Over time she realised they each had a subtly distinctive tone. The Beaconsfield bell differed from the two for Wycombe Middle. To that box, platform line, it sounded more like an alarmed blackbird, while for main line it was deep and melodious. The bell for trains going over the branch had a timid sound as if when it first rang it was saying 'excuse me'.

At one point in the evening the signalman answered the phone from Beaconsfield and when he replaced the receiver he turned and said, "Our mate wants to know who our visitor is."

Bobbie looked surprised and asked how did he know she was there. "It's how you ring the bell, I expect", the older Bob replied. "You just know when it's a different hand on the tapper."

Bobbie coped with the levers better than she imagined. Some were harder to pull than others and, naturally, she had neither the grace nor economy of movement that her experienced colleagues possessed. She 'changed the road' and 'pulled off' for the 9.45 a.m. Aberystwyth, and the following 11.45 a.m. Birkenhead, and going in the opposite direction, belled the down 'fasts' from Paddington. Sadly missing were the Pullman services. The units ran Mondays to Fridays only, and spent the weekends resting at Cannock Road carriage sidings or on

Tyseley Loco. But what Bobbie considered was the highlight of the evening was being trusted to hand up to the driver of the 5.24 p.m. departure to Maidenhead the token to allow him over the single line.

Bobbie's visit lasted much longer than she anticipated, a combination of her reluctance to leave and the continued hospitality shown by the two railwaymen. Bob the signalman, shared his sandwiches with her, and the younger Bob made numerous cups of tea.

The 6.02 train home left without her so Bobbie made up her mind to catch the next at 7.24, but before that she was party to an amusing interlude. Around seven o'clock the booking boy seemed to be listening out for something or someone, and when he stood in the shadows at one end of the box, despite the cold air, he slid the window open a few inches. Sure enough, after a minute or two a voice could be heard that grew louder as the moments passed. Bobbie realised it was an evening newspaper salesman offering sporting news and placing great emphasis on the last syllable of his call. The boy provided an echo and the interchange went something like this.

"RacingandfootballreSULTS!"

From young Bob, "—ZALTS!"

"RacingandfootballreSULTS!"

"—ZALTS!"

"RacingandfootballreSULTS."

Bobbie Gherardini had tears of suppressed laughter in her eyes and just had to join in on the fun. "—ZALTS!" she echoed.

"Racingand ... if I come up there someone's going to get 'urt!"

At this point the boy decided that the game was over and slid the box window shut, but the vendor could still be heard as he moved along Gordon Road.

"I don't think anyone ever buys a paper from him," the booking boy said. "I saw him in town once. He's a scary old git with a glass eye."

Bobbie finally thanked her hosts for making her welcome and left to catch her train. Fireworks illuminated the sky as she went but, overall, she considered it had been an unusual Guy Fawkes Night.

Armistice Day of the Great War fell during the following week, and Bobbie sought a poppy to wear as she had done from as long as she could remember. This year there was no mistaking the poppy seller she met in town. It was the newspaper vendor. One eye stared sightlessly while the good one surveyed her menacingly. The situation with her father, together with a fascination for the commemorative names applied to LMS Royal Scots, gave Bobbie a knowledge of both world wars and military memorabilia unusual in a young woman. Having given the vendor a florin she would have taken her poppy and and moved on, but she noticed a particular medal among the array pinned to his blazer.

"Is that a Victoria Cross?" Bobbie asked. The man, with typical modesty, merely nodded. "What did you do to earn it?"

"Nothing much really," came a growl of a reply. "My mate deserved it more 'n me. But he never came out of it. In some ways it makes up for losing a leg."

Bobbie looked closer at the man in astonishment. But without doubt nothing was to be seen below his right trouser leg. The stout walking stick he had was obviously an essential means of support.

Bobbie generously gave him a half-crown more for her poppy and, like a scene from 'Beauty and the Beast', kissed the war veteran on the cheek. She felt so ashamed that she had taken part in ridiculing the man on November 5th.

The days became so short that Bobbie needed a torch to open her hut in the mornings. One particular morning she was startled by some creature fleeing out of it as she went in. It wasn't a dog and rather too big for a cat. The same thing happened the next morning and, being less nervous and more observant, Bobbie realised her nocturnal visitor was a fox. He, or maybe she, clearly gained entry through the gaps in the woodwork where the walls no longer met the floor. She never knew from where it came but on each occasion it would dash away along the up extension before disappearing down the embankment. Bobbie would leave food for her 'pet' and named it Skimbleshanks from the railway poem by the recently deceased T.S. Eliot.

On the day of the winter solstice Bobbie Gherardini was startled by a much larger creature of the human kind. Preparing for a visit to the signals at Saunderton she jumped in alarm when Jon Rice appeared beside her.

"Oh! I-I-I didn't hear you come in."

"Obviously not," Rice sneered in reply. "I'm just passing, but I thought I'd remind you that Christmas is coming and that you Italians might be thinking of a present for my mate." He grinned menacingly." 'Course, I'd love to have you in my stocking on Christmas morning. Or rather, I'd love to have you in stockings!" Chuckling to himself, he left as quickly as he had come.

Poor Bobbie was quite shaken and remained in the hut longer than she ought and missed her train. Waiting for the next one gave her time to consider what Jon Rice had said. But it was the principles involved that made her adamant not to succumb to threats. She thought how happy she had been a year previously. She had anticipated a possible romance with the booking boy but he had plummeted in her estimation since the episode with the newsman. Oh, how she missed Pete Vere, but she had not seen or heard of him since their dismissal. It was going to be a miserable Christmas. But salvation came from an unexpected quarter.

A present from Bob (the signalman) lifted her spirits enormously. It was the chart hit 'Morningtown Ride' by the Seekers, a gentle song with a railway theme, and destined for the No.1 spot had it not been for the Welsh tenor Tom Jones. Christmas 1966 turned out to be a happy time after all, even if the season of goodwill was short.

Arriving for work on Monday 2nd January, Miss Gherardini was met by the local fire brigade who showed her the smouldering remains of her hut. Ironically the only thing to survive was the cast iron 'Smoking Prohibited' sign which lay among the ashes. And what of the fox? Only Bobbie saw the charred body still tied by wire to a 56lb rail chair. She knew the score.

Chapter Fifteen

It was not a particularly happy start to 1967 for the crossing keeper's daughter, and as she was known to smoke, she had to accept the responsibility for the blaze. Her more knowledgeable colleagues, however, reasoned that if a cigarette smoked on a Friday afternoon had caused the fire, why did it wait until Monday morning to flare up?

A working area and bench space were hurriedly provided in the S & T cabin and the two technicians joked that the replacement hut should be re-sited back to its original position at the other end of the station beneath the water tower!

Nor did the second week of the new year show any improvement to Bobbie's well-being, as she had the misfortune to fall from a signal. At a height of twelve feet the up branch starter was not a particularly tall example, but nevertheless she was very lucky to escape injury as she fell not onto the track, but on the relatively soft ground at the top of the embankment. However, she was quite shaken and sat for a moment to recover, but was soon chilled from the effects of shock and the falling air temperature. She cursed herself for reaching to clean the signal arm just as it moved—she knew the timetable, after all—and for ignoring the frost that had lingered on some signal post footboards all day.

As she struggled to her feet she heard someone shouting. "Bobbie! I saw you fall! Have you hurt yourself? Are you OK?" It was Bob the signalman from the South box running to help her. "I pulled off for the Maidenhead—looked to see that the signal had obeyed the lever—and saw you go." He broke off to ensure they both stood clear of the track as the branch line train responsible for the incident motored past them. "Are you sure you're OK?"

"Yes," Bobbie answered weakly. "I'm alright—no need to worry."

But the signalman continued to be concerned for the girl's welfare.

"You're shivering! Here, have my coat and I'll walk you back to the box. I'll make you some tea and you can sit by the stove for a bit." Bobbie accepted his assistance gratefully, but found that when they reached the signal box steps she was quite unable to mount them. The signalman's anxiety increased as he wondered what best to do. "You'd better let me run you home," he decided. "If we go now I'll be back before the rush hour. The boy won't mind looking after things. You go to my car—the blue Mini over there—SKX something or other, and I'll nip up and tell him what I'm doing."

Five minutes later the signalman was in his car ready to leave. "Right away, Juniper Crossing!" he told his passenger.

On the way, the signalman confessed an ulterior motive for taking Bobbie home: he had forgotten his supper so intended to get himself something to eat on his journey back. It was only on arrival in Juniper Lane that he also discovered that he had no money on him either. Bobbie gave him a ten shilling note and suggested he bought himself fish and chips, when he got back, from the 'chippie' a few minutes' walk from the signal box.

"You can let me have the change another time," Bobbie said. "Thank you ever so much for bringing me home. You're my hero."

"You're welcome, and thank you too for saving me from starvation! We must sound like a mutual appreciation society, but seriously now, I would take tomorrow off and rest."

Bobbie intended taking the advice, but once her hero had gone she realised she was still wearing his coat, so no matter how difficult the climbing of signal ladders might prove to be, she resolved to be back at work the next day.

To Bobbie's credit she almost kept to a normal routine. On account of working more slowly it was only because the days were still short that prevented her from fully completing her duties. Before she went home she called in on the signal box men and thanked them both for their kindness. She also gave the signalman back his coat, but, alas, she did not get her change from the ten shilling note. Instead, while the booking boy went to retrieve the token off the 3.39 p.m. Bourne End, the signalman used the brief two minutes to invite Bobbie up to the box on Saturday night for a fish and chip supper together. When the boy returned the signalman carried on speaking to Bobbie, but his words were cleverly designed to give her essential information while giving nothing away to the boy.

"Yes I'm on 12-hour nights over the next weekend—6 p.m. 'til 6 a.m. But the boy here will be off as usual at 9.16 in the evening."

"What an odd time to finish," Bobbie remarked, innocently.

"It's something," the booking boy himself replied, "to do with the laws of employing juveniles, I think. On early turn I do 6.44 'til 2 o'clock in the afternoon. It works out at 7 hours 16 a day." The signalman looked at Bobbie enquiringly as he saw her out of the door, but she smiled and discreetly nodded her head as she left.

Saturday January 14th saw Bobbie Gherardini carrying to the South box a hot supper for two tightly wrapped in a Daily

Telegraph, but had he not been whistling the new Top Ten hit by The Monkees, she would have almost certainly have bumped into the booking boy. By her watch Bobbie saw it was 9.30 so the boy was leaving much later than anticipated. As it was, Bobbie ducked down beside a familiar blue Mini and waited until he'd gone. Once she could no longer hear I'm a Believer' she made her way up the box steps.

"I thought he'd never go," her host admitted as he helped her off with her coat. "And don't you look a picture too! I've never seen you in a dress before."

"It makes a change from my smelly jeans."

The only light on in the box was that over the train register desk, creating an almost romantic setting, and once the last up 'fast' of the day, 9.38 p.m. to Paddington (4.30 Birkenhead) had departed, the couple were able to enjoy their meal without interruption.

As they ate, Bob the signalman outlined some of the changes they could expect in March when a new timetable would take effect. The majority of expresses would be lost to the electrified services operating out of the new Euston Station, and of the few that remained none would go further than Birmingham. There would be no more 'Birkenheads' like they had just seen, nor blue Pullmans as those units would be transferred to the Bristol and South Wales routes. Closer to home, Wycombe would lose its resident pilot, the 0-6-0 diesel shunter, as the engine off the Acton goods would be diagrammed to shunt and trip locally instead.

Just before 10 p.m., the Beaconsfield bell rang 'call attention' and the signalman there announced that he was 'switching out,' that is to say, closing his box. Following the one beat on the bell came a rapid 5–5–7 which Bob at the South acknowledged before being called to the telephone. He bade his homeward-bound colleague a good night then entered into some banter with his counterpart at Gerrards Cross to whom he was now connected. At Beaconsfield the points would remain set for the platforms and the signals remain 'off' until the box was next switched in.

The Gerrards Cross man belled the 9.20 out of Marylebone (a 3–1) and sent the 'train entering section' at the same time. This particular train, Bob explained to his young friend, would be some time coming, owing to the longer section, but would terminate at High Wycombe. Once it had arrived and all passengers had alighted, the 4-car set duly shunted back into the up platform line extension. With the unit ticking over directly opposite the signal box, Bob asked Bobbie to remain seated in order not to be seen by the any of the traincrew.

The extension to the up platform line was a useful addition to the layout dating from 1943. Effectively it formed a loop parallel to the up main. Using the facility as a stabling point enabled empty DMUs to simply back into the up platform when necessary to form a service. As he changed the points and cleared the disc signal to permit the shunt, Bob explained that it was the last up passenger train that day. A little later, at 10.40, it departed on time for Marylebone, and as it passed the box the 'Control' telephone rang with a message that a Newhaven–Knowle and Dorridge return empty car-flat special could be expected following the 10.20 down from Marylebone. Bob made a note to the effect in the train register book before being summoned to the bells again. This time it was the turn of Wycombe Middle to 'switch out'.

Once more there was the cacophony of sound as the 5–5–7 rang out again, followed by some customary words over the telephone to greet new nocturnal neighbours.

"Right," said Bob, "we're through to Gerrards Cross now

on the up, and Risborough North going down. Wycombe North is only open on weekdays, and Risborough South is already out. I feel this is where the night shift really begins."

The signalman made his work sound so absorbing that Bobbie was disappointed that she would not be able to stay for much longer, it being arranged that Mr Gherardini should collect his daughter at 11.30 p.m. As it happened he'd parked his Fiat in the former goods yard next to the signalman's blue Mini as the 10.20 p.m. Marylebone was signalled into the bay platform a little before 11.15. Back in Wycombe South Box, Bobbie was witnessing a dilemma for her signalman friend.

"I'm not sure what to do," he said. "This chap"—pointing at the DMU approaching them—"goes back 'empty stock' and it's usually a quick turn-round. But if I set the road for him I'll not be able to pull off for the car-flats and I'll delay him."

Bobbie, thinking of the driver of the special being stuck behind the local train all the way from Northolt Junction, suggested that it should have preference. But the signalman disagreed. "I'll make a signaller of you yet! But for exactly that reason I'll let the stock go first as one last check to the freight won't really hurt him."

As he belled the empty 4-car set (2–2–1) to the Gerrards Cross man, so the driver of the unit was 'blowing up' to be let out, and within a minute the DMU was returning home to London; the cab lights came on momentarily and the guard, seated next to his driver, cheerfully waved as they passed the box.

Having had the special freight accepted by Princes Risborough North some minutes before, immediately the empty DMU was away Bob heaved over the points and cleared his signals for the car-flats. There had been no braying diesel horn so Bob was confident that he hadn't actually stopped the special, but the manner in which the locomotive was now accelerating suggested that the driver had seen the signals initially against him.

Unusually, the locomotive was a Western class diesel-hydraulic. "You don't see many 'Thousands' down this way nowadays," Bob remarked. "I can't believe it's worked through from the Southern. They must've changed engines at Acton, and you can bet your old Grannie's savings they won't want it at Tyseley so it's sure to come back light engine."

Standing together, Bob and Bobbie watched the long train of bogie flat wagons snake by and away through the station, both looking for a possible hot axle box or other defect as it passed. Owing to the darkness neither had been able to determine the locomotive name. "It was a short one," Bob said. "Western King, or maybe Duke." Bobbie slipped her arm around Bob's waist and suggested Hero. Mr Gherardini saw the train pass too as he sat in his car waiting for his daughter. She did join him eventually, apologising profusely, but the nocturnal world of signalling had left such an indelible impression on her that she had been quite reluctant to leave it; consequently, a second invitation to supper in the near future was readily accepted.

Chapter Sixteen

O n a number of Sundays during February 1967, owing to engineering work on the new line, trains beyond Princes Risborough were being diverted along the Thame branch to join the original GWR route north to Birmingham via Oxford. Passenger services ceased from January 1963, but considerable freight traffic still used the two ends of the link (Princes Risborough to Thame, and Oxford's Kennington Junction to Morris Cowley), and the line was currently extant throughout. Bobbie was guest once more in Wycombe South Box on the Saturday night of February 18th, her host making her especially welcome by providing not only a table cloth and serviettes but a bottle of red wine already opened and 'breathing'.

Once again a Newhaven car-flat special was imminent, and Bob made a comment that it should become a regular feature in the timetable. However, it was rather earlier than before and able to enjoy a clear run through. Bobbie signalled the train herself and stood patiently at the levers waiting for the train to make an appearance. Surprisingly, it again had unusual motive power. This time it was the turn of 1Co-Co1 diesel D294, surely doing more than the maximum speed of 45mph permitted through High Wycombe.

It was a little later that Bob asked his nubile assistant when her father was coming to fetch her. She surprised the signalman by replying that her father would not be coming at all!

Meanwhile another extra freight was expected, Control informed them, bound for where the engineering work was actually taking place. Surprisingly, this train, consisting of bogie bolster and 'plate' wagons for the recovery of redundant permanent way materials, could not be accepted by the signalman at Princes Risborough North because he still had the Newhaven train with him. Locomotive D294 had raised a number of questions.

Apparently the driver did not 'know the road' over the Thame branch, and the pilotman, who would be his conductor over the route, was not familiar with the D200 class. It was further rumoured that the 133-ton English Electric diesels with their massive 8-wheel 1Co-Co1 bogies were not permitted over the branch anyway. So while the telephone wires were buzzing between Control and Princes Risborough, the freight for the engineer's possession site drew to stand at Wycombe South Box. The signalman anticipated that the locomen might carry out Rule 55.

"You'd better hide yourself, love," he advised Bobbie. "Stay in the loo until he's gone. If he wants a pee I'll say it's out of order."

The engine on the freight, D1654, was single-manned so it was the driver himself who got down off the footplate and made his way up into the box. The driver did not say "Good evening" (it would have been better if he'd had), but instead used the old familiar term for signalmen.

"Alright there, bobbie?"

"Yes, thanks!" piped up a voice from the toilet.

The driver stared at the signalman in amazement and the signalman stared back in horror. Then the face to whom the voice belonged peeped out of the cubicle. "Has he gone? Oh!" In stunned silence the signalman passed the driver a pen, and the driver, chuckling to himself, duly signed the train register to fulfil the requirements of Rule 55. While he did so, the signalman felt that an explanation of some sort was necessary.

"Er, this is my landlady. I mean, lamplady! She's checking to—to see how well her lamps show up at night!"

The driver laughed. "Look, mate, just give us the road—none of my business what you get up to!"

A more composed signalman told the driver the reason for the delay, yet the moment he finished speaking the Risborough bell rang 3–2 accepting at last the waiting train.

Bob was pleased to tell the driver he was now 'right away' and with considerable relief watched him rejoin his train. Back in the cab of D1654 the driver pulled down his window for a final jovial comment. "Tell her to join the loco!"

Bob waved and nodded in agreement, and watched as the driver moved his master handle from the 'engine-only' position to 'forward' and opened the controller. Some 2750hp of Sulzer engine responded, and with the air heavy with exhaust smoke the special freight drew slowly away.

No. 87 was generally considered the most difficult lever in Wycombe South box. It was not only responsible for the advanced starter at the end of the down platform line, it also operated a banner-repeating signal that co-acted with it at the entrance to the platform. The sheer length of signal wire and the curvature of the platform made No.87 a formidable lever to pull.

Endeavouring to lower the signal for D1654, Bobbie needed several attempts to get the lever over. The signalman, shaking his head in amusement, went to help but had to get behind her to assist. Once No.87 was securely over, the signalman found to his surprise that he had the girl in his arms. She made no attempt to escape but simply turned around within his grasp to face him. For several seconds they looked at one another in silence, eyes searching for the other's innermost thoughts. Then they kissed, gently at first, then passionately, and from that moment their friendship took on a whole new meaning. It was not uncommon for the local beat police constable to seek the warmth of a signal box if the night was cold and his shift uneventful. It was customary, too, for the officer to go up quietly in case, as sometimes happened, the signalman had got his 'head down'. By necessity, the upper floor of a signal box was glazed on at least three sides, so even from the entrance and with only a single lamp burning the whole operating area could be seen. But on the night in question the officer went no further than the top of the signal box steps as he was astonished at what he saw within.

The signalman was ensconced in the armchair as expected, but sitting on his lap with her arms around his neck snuggled a young woman. The man had her breasts out, and the hem of her dress was rolled up way beyond the tops of her stockings. Whatever the man was doing, the constable realised that comfort from the signal box stove and intelligent conversation were out of the question, and instead sought a cup of tea back in the 'nick'.

The crossing keeper's daughter spent the whole night in the signal box, it being her desire to experience railway work at night, but there was little to disturb her, and the copious amount of red wine she had drunk ensured that once alone in the armchair she slept quite soundly. The signalman made himself as comfortable as best he could at the train register desk. He glanced at the sleeping figure from time to time, and wondered how easy it would be to have sex with her but he did not want to push things too far too quickly. Bobbie had made it quite plain that she intended to be gone before the next signalman came on duty.

As it happened, a noisy 'Hymek', going down to the 'possession' to provide relief for the enginemen there, passed and woke Bobbie soon after 5 a.m. The signalman, still playing the role of host, made a pot of tea and shared his toast with her too. He did not envy her long walk home, but keeping to the railway line Bobbie's journey wasn't at all unpleasant. Numerous rabbits stamped their hind feet and hopped away as she approached, and the dawn chorus was in full song within Fennel's Wood as she passed between the beeches and her old alma mater.

It was fully light when she took a rest on the platform seat on Loudwater Station. She was aware that her father had sat on that very seat years before, and it was difficult to imagine that the station had once been at the heart of village life. The signal box was closed, but at least it would re-open again on Monday morning. Looking at it, Bobbie realised how much she wanted to work in a signal box herself. If her father lacked ambition, there was no need to follow his example. During the past winter she had envied the men in their cosy cabins while she tramped the frosty sleepers.

Friday March 3rd was a day of mixed emotions. The major changes to the timetable came about and the Birmingham diesel Pullman ran for the last time, but it was also the day that Bobbie Gherardini applied for the vacancy at Wooburn Green Signal Box.

Chapter Seventeen

The inauguration of the new electric services from Euston Station were sadly marred by tragedy on other parts of the system. It began on Tuesday February 28th when BR/Sulzer diesel D5002, running round its train of ballast wagons, fouled the main line in the path of a Manchester–Coventry electric multiple unit at Stechford. Nine passengers in addition to the driver of the express were killed. The breaking of several rules and general incompetence throughout the shunting move caused the accident.

More mysterious, however, was the disaster at Conington in the flat Fenland countryside on the night of March 5th where five more people died. How a signalman could wilfully move the points under the 10.30 p.m. from King's Cross hauled by Deltic D9004 was much debated.

Easter beckoned, but to Bobbie's dismay when out shopping with her mother in Marlow, she met Jon Rice again. Permanent waymen were doing some preliminary work prior to the station being re-sited, and Mrs Gherardini spoke to the gang which gave Rice an opportunity to accost her daughter and speak to her alone.

"It was a pity you forgot my mate last Christmas, but you could oblige him on his birthday, in May—just before he emigrates to Australia. From what I hear you can be very obliging, especially to signalmen!" Poor Bobbie blushed and was glad her mother could not overhear. Just what Rice was aware of, or to what he was alluding, she could only guess.

March 24th was Good Friday, and as usual a Sunday service was anticipated, and with no trains running over the branch the booking boy would not be on duty. Bob the signalman quietly mentioned to Bobbie that he was on late turn that day and invited her up for hot cross buns; after all, if she were destined to take charge of Wooburn Green she should have tuition on signalling rules and regulations. Bobbie envisaged that she could be a signalwoman by the summer. She knew that the booking boy was also expecting to become a signalman himself. Now eighteen years old (the minimum age), the boy had set his sights on Greenford West a few miles up the line from Northolt Junction.

However, as things turned out, the boy decided against the prospect of working so far from home, and instead also chose Wooburn Green. To Bobbie's chagrin he was successful. The railway management, without apology, wrote to Miss Gherardini, offering her the position of telegraphist, but Bobbie decided to wait for another opportunity to have her own signal box.

It was Monday April 10th that Bob Gillespie came on duty beaming from ear to ear. Over the weekend he had picked the 100–1 shock winner of the Grand National at Aintree. For a five-shilling win and each way bet he'd won over £30. The scale of his luck became apparent when one read news reports of the race. A horse, already riderless, finally refused at the twenty-third fence and, trotting along the length of it, stopped the majority of the following runners. John Buckingham on the rank outsider Foinavon was so far behind the rest of the field that he was able to avoid the chaos and go on to win.

Bob decided to spend his windfall on taking a short break. He often went off by himself fishing but this time he booked a visit to Crewe Works organised by the Motive Power Club open to both members and non-members alike. Bob also decided that he would not go alone. In addition to Crewe, a number of engine sheds around Manchester where steam could still be seen were on his agenda. He told Bobbie Gherardini of his itinerary—and his invitation.

The girl had never been away from home before so it was with some trepidation that she accepted the signalman's offer. What to tell her parents on the Friday afternoon of her departure she had no idea, so she simply told them to expect her back on Sunday and hurried out.

The holidaymakers met in Wooburn Green, but it was only when they were on the M1 motorway that they relaxed and began to enjoy the excursion. Crewe was reached via the M6 later that evening where they booked into a small family-run guest house.

"You are married, aren't you?" queried the proprietress. "I don't allow any hanky-panky here. Mine's a respectable establishment!"

Bob Gillespie had expected a reception such as this and assured the woman that she was not to worry, and Bobbie offered her left hand for inspection where a ring on the appropriate finger could be seen. The landlady showed her guests to their room, but as soon as she had gone Bob locked and bolted the door behind her. He didn't want her coming back with anything so mundane as instructions on what to do in case of fire—not for what he had in mind.

The room was small so the double bed took up most of the available space; Bobbie was sat on it contemplating unpacking, but Bob flopped down full length on it, testing the quality of the mattress. The mattress was fine but the bed creaked and groaned with his every move. Throughout the long drive up the motorway he had thought of little else but having the girl in bed; but now, as he pulled her down alongside he knew he could not wait any longer. It was twenty minutes before Bobbie finally unpacked.

"Now I know," she remarked, "why you're called 'Big Bob'!"

"And now I know why they call you 'Finsbury Park'."

"Finsbury Park?"Bobbie queried. " Why on earth—?"

"34G! Think about it!"

"Oh!" she laughed, "but I'm only an 'E'!"

After their long journey the couple chose to eat in, and it was with a glass of champagne, no less, with their meal that Mr Gillespie toasted not only his young 'wife' but also the origin of his winnings. "To 'Popham Down'," he said. "What a wonderful name for the nag that caused all the mayhem in the National."

Their evening meal was adequate, but champagne effectively made it 'haute cuisine', as well as being a powerful aphrodisiac so much so that later, back in the privacy of their room, it was of little consequence that neither had brought any nightwear. Some animal-like desire had been spent earlier so once in bed the couple enjoyed considerable foreplay before they were strenuously making love again; and as the pace increased, their expressions of delight became louder and more frequent until the inevitable occurred and both breathlessly took a rest from their exertions.

It took them some moments to recover so Bobbie reached into her satchel for her cigarettes and, ignoring the 'Strictly No Smoking in Bedrooms' sign, lit up and shared one with her lover. Bobbie's soapdish became a suitable ash-tray, but a banging on the adjoining wall and a woman's voice shouting startled them both.

"I hope you've finished in there, decent folk want to get some sleep!" Bobbie and Bob looked at one another for a moment, then laughed,

"We'll have to do it on the floor then," Bobbie whispered.

Bob Gillespie was amazed at the girl's sexual appetite and doubted his ability to perform again. But Mrs Gillespie had never ventured away from the missionary position so it was a new and very arousing experience for Bob to lie on his back in a reversal of roles, particularly beneath a well-endowed female, so his stamina was never in question. But it was fortunate that only he saw the amount of dirt under the bed and something small, brown and furry dart away to safety. So much for a respectable establishment.

The next morning, after a hearty restorative breakfast, the couple met with some thirty others at the Nantwich Road entrance to Crewe Works. Without doubt the tour of the Works was interesting, but overall it was rather a disappointment. The escort was more a shepherd to a flock of sheep than a guide. No mention was made of the history of Crewe, nor anything said of the great engineers or famous locomotives built there. Sadly, it was little more than a number-taking exercise for the trainspotters among them.

Nevertheless, information could be gleaned if one had the audacity to stop the tour and ask questions. February 3rd, for example, had seen Britannia class 70013 emerge as the last steam locomotive to receive a major overhaul there, and the 750v dc E5000 class locomotives from the Southern Region were there for conversion to dual-powered Electro-Diesels E6101–10.

Not surprisingly a number of steam engines stood rusting and silent, but several diesels also awaited a decision on their fate, the future for members of the unorthodox Metro-Vick

Co-Bo D5700 class looking particularly bleak. One locomotive, not part of any rationalisation plan to eliminate non-standard classes, was English Electric Type 4 D322. The remains of this diesel, which suffered collision damage south of Warrington when hauling a Euston-Stranraer express in May 1966, attracted a considerable amount of macabre attention.

Although several Brush Type 4s were in for repair, no new members of the class were being built there as Crewe had completed D1111, the last of its allocation of 302 locomotives, in February. Numbers for the class ran out at 1999 (from1500), and because diesel mechanical shunters occupied numbers D2000 onwards, the last dozen became D1100–11. Someone on the tour asked why the numbers were not allocated backwards, as was the case with the Stanier 'Black 5's, and beginning from 1499, but the guide had no answer to give. All he did say was that both D1960 and 1961, the final two locomotives of the class of 512, were still under construction at Brush.

Once the tour was over and back on the streets of Crewe many of the party were observed seeking admission to other establishments. From what was overheard the electric traction depot was top of the list, but great was the indignation when they were refused entry. Having experience of working only on the Western Region, Bobbie was intrigued by the proliferation of upper quadrant signals. She noticed too that the lamp associated with the arm was to the left of the post instead of the right. Also there was no ornate finial to the post; a simple cap sufficed. Signal box nomenclature on the LMR was equally fascinating. There was no South, Middle or North on the ex-LNWR lines but a numerical system used instead. Bobbie saw this for herself when at one point, parked in a lay-by to get their bearings, they could see Crewe Gresty Lane No.6.

"There must be five others in the vicinity then!" Bob commented.

For the afternoon Bob remembered something of his itinerary, and the couple drove to Manchester to see again some steam. 9B Stockport Edgeley was the shed Bob headed for but never managed to reach, and so poorly did he cope with city traffic that, intending to visit 9E Trafford Park, the pair eventually ended up at Patricroft—achieved by patiently following a bus bound for Eccles!

Bob explained that he would do all the talking to the shed master. "With all their loco experience they deserve some respect. You're my daughter, now, by the way!"

"Make your mind up!" Bobbie laughed.

As Bob predicted, the shed master was amenable to their visit. "Just let me know when you're done", he said.

Patricroft was unusual in that the LNWR shed of 1885 was added to some twenty years later by an extension built at right angles to the original, and reached by a different set of tracks thus creating an L-shaped depot with a turntable within the angle. However, Patricroft that day was similar to the majority of surviving steam sheds in the north-west with dilapidated buildings, piles of ash and weed-infested redundant tracks. But morale was high even though the shed would close the following year, and without exception every engineman they encountered had a cheery word for them.

Engines seen that day were predominantly Stanier class 5s and 8s together with Standard 9Fs and 5MTs, one of which, 73128, they saw being turned. All were desperately in need of a cleaning rag.

A number of diesels were present. One in particular, inside the shed, Bobbie pointed out to her companion, was 1Co-Co1 Type 4 D326.

"Of course!" Bob remembered, "the 'Great Train Robbery' engine."

A passing locoman gave them the information they sought—which way was D326 facing on that night in August 1963?

"The driver and his mate were at the radiator end. Number 1 cab is always the rad end. Go on up if you want, lass. It's not locked."

For Bobbie the passing years had failed to dim any fascination of that fateful night. Climbing up into the correct cab, she first sat in the seat once occupied by secondman David Whitby before moving over to the driving position. With her hands on the controls that Jack Mills would have used, she imagined being stopped by a red signal at 3 a.m. in the morning, having presumably heard an AWS bell ring for a clear distant signal which had showed 'caution'. It was also apparent how easily one could be overpowered within the confined space of that particular footplate.

At the conclusion of their visit the two enthusiasts thanked their host, and while Bob went to the gents, the shed master offered Bobbie the paperweight from his desk. It was a 26F shed code plate.

"I was keeping this for myself," he said, "but you may as well have it."

To his surprise Bobbie refused it, saying she would have liked a 9H (for Patricroft) plate instead. The shed master grunted something inaudible and returned the plate to his desk.

The drive back to Crewe was straightforward and the couple decided on the cinema for the evening. The classic film *Brief Encounter* was showing, starring Trevor Howard and Celia Johnson. They had drinks in their guest house bar later, and rounded off a very pleasant day by enjoying each other's intimate company one more time. Yet somehow a little of the magic of the previous night was missing. Bob wondered if the emotions raised in the film had aroused a mixture of feelings about their own relationship. Watching the doomed love affair between Dr Harvey and Laura Jesson perhaps had been a mistake. A bawdy 'Carry On' film might have been more suitable.

On the journey home, Bobbie spoke to her companion of the dilemma she faced regarding the 1933 penny and Jon Rice. The signalman was disappointed that she had not confided in him before, claiming that he would've sorted the blighter out from the first. But as to a solution he was less vociferous. Options open to her were few. Out of the question was the thought of handing the coin over, but retaliating in return, Bob considered, might well frighten him off.

"Tell him you'll call the police if he threatens you again. That very often works. Or say you're going to get a solicitor; he won't know whether to believe you or not. Better still," he concluded, "tell him you've got an Uncle whose a don in the Mafia!"

When Bobbie arrived back home she realised that she still lacked an explanation to give her mother and father for her absence. However, in the event none was needed as her parents greeted her excitedly and gave her a letter to read, which inexplicably had been addressed to Mr Gherardini who had quite innocently opened it. Mr and Mrs Gherardini knew before their daughter that she had been offered the post of signalwoman at Loudwater Signal Box

Chapter Eighteen

In the new timetable for March 1967 Paddington-Birmingham services no longer used Birmingham Snow Hill. Trains left the GWR main line at Bordesley and traversed twenty-six chains of the Midland Railway Derby-Gloucester route before joining the original London and Birmingham Railway line into New Street Station. Devoid of main line services, Snow Hill became the largest unstaffed halt in the world. However, on a positive note all trains in both directions called at High Wycombe and many at Princes Risborough, giving residents of those towns a level of service never previously enjoyed. The motive power employed was, as before, the ubiquitous Brush Type 4, but one interesting diagram was the first up express in the mornings which originated from Banbury and invariably produced a 'Hymek' Type 3 D7000 class.

The new services also included a connection to London Airport. Jet-setters alighting at High Wycombe would find a coach waiting to drive them directly to Heathrow. Bobbie witnessed this for herself one morning when the 10.17 arrival from Birmingham drew into the up platform. It was not the number of passengers that overwhelmed the porter, but the quantity of luggage.

In an attempt to minimise delays, Bobbie took charge of a 4-wheel barrow herself, thereby saving the porter having to make two trips from platform to coach with his own. But it was no easy task. Platform three to the forecourt was a considerable distance from one side of the station to the other, and the subway meant effort was required to prevent the barrow from running amok down the slope. Once having passed under the four-track layout, strength was again required to pull the barrow up the other side as well as ensuring that no suitcases tumbled off.

Far from being grateful for her assistance, the surly porter made it clear to Bobbie that in future she should mind her own business.

"I'll thank you not to interfere with my duties. You stick to selling your Mars Bars or whatever it is you do these days."

Bobbie soon discovered the reason for his hurtful comments, as once the luggage was safely on the coach the passengers felt obliged to show their appreciation in the usual manner. Many of the transferees were wealthy businessmen, and it was small wonder that local signalmen, Bob Gillespie included, were not adverse to being asked to cover portering duties in addition to their regular box work when a need arose.

Bobbie and her lover continued to meet whenever he had a late turn on a Sunday, which equated to one in every three weeks. She knew that what she was doing was wrong, but he satisfied her in such ways that she could never achieve herself. He in turn needed her for fulfilment that was lacking within his own marriage.

As predicted, the sparsity of the new express service confirmed the rumours that the 'last main line' would be reduced to a single track, and indeed the service was actually timed to reflect the limitations of Bicester being the only station en route to provide a passing facility. Other candidates for similar rationalisation were the 'Berks & Hants' route (Reading to Westbury), and Plymouth all the way to Penzance. The feasibility of these projects was determined from the experience gained by singling the main line between Salisbury and Exeter on the

Southern Region.

In the London area there was considerable modernisation going on. At Old Oak Common a new panel signal box would assume control of Paddington Station and twelve miles westwards to Hayes from where control would pass to the existing panel box at Slough. The Old Oak Panel was replacing an earlier example commissioned as recently as 1962. Thirteen signal boxes had been closed then, including the WR's busiest and second most busy boxes, Old Oak Common West and Ladbroke Grove respectively. Around High Wycombe, rumours of a panel box being constructed there abounded—either that or Old Oak Common would take in the GW/GC line as well.

In the event the fears were not substantiated, but a panel of sorts was installed beside the manual frame in Princes Risborough North. Here the modernisation was incorporated within the plan to single the 'new line' and culminate in the closure of Ardley, Bicester North and Princes Risborough South signal boxes.

Bobbie's main source of information for technical development was the two signal and telegraph men. Since the destruction of her lamp hut her facilities had been transferred to their cabin. The situation was not ideal as Bobbie was not permitted to have her own key, but overall it was a satisfactory arrangement.

One afternoon the threesome were outside the cabin, waiting to cross the lines while a DMU made a shunt, when one of the men remarked, "I hear Bob Gillespie's leaving us. He's got a reliefman's job, up in Manchester. Apparently he and some tart had a dirty weekend up there in April just after his big win." Bobbie, rooted to where she stood, could hardly believe her ears.

"Yes," the second technician added. "He goes at the end of May. But we're losing a good bloke."

Signal wires whistled and point rodding rattled but Bobbie heard none of it. She continued to stare at the men in amazement. "It's like this," the first went on. "His wife learned about his affair and kicked him out. Apparently the booking boy saw the mistress hanging around outside the box in January and once he'd moved to Wooburn Green felt he could tell on his former mate. Some mate!" Bobbie just wanted the ground to open up beneath her as shock, embarrassment and humiliation—the whole gamut of human emotions—invaded her senses.

Once the S&T men had left, Bobbie headed for the branch distant signal, and even though she had attended to it only the day before she climbed the ladder to the lamp at the top and found solace in her lofty eyrie from the nightmare she had just experienced. Smoking cigarette after cigarette consoled her, and when she finally descended from the signal she felt more able to face the world. Needless to say, the next time she saw her signalman friend it was an emotional meeting. It was not a time for recrimination, and in fact few words were spoken within the short time they spent together. Bobbie was in tears as she descended the box steps but it was a sad signalman too that she left behind.

By the middle of June Bobbie learned that the Loudwater signalman had left and so fully expected to be summoned to replace him, but a relief signalman was booked to cover the vacancy. Upon making enquiries Bobbie was informed she would have to continue as lampwoman until a replacement for her own work was recruited.

Later in the month came some sad news for Mr Gherardini. By letter from the surviving family, he learned that his old friend Ted Davies had passed away and the Gherardinis were invited to the funeral. Owing to the distance involved, the Gherardini family accepted the invitation but arranged to spend a night in

Cardiff in order to attend the service early the next morning in Caerphilly. Thus it was with sadness that Mr Gherardini drove again to Wales in his Fiat Multipla, for despite knowing that the couple had become increasingly frail, he regretted not visiting his old mentor beyond the one occasion in 1965. The Gherardinis were glad they'd made an effort to attend as neither Ted nor his wife had any siblings, the family was small and the number of relatives few. Despite barely a dozen in the congregation (including the organist) there was a stirring rendition of Hughes's 'Cwm Rhondda', fortunately sung in English.

On the journey back the Gherardinis visited Barry Island, and leaving Mrs Gherardini sunbathing on the promenade the father drove his daughter to show her the withdrawn steam engines in the dockland sidings nearby. Bobbie had tears in her eyes as they walked among the rows of locomotives that Dai Woodham had bought for scrapping. Somehow it seemed the right place to be following a funeral.

Later, having collected Mrs Gherardini from the beach, Ben lost his way around Newport and ended up passing Cashmore's scrapyard. This was in some ways more astonishing than Woodham's, as while only a few engines were present (all 4-6-2s of the West Country class, 34005/9/24 and 32), behind them was an absolute mountain of locomotive fragments. Ben stopped the car for a closer look and was soon approached by a man holding a large Alsatian by the collar.

"Lost are you, boy?" the man asked.

Ben admitted he was, and not at all intimidated, asked for directions. Glancing in the car at its occupants, the security man soon came to the conclusion that the Gherardinis were not scrap metal thieves and described the best route for them quite amicably. He also suggested that as steam was still running on the Southern Region, they should go and see it while it was, in effect, on their doorstep. Scrutinizing Ben's ageing Fiat, the security man added as a parting shot that the next car the Gherardinis bought might well contain several elements of a melted down Bulleid Pacific.

Back at work on the Monday morning, Bobbie made some enquiries, and what they had been told at Newport was confirmed: steam on the LSW main line from Waterloo would end on July 9th—a week hence.

Ben Gherardini took his daughter to the lineside at Brookwood near Woking that Sunday, and although there was little steam about they did witness, with crowds of others on that warm afternoon, Merchant Navy 35030 *Elder Dempster Lines* storm past them on the 2.07 p.m. from Weymouth. Once the cheering had subsided, everyone began packing up their cameras and tape recorders and the Gherardinis realised that there was to be no more steam. Someone turned up the volume on his radio as 'Waterloo Sunset' by the Kinks came over the airwaves. It made a fitting end to the demise of Southern steam.

With still no intimation of a starting date for her signalling career, Bobbie Gherardini had to continue to be patient, the consolation being that it was the best time of the year to do so. She spent many a happy hour out in the country. Basking in the sun when out at the branch distant signal one afternoon she realised how much she would miss her signals and the relative freedom she enjoyed.

The weeks passed and the humid August nights were replaced by chilly evening dews as the days lengthened and Autumn came. Finally, one week after her nineteenth birthday, Bobbie received the letter for which she had waited so long. A replacement lampman was to be employed imminently and she would commence duties at Loudwater a month hence. In the meantime she was to attend Paddington for a medical examination at her earliest convenience.

It was for that reason that Bobbie waited patiently on platform three at High Wycombe for the 1.24 p.m. departure for London. Her train, the 11.40 a.m. from Birmingham New Street, the station announcer warned, was running twenty minutes late. Bobbie frowned with annoyance but was glad that she had allowed herself extra time in which to keep her appointment. The delay was no surprise, as ever since the Brush 2750hp diesel-electrics had been substituted by the NBL Warship class, the timetable had gone to pieces. At 2200hp the twin-engined diesel-hydraulics were not only less powerful but also much less reliable.

At 1.50 the train arrived having clearly lost yet more minutes. The secondman was in the open cab doorway making signs to the platform staff: one thumb up, the other down, which meant they were running on one engine only.

The ailing locomotive was *Ramillies*, D837, and to make matters worse, it was also in deplorable condition externally. The solutions used in the carriage-washing plant to clean the locomotive were obviously too harsh as the maroon livery was peeling away to reveal both the original green, grey primer, and even bare metal.

But the 1100hp still available to the driver proved adequate for the task, and Bobbie did arrive on time for her check-up at the Divisional Headquarters of the Western Region after all. On her way to the medical centre she was aware of the many powerful individuals who had attended historic meetings in the offices she passed. Some she recalled were those commemorated by Castle class namings such as *Sir Felix Pole* (5066) and *Sir James Milne* (7001). Nor could she pass without admiring a large painting of the Brown-Boveri A1A-A1A Gas Turbine No.18000. A decision had been made in 1946 to try a novel form of propulsion, and the Swiss-built locomotive was joined later by No. 18100, a Co-Co example from Metropolitan-Vickers of Manchester as the motive power of the future.

In the medical centre Bobbie was met by a Mrs Glenys Watson who introduced herself as both the nurse and receptionist, and sending Bobbie through to the examination room, announced her accordingly.

"Miss Roberta Gherardini to see you, Doctor Goode."

The doctor welcomed his patient and put her at ease by joking that she was easily the best-looking signalman he'd ever examined. The first part of the proceedings was visual. Bobbie stood at one end of the room and recited the usual letters from the wall chart. This was followed by the Ishihara colour-blindness test. She passed both.

Bobbie was then instructed to undress, and as no modesty screens were available, she had to strip in front of the doctor. Once she was naked on the couch, he checked her reflexes and, palpating her abdomen, checked her internal organs. He also checked her pulse rate.

"I shall need to take your pulse again," Dr Goode said, "after some exercise. So go to the end of the room please and hurry towards me." Bobbie was surprised by the request but he was the professional in the white coat, so she obliged. "And once more please, Miss."

Bobbie was becoming acutely embarrassed as she was still naked, but again she complied with the doctor's wishes.

"Thank you, Miss. Excellent. I'll take your pulse again now." She stood before him and he raised her breasts to feel the beating of her heart. He seemed pleased with the results.

Somewhat later, Nurse Watson entered the room and was surprised to witness Dr Goode concluding his examination by holding a tape over the girl's breasts, allegedly measuring her for uniform, and had she been a moment earlier she might have seen how carefully he checked the girl's inside leg measurement. Bobbie eventually returned fully clothed to Nurse Watson in reception.

"Do you always undress so readily?" she asked.

"Well," Bobbie replied. "I just did what the doctor wanted me to do."

"I see, because I need a girl who doesn't mind taking her clothes off. My husband and I run a club and we always need girls like you to dance for us. How about joining us in your free time?"

Her transistor radio was playing softly, but she turned up the volume so that the Bee Gees could be more clearly heard.

"Let me see what you can do with 'Massachusetts'."

Bobbie obeyed the request and gyrated around a bit to the music. Nurse Watson seemed satisfied and commented that someone so voluptuous would make a great addition to the team."

Bobbie listened to what she was being offered and found herself in the same situation, she recalled, when having first met Pete Vere, making her mind up to say no, but agreeing to the proposal.

"Excellent, dear!" Mrs Watson said. "I'm sure you've made the right decision. Take my card. The pay isn't brilliant, but the tips? Wow!"

On her journey home, Bobbie tried to quell the misgivings she had about her new 'career'. She had never considered dancing before, and what was it said about taking clothes off? She decided she would not mention the club to her parents, but only report that the doctor had passed her as A1.

Chapter Nineteen

Bobbie Gherardini, eager to begin her career in the signal box, waited patiently for the letter confirming a starting date for Loudwater. However, a dismal lack of communication meant that time passed and no official letter was forthcoming, and she knew from what her father said that the box was being worked by relief signalmen on both early and late turns. Throughout much of November and December, Bobbie made numerous telephone calls, all of which proved to be fruitless, until she was finally informed by letter immediately after Christmas that her signalling career could not be considered until a new lamp-man had been recruited—and this after having heard previously that a replacement for her was 'imminent', and of course being passed as medically fit to manage a signal box. Bobbie's patience fortunately was unlimited.

Early in 1968, Bobbie and her father both recalled the words of old Jim Kendall that the gates at Spicer's Crossing could easily be replaced by automatic unmanned barriers of the type particularly common on railways in Europe. Juniper Lane had not succumbed to that indignity, but the lane to Hixon off the A51 in Staffordshire tragically had.

On the morning of 6th January, a massive low-loader crept over the crossing there so slowly that when the warning bells rang and the barriers came down, the huge vehicle, with its 120-ton transformer load, was still moving across the tracks as the 11.30 a.m. Manchester-Euston express approached at

75mph. Disaster was inevitable, and both enginemen in the cab of AL1 locomotive E3009, driver Stanley Turner and his secondman James Toghill, were killed. Another driver, unfortunately riding with them, also died along with eight passengers from the wrecked coaches.

In many ways the Hixon collision prompted second thoughts on the progressive introduction of continental-style crossings, and allowed Ben Gherardini's railway career to continue. Without doubt, had Hixon been manned the accident would not have happened.

Nearer the end of that first month of 1968, Bobbie unusually worked a Saturday morning herself (she had been unwell earlier in the week and was catching up with her lamps) and she was fortunate to see the new diesel prototype '*Kestrel*' pass through High Wycombe. A number of off-duty staff had also turned out to see the locomotive on its demonstration run from Marylebone to Princes Risborough. HS4000, in striking brown and yellow livery, was a development by Hawker Siddeley of the Brush Type 4.

To Bobbie's dismay, however, one of the railwaymen watching was Jon Rice, and he saw her before she could take evasive action. As he took her arm she could only mutter obscenities under her breath for her lack of vigilance.

"Still trainspotting, I see!" was his greeting.

Bobbie sought solace from the other men present but they seemed oblivious to her distress. They were discussing the folly of constructing new diesels when clearly the future was for electric traction. Proof of their argument they claimed was the recent scrapping of all five of the original D600 'Warships'.

Abandoning attempts to join in the conversation, poor Bobbie turned her attention to Rice.

"How—how are you?" she gasped. A confrontation with

him inevitably made her breathless, and the heaving bosom did not go unnoticed.

"Fine! Been busy disconnecting the siding points at Wooburn Green." Then, with almost divine intervention, Bobbie was saved any further harassment by a cry from the group that the last man through the door of the 'Flint' bought the drinks. Without another word Rice pushed Bobbie away from him and hurried after his colleagues.

With a heartfelt sigh of relief Bobbie went about her business and thought about her father's 1933 penny. Was it really worth much? She wished she'd never set eyes on it. If Rice was working locally again she would see more of him, and she had no Bob Gillespie to help her. His advice to retaliate or threaten in return was forgotten in the anxiety of the moment, and she did not want to upset the man and make a difficult situation even worse.

Before Bobbie finished her work, she saw the magnificent 'Kestrel' return London-bound, then reflected on the conversation she'd heard earlier; if diesel traction was as dated as suggested then it was only history repeating itself, as literally hundreds of steam engines were built after publication of the 1955 Modernisation Plan which stated that steam should be eliminated. The majority, of course, were BR Standard classes, but looking back, it would appear to be a case of gross mismanagement, particularly by the Western Region because as late as the summer of 1956 they were still introducing GWR-designed pannier tanks, by which time hundreds of 0-6-0 diesel shunters were on the scene.

Had Bobbie been in her usual rude health, this same Saturday would have been her first night at the Caboose Club. So it was for the next weekend that Bobbie's parents believed she would be visiting friends in London and not back until the Sunday morning. They had been puzzled and rather annoyed that she'd played the same few records over and over in her room. But those were the ones sent to her by Mrs Watson, to which Bobbie was to choreograph a dance routine.

As Bobbie went to bed that night she pondered on what the sleeping arrangements might be at the Club. An overnight stay was essential as it did not close until the the early hours of the next morning. What time it did close Bobbie didn't know, and she realised there were many questions she ought to have asked but could not do so now without appearing foolish. Maybe, she thought, as she drifted off to sleep, if she was lucky, Mrs Watson would be like the Mother Superior from the bakery.

Monday morning brought flurries of snow but not enough to cause disruption to services, but as Bobbie prepared to attend to the first of her signals Jon Rice came into the cabin.

"I'm sorry I didn't have much time for you on Saturday. I wanted to discuss our little arrangement. You remember, yeah? Where you hand something over to a mate of mine, I get a nice commission and everyone lives happily ever after!"

"Look," Bobbie protested, "I don't have anything to give you."

"But you are so wrong! There's a lovely little guest house just up the hill. Very discreet. I'd keep you snug these cold nights!"

Fortunately for Bobbie their conversation was interrupted once again, this time by the return of both signal and telegraph men. Jon Rice promptly left the cabin, and a few minutes later Bobbie followed after first making sure the coast was clear—an action that did not go unobserved by the elder of the two men.

"Was he pestering you?"

"No, no!" Bobbie replied, not wanting either of them to get involved in in the situation. "It's OK, really it is."

She walked to the up platform just as the 7.35 a.m. Banbury drew in, and such was the popularity of this train (8.27 departure, non-stop to Paddington) that literally hundreds were waiting to board. Bobbie made no attempt to weave a way through the throng of passengers. The driver greeted Bobbie cheerfully then pipped the horn of his blue 'Hymek' to acknowledge the 'right away'. D7017 then made a typically noisy departure, and by the time Bobbie had reached the first of her signals for attention, those belonging to High Wycombe Middle Box, the up platform was already reoccupied by an 8-car DMU forming a stopping service to Marylebone.

As the morning wore on the weather seemed to turn colder although the snow showers had passed. It was not practical to wear gloves when seeing to the signal lamps so by mid-morning Bobbie took advantage of the warmth in the Middle box at the quieter end of the station. It was a morning such as this when she thought wistfully of having her own signal box at Loudwater.

Lunch break was taken back at the S&T cabin. Neither lineman was present, and as the key was in the door Bobbie took the precaution of locking herself in. Delving in her satchel she searched for her timetable to find a train to take her to her first session at the Caboose Club. She had begun this earlier, but stopped when interrupted by Jon Rice. Now she realised she had mislaid the card Mrs Watson had given her. On it was a lot of personal information, but though she searched for it, even emptying out the S&T men's rubbish bin, it was to no avail. Fortunately, most of the details on the card she could remember.

Luncheon over, she returned to finish the signals for the Middle box and make a start on those for Wycombe North further down the line, which controlled the goods yard. Years before, the signal box there had been open twenty-four hours a day, but those busy times had gone and a single weekday shift only sufficed. Nor was there a night turn at the Middle; only the South box was open continuously.

The week passed all too quickly, and with mounting trepidation Bobbie found herself at High Wycombe Station on Saturday evening catching the last up express of the day. Arriving in Paddington, she had two hours before she was due on stage for her first dance at the club. It was a burly doorman who ushered Bobbie along to Mrs Watson's office. He must have detected Bobbie's nervousness as he left her.

"Don't worry, sweetheart, the guys'll love you!"

Bobbie could hear a band playing, with intermittent applause followed by much whistling and cheering at the conclusion of the piece. She did not have to wait long for Mrs Watson, but she hardly recognised the woman. Glenys the proprietress looked nothing like Glenys the nurse; the most startling difference being the bouffant red hair that was surely a wig. Bobbie also learned that despite wearing her best dress that evening, she was to change into clothes provided by Mrs Watson. For Bobbie it was yet one more misgiving.

"What if they don't fit me?" she protested.

"Don't worry, darling. It's never been a problem yet!" Before Mrs Watson left Bobbie to prepare herself, she reiterated the doorman's words of how popular she was surely going to be.

The layout of the stage and side wings created, in effect, a one-way system which in many respects was an unfortunate arrangement, as those going on stage did not meet those coming off. Thus it was that Bobbie heard the rapturous applause for the girl billed before her but did not see the girl in person. Had she done so, Bobbie might have been more aware of what was expected of her.

Chapter Twenty

Bobbie's first number was 'A Whiter Shade of Pale', a big hit from May 1967 and a wonderfully andante piece for an organist. Mrs Watson came to escort her protégé to the stage, and Bobbie, only dimly aware that she was announced, heard none of the applause—only the music—from the small band as she was propelled across the stage into the dawn of a new career.

It was impossible to tell how many were in the audience. The spotlight was dazzling, and much of the club hidden by subdued lighting and cigar smoke. The duration of the Procol Harum hit was extended to five minutes but to Bobbie it seemed more like fifty. Yet the band behind her played well, and the performance by the organist so near a match to that of Matt Fisher that Bobbie had no problems with her routine, but she could not help but notice that men at the bar away to her left were paying her little attention and concentrating more on their drinks. Undaunted, Bobbie continued her dance and finally, to rather meagre applause, thankfully left the stage and returned to the antechamber. She could have sworn that she'd seen Jon Rice in the audience, but convinced herself that she must have been mistaken.

She was not due on again for half an hour so Bobbie, for the first time since she'd arrived, relaxed a little and enjoyed a smoke. Later she took the opportunity to explore the room. A fur coat lay over the back of a chair, and she discovered a number of doors led off into what were tiny bedrooms. They were little more than cupboards yet there was space for a made-up camp bed, and Bobbie was relieved to find in one a note pinned to a pillow with her name on.

For Bobbie's second appearance on stage she was to dance to the song 'I Love How You Love Me', a minor chart success for Maureen Evans in 1964. Mrs Watson's sister would be the vocalist. The routine began quite straightforwardly, but after just the opening chorus the singer came to Bobbie's side and, like a ventriloquist addressing a dummy, told her to go and see the bartender. Puzzled, Bobbie did as she was asked and walked straight into the arms of Mrs Watson who, with her colleague assisting willingly, stripped the protesting Bobbie naked behind the bar. Mrs Watson almost snarled her instructions.

"Now get back out there and do what I'm paying you for, and just you remember to keep a hand over your fanny, I don't want to get closed down; and another thing, next time I tell you to give yourself a trim, do it—unless you want Jack here to do it for you!"

The band resumed playing as Bobbie, wearing only a red choker and matching high heels, was propelled onto the stage to continue her act. Blinking back tears of indignation she peered again into the haze, but as if to welcome her return there was loud applause and whistling, those at the front tables rising to their feet and clapping the most. Lewd suggestions followed as Bobbie's performance restarted, and almost immediately money began to appear on the stage. Owing to the interruption Bobbie's routine was short, and Mrs Watson soon came forward to usher her away and gather up the rewards.

"I'll take care of these," she said. "You get back here in half an hour."

Offstage, and only bothering to slip on the discarded fur

coat, Bobbie wept over her own foolishness and tried to come to terms with her humiliating experience. There were sounds coming through the thin walls of a couple having a good time in one of the small rooms, but Bobbie paid them no heed; nothing about the Caboose Club surprised her any more. When the noises stopped no one appeared, nor did anyone else materialise, certainly not Mrs Watson with the tips which Bobbie realised she wasn't going to see.

As she chain-smoked, the nicotine gave her some clarity of thought and much of what she previously had only half-understood became blindingly obvious. How could she have been so naïve? She decided therefore that her next number 'Move Over Darling' (Doris Day 1964) should be one to remember as it would be her last. Wearing only the fur coat, Bobbie returned to the stage for her third routine and, buoyed by indignation, flung off the coat to a rapturous cheer of delight from the crowd. Such nudity was generally confined to the final moments of a song so Bobbie was providing much more than the usual quota. Their appreciation encouraged her to the extent that although she obeyed Mrs Watson's order and kept a hand discreetly in position, what the good lady could not see was how Bobbie spread her fingers so those directly in front of her saw much more than they should have done! The roar of approval was deafening.

Bobbie could see Mrs Watson watching her suspiciously and perhaps wondering if she should intervene, but good money was being thrown Bobbie's way so she let things be. It was only when Bobbie took her routine to another dimension that the woman began to take hesitant steps forward.

The club had a strict 'no touching' policy but Bobbie didn't care. She ceased bothering to dance and waving both hands defiantly at Mrs Watson knelt at the front of the stage where she allowed one man immediately below her to reach and fondle her breasts. The crowd went wild as they pressed forward to share the experience while banknotes fluttered around like confetti. Someone, the worse for drink and keen not to miss out on the fun, was even standing on a table.

"Save your money, you can shag her for tuppence! The eyetie bitch!"

The words chilled Bobbie's heart as she recognised the voice of Jon Rice and realised that he was in the crowd after all, and that it must have been he also who stole her card and traced her movements. Such was his enthusiasm that the table on which he stood collapsed under his weight, yet he got up from the broken glasses and spilt drinks to mount the stage, unzip his trousers and pull out his fierce erection. Egged on by the crowd, he was clearly intent on raping the girl on the spot.

The bass player was first to respond. Leaving the band he felled Rice with a single swipe of his guitar and then kicked the prostrate body off the stage. Outraged at this assault on a member of the paying public, other men from the crowd stormed the stage in protest. While some went for the bassist, others picked on whoever happened to be nearest. It was complete mayhem but Bobbie, keeping on the outside of the melee, had the presence of mind to retrieve the fur coat and stuff the pockets with as many of the banknotes as she could before fleeing.

There were shouts for her to return at once, but she was resolute in her decision to be gone. With no time to lose she bundled her own clothes into her satchel, wrapped the fur coat closely around her and hurried out into the street. As she paused to get her breath back in a doorway of a shop opposite the club, she lit a cigarette and saw the first of several police constables arrive. Bobbie approached one of them with as much nonchalance as she could muster for directions to Marylebone Station.

"You have to pass 'GO'! Sorry, love, get someone else to help you." At 3 a.m. Bobbie thought that unlikely, but she recrossed the street to observe the aftermath of the affray. An ambulance arrived and one of the individuals helped into it was Jon Rice, and a woman led away in handcuffs was surely Mrs Watson. To Bobbie's surprise her medical examiner, Dr Goode, was also being taken away. At that point Bobbie concluded she had had enough of the Caboose Club and her one remaining desire was to get back home.

She would never have imagined herself walking the streets of London in the early hours of a Sunday morning, but after the humiliating and degrading experience she had suffered she felt wonderfully free. She was surprised how busy the city still was. More or less by luck she managed to get on to the Euston Road and, from an earlier visit to Madame Tussauds, knew if she headed westwards and turned right soon after crossing Baker Street she would find Marylebone Station. It was nearly 4 a.m. before she reached that sanctuary only to discover no hot drinks available nor even a waiting room open where she could dress herself properly and rest. She realised she had little choice but to wait as patiently as she could for the first train of the day to High Wycombe.

There were few railway staff about but inevitably Bobbie caught the eye of a British Transport policeman. She watched his progress but he seemed to take little notice of her, and for a fleeting moment she considered opening her coat and getting herself arrested just to enjoy the warmth of a police cell, but instead she pulled the fur coat all the more tightly around her body as the officer disappeared the way he had come.

She remembered the policeman she had spoken to outside

the club and his reference to Monopoly. Wondering how much money she did have she inspected the contents of her satchel to discover a number of ten-shilling notes, several pound notes and a lot of American dollar bills. As Bobbie put the money away she looked up to find herself being observed again by the railway policeman. He had returned, accompanied by a female colleague. It was she who spoke to Bobbie.

"What are you doing here at this hour of the morning?"

"I'm waiting for a train," Bobbie replied simply.

"Well, we've had numerous complaints concerning this station being used for prostitution so I'm afraid I must ask you to leave."

Poor Bobbie was horrified, still smarting from her ordeal and chilled to the bone. Sex was the last thing on her mind.

"But you don't understand," Bobbie argued. "I just want to get home. I was working in a club earlier, as a dancer, but I've quit, and the the money is tips." Neither officer looked particularly convinced so Bobbie continued to explain. "I know I've a long wait, but I work on the railway myself and I really am waiting for a train."

"Well, what do you do on the railway?" the policewoman asked.

"I'm the lampwoman for the signal boxes at High Wycombe." The male officer then asked what the names of the signal boxes were and Bobbie frowned for a moment before she understood the question and realised it was question designed to catch her out.

"Oh," she replied. "South, Middle and North." To Bobbie's relief both officers were satisfied with her answer and left her alone to resume their beat duties.

On weekdays the first train in the morning from Marylebone was the unadvertised (not in the public timetable, that is)

4.00 a.m. departure, commonly referred to by dint of what it primarily carried: 'The papers'. On Sundays, however, the first train down was considerably later, at 6.53 a.m., and appeared in both working and public timetables.

When the transport police left Bobbie the time was 4.45 a.m., and as it was too cold to sit still for long Bobbie paced around reading the many advertisements and studying the timetables, both her own and that for the Amersham line. But fortunately Bobbie did not have to wait as long as she anticipated.

Around 6 a.m. she noticed a DMU running in, and was overjoyed to see the destination blind being wound around to read 'High Wycombe' by the guard who was riding with his driver.

When they'd stopped, the driver began walking to the other end of his unit while the West Indian guard busied himself first checking, then attaching, a tail lamp. He turned to Bobbie as she approached.

"You want my train, lady?" he enquired.

"I think so. Will you be the 6.53?"

"Yes, Ma'am. You get right on in!"

Thoroughly chilled, and never more glad to climb into a railway coach, Bobbie first sat appreciating the warmth, then regardless of the well-known notice took advantage of the toilet facilities and the opportunity to dress properly. Returning to her seat she was soon asleep and roused only when the train started, and again later when negotiating Northholt Junction where trains from Marylebone passed under the Great Western direct line to Birmingham, and came up to join it after a short distance, from which point they were on the 'new' joint line. Once on familiar metals Bobbie became more relaxed and oblivious to the progress of her train; whether it stopped anywhere en route she neither knew or cared. But the same guard kindly tapped on the carriage window to wake her when they arrived in High Wycombe.

There was no bus home scheduled at that hour on a Sunday morning but Bobbie, refreshed after her sleep, was content to walk and reflect on the events of the night before and the inevitable retribution from Jon Rice. She didn't expect any from Nurse Glenys Watson. How different the woman was out of uniform. And whose fur coat did she have? Was it Mrs Watson's? Bobbie would of course send it back. In the meantime she was going to report both her and Dr Goode. The thought of them both being 'struck off' was a comfort to Bobbie, still incensed over the way she had been treated.

Chapter Twenty-One

Daybreak on Monday morning witnessed one of the rare occasions when Bobbie Gheradini really did not want to go in to work. She was dreading the inevitable confrontation with Jon Rice over the unfortunate events of the weekend. She knew that none of it was her fault but did not think that he would to see it that way. However, she need not have had such a sleepless night, because when she arrived for work, she learned from her S&T colleagues that Rice had reported sick, nursing a fractured shoulder blade. Said one of the men, "In a fight in some seedy strip joint, I've heard." Bobbie winced with embarrassment but said nothing.

It was a somewhat withdrawn Bobbie that continued to do her work as diligently as before, but with still no prospect of becoming a signalwoman she felt more than ever before that she should get away and leave everything behind her.

Normally Bobbie kept her own counsel but, without quite knowing why, she confided in the young newly-appointed signalman at the Middle box. A mug of tea and warmth from his stove was all she knew she could expect from him as his youthful charms were directed at those of the same gender as himself, but nevertheless Bobbie appreciated his encouragement for a change of career. However, she came to a personal decision herself during an incident that occurred one morning in the middle of February.

A lone Brush Type 4, D1728, for Tyseley, was momentarily

stopped at the Middle's down main home. The engine was eventually allowed to continue on its way, but the driver interrupted the progress and pulled up right outside the box, left his cab, and came stomping up to belligerently insist the signalman telephoned Control immediately. Taken aback, the signalman obliged but, once a voice answered, the driver snatched the phone away and informed the poor Control clerk in no uncertain terms that unless he was guaranteed a clear run back to the West Midlands he would leave the engine right where it was and return 'on the cushions' with the next down 'fast'. His wish must have been granted as, with an emphatic grunt, he terminated the call. Bobbie and the signalman looked at each other and at the driver but he simply muttered something unintelligible and left to rejoin the footplate, while his poor secondman looked as if he was on the verge of tears. Bobbie felt sorry for the lad, as even being given priority status, it would likely be two hours at least before he would be able to book off from his ill-tempered mate.

It later transpired that the pair had brought up an overnight freight to Acton. Starting from Bescot the trip was bedevilled with problems: a wagon with a 'hot axle box' was detached at Leamington, and yet another at Banbury; it was while waiting in the up loop at Banbury that their engine, D1714, was commandeered to take over from an ailing 'Peak' on a freightliner scheduled for a container ship waiting to sail from Southampton. No spare locomotive at Banbury or Oxford meant the pair had to wait for D1728 to come from Tyseley before they could hook on and continue.

It was the plight of that secondman that made Bobbie realise she no longer wanted to be part of the railway operating scene. During her lunch break she wrote out her letter of resignation, but having some misgivings about the wisdom of her actions did not post the missive that day. Nor did she do so the next. On the third day, with it still in her satchel, the same Wycombe Middle man happened to mention that his heavily pregnant elder sister was leaving her job as train announcer at Twyford.

Earlier Bobbie would have laughed at the thought of using a public address system but she instantly felt that that was the role for her. The letter of resignation developed into one of application, the risky step of giving notice—necessary, Bobbie thought, to avoid the possibility of a transfer again—being delayed until a replacement was found. But she was blessed with good fortune, and following a successful interview at Western Tower in Reading, the London Division's new provincial offices, Roberta Gherardini became a train announcer for Twyford based in the recently constructed signal box there.

Twyford in Berkshire lay, give or take a mile or two, midway between Maidenhead and Reading on Brunel's main line west to Bristol. The new panel box was the result of singling the 4½-mile branch line to Henley-on-Thames and taking over the work of both Twyford East and West signal boxes on the main line as well as six others in the vicinity. Yet despite being a new installation, the box also incorporated a mechanical lever frame to control movements locally, in particular those over the branch line.

Two train announcers were employed at Twyford, working between them a 12-hour day from 7 a.m. to 7 p.m., changing over at 1 p.m. On the morning of Monday, February 20th 1968, Bobbie was met by Mrs Molly Davies, herself on late turn, but covering both shifts in order to show Bobbie her responsibilities and escort her to the signal box situated in the 'vee' of the junction of the Reading and Henley lines. To Bobbie, Mrs Davies was the spitting image of the Mother Superior from the bakery, both in appearance and demeanour.

Twyford box was open continuously, and the early-turn signalman to whom Bobbie was introduced that morning was Henry Collinson, a short thick-set middle-aged man, bespectacled with greying fair hair. His role looked deceptively easy in contrast to High Wycombe. The Twyford signalman stood at a panel upon which was depicted a plan of the area in the style of Harry Beck's London Underground map. By turning an appropriate switch on the diagram at the 'entrance' to a route, and simply pressing a button at the 'exit', electrically operated points moved and colour-light signals cleared for a train to proceed. That a route was correctly set was confirmed by a series of white lights on the diagram. These lights changed to red as the train occupied the relevant track circuits.

What was completely new to Bobbie was the emphasis placed on train description. The four-character head code carried by the DMU or locomotive was also represented on the console. For Bobbie, having been raised as it were on a branch line, and having watched the decline of the Paddington-Birmingham route, the West of England main line seemed extremely busy. But, inevitably, Henry was quick to point out how much busier it had been in days gone by when, interestingly enough, he had manned some of the signal boxes closed on account of the resignalling work, such as Kennet Bridge, Ruscombe and also Sonning, the box at the western end of the much photographed cutting.

For Bobbie's first day, and indeed for the second, she was granted the luxury of office-like hours of 10 a.m. until 4 p.m., her regular early turn not due to commence until Wednesday. Both Henry Collinson and Molly Davies treated Bobbie as if she were a favourite niece and, anxious that she should have an easy first day, insisted that initially they should do the work for her while she acquainted herself with the timetable and, just as importantly, with the kettle! By comparison with her colleagues at Reading where the majority of trains called at a large number of platforms, Bobbie knew her task was straight-forward. Main line trains that called at Twyford were few, and the only additional suburban service was that along the branch to Henley. The signalman said he could give her a cue when a train needed to be announced but added that she only need observe the console to learn that for herself.

"If in doubt," he said, "ask, and if I don't know which train is what, just leave the bloody mike off!"

As he finished speaking, a local train (2A14) 'struck in' on the up relief. He cleared his throat and stated that he would announce the train himself. He flicked the microphone on, and a red warning light glowed beside the switch as a visual reminder.

"Station announcement. The next train at platform number four is the 10.50 departure for London, calling at Maidenhead, Taplow, Burnham, Slough, Ealing Broadway and Paddington." The signalman finished his speech, but Bobbie failed to see the red light go out. She was astonished when the signalman spoke again. "Oi you, you fat bastard! Put that cigar out! You're getting in a non-smoking compartment!" Bobbie could not believe what she was hearing, but soon laughed when she realised her leg had been pulled.

Henry then moved back to his console, allowing Molly to resume her position at the announcer's desk. She then spoke herself as almost simultaneously another DMU was arriving from the opposite direction.

"Station announcement. The train approaching platform three is the 10.50 to Reading. Reading only train platform three." She switched off the microphone and the red light went out.

"There you are, two slightly different ways of passing on information. If you can, it helps to use the word 'approaching'. It gives passengers a chance to get their bags together, kiss one another goodbye—all that sort of thing. Do remember the 'Station Announcement' bit; it's like a 'listen here, you lot, pay attention', and don't forget to repeat the main part of the message again, and please, use the 24-hour clock system. Have a go yourself whenever you like."

Bobbie thanked her mentor and agreed that she would announce the next train along the branch line. Almost stealthily, while they had been preoccupied with the more prestigious services, a single unit rail-car had arrived from Henley-on-Thames and now waited patiently in the bay platform, number five.

Shortly before W55029 was due to depart back whence it came (to Henley) Bobbie kept her promise by intending to announce it but, to her dismay, not a word came from her lips. She could not speak but let out a wail instead. Quick to respond, the signalman left his panel and spoke into the microphone.

"Ladies and gentlemen, I do apologise, I trod on the signal box cat! The train at platform five is for Henley-on-Thames. All stations to Henley, platform five."

When he finished the announcement and turned to Bobbie, he saw only tears of laughter in her eyes. "Do we have a cat?" she asked.

"No, no. Mind you, there was one once in the old West box. Now," he continued, "imagine you're only speaking to Molly here."

So Bobbie tried once more. "Sta... sta... sta... ," she stammered.

Again it was Henry who saved the day. Bobbie was looking at Molly, but she was insufficient as the focus of attention so

Henry joined her, and as they posed like a happy couple having their photograph taken at the seaside, Bobbie managed to speak over the air. "Sta… tion announcement. The train at platform, er… ,"—Molly waved a hand extending all the digits—"five," gasped Bobbie, "is for Henry—sorry, Henley! Henry—Henley, train platform five!"

Molly chuckled, and the signalman, looking out of the window, added, "Well done, love, pity it's already half way there!" But Bobbie was pleased she had actually done the announcement, and her fear of the microphone subsided. Molly suggested that for the future she should bring in a photograph of a boyfriend and use him as a person to address. She seemed surprised when Bobbie said she didn't have one.

However, Bobbie accepted the advice, and the next day brought with her a photograph of The Searchers in addition to a framed print that had once graced the walls of the S&T cabin in High Wycombe, and been presented to Bobbie as a farewell gift on her last day as lampwoman there. It was the photograph of the famous gantry at Rugby. Her lamping mentor, Joe with the unpronounceable surname, had come up from Princes Risborough especially to see her and wish her well, and the mystery of where the Rugby print had disappeared to was explained! Joe had taken the trouble to both clean and frame the picture. They'd had a lunchtime drink together in 'The Antelope' pub in Church Square, and then later walked to where his old Austin A50 was parked in Wycombe North yard to continue their conversation. Bobbie remembered Joe's remarks about paraffin and that the only friends she would have while lamping would be the signals, and he had been right.

Meanwhile, that afternoon the coalmen were attending their business loading up their lorries from the 16-tonners shunted in earlier. The signalman was in his box, and ticking over in a siding was D6342 on the already made-up 4.05 p.m. for Thame. Although departure was two hours away, the locomotive had been left idling since its earlier duties as few drivers shut a diesel-hydraulic down in wintertime, particularly if the batteries were suspect, for fear of being unable to start it up again.

It was in his car that Joe admitted he'd forgotten to bring the list of lever numbers in connection with the Rugby signals. To rectify this, Joe suggested that he and Bobbie met again in the 'The Antelope' the following evening, a proposal to which Bobbie readily agreed. Wycombe North box was 'switched out' and the yard dark and silent when Joe parked his car once again among the sidings. No one was around to witness him and his companion climb into the back seat nor observe later the old car rocking on its suspension.

Chapter Twenty Two

In order to be on duty for 7 a.m., Bobbie had to begin her journey to work by bus as there was not a suitably early enough train along the branch for her to catch the 6.41 from Maidenhead which arrived at Twyford at 6.50.

Bobbie's Twyford station dated from the 1890s. Originally the route was double track only, but those early metals became the relief lines when the main lines were added and additional platforms provided. The footbridge linking the platforms was the ideal vantage point, and from it, so straight were the four tracks, one could see for miles in either direction. Bobbie tried to imagine the scene in Victorian times and the rails laid to Broad Gauge and 2ft 3¾ins wider apart. From the footbridge one could plainly see the slight deviation the later lines took around the original downside building which became an island platform.

Of the station's earlier signal boxes, Twyford West had once stood on the Reading end of the island platform. The site of the East box was beyond the roadbridge carrying the A321 to Wokingham. Legislation for mechanical signal boxes dictated that 350 yards of rodding was the maximum permitted between lever and points, and this explained the existence of many such boxes. However, the spread of modern signalling technology was nothing new. Power-operated points had been installed at Beaconsfield on the GW&GC joint line as early as 1923, permitting the closure of the West box there. Gerrards

Cross too was similarly modernised.

Yet, overall, the 'new line' was generally untouched by the hand of progress. In contrast, signal boxes on the GWR main line to Bristol had been decimated. Excluding Twyford, just five boxes—Old Oak Common, Slough, Reading, Swindon and Bristol—would be responsible for Brunel's original line. Until a few years ago, five signal boxes were essential in and around Slough alone.

It would be easy to question why there was a new box at Twyford at all. Slough (or Reading) panel had the capacity to control it, but, in fact, Twyford preceded both by a number of years. Bobbie knew that she was going to be very happy at Twyford. It was a comfortable indoor job, a great team and no likelihood of meeting undesirable individuals off the permanent way. One thing which did impress her was the speed at which the trains passed. Even in their heyday the Birmingham trains that had not stopped at High Wycombe passed at only 45mph due to the curvature of the layout. At Twyford, expresses hammered through at 85 or 90, and given a late running service coming up, with a driver anxious to get finished, speeds of 100mph were not uncommon.

One needed to be at Twyford little more than an hour to see the whole of the WRs locomotive fleet engaged on principle duties: the Brush Type 4s and both B-B and C-C varieties of diesel-hydraulic. It was interesting to see the Pullman multiple units again; the Bristol and South Wales services ran regularly in competition with the M4 motorway but gone was the distinctive blue and white livery in favour of an uninspiring grey with all-over yellow ends. But if Bobbie had wondered what had become of the Birmingham Pullman set she'd once known, it had not been transferred to the LM Region as originally planned, but now provided a service to Oxford.

With the exception of the Pullmans, the best or fastest trains on the WR were virtually anonymous, carrying neither head-board or coach roof boards as a means of identity. However, some famous names from the past were still perpetuated by the older railwayman; as an example, the 18.00 Paddington-Swansea continued to be referred to as the 'Dragon'. Now hauled by a D1000 class, even Bobbie could recall the 'Red Dragon' storming through Maidenhead behind a Britannia Pacific, one of the batch 70015–29 then allocated to the WR. Train reporting numbers were a major feature of modern signal-ling, but the Western had long developed its own identification codes for express trains using a set of three numbers carried in a frame fixed to the handles of the smokebox door.

The first number, from zero to 9, gave a clue from where the train had started. 1, for example, indicated Paddington, 7 meant Wales (the Red Dragon carried 720) while 9 was Birkenhead. These WR headcodes were used in conjunction with the tradi-tional headlamp code, but were always a source of annoyance to trainspotters as they very effectively hid the smokebox numberplate. With the dawn of the diesels the old lamp codes were perpetuated by unfolding a disc on the front of the loco-motive which also allowed a white light to be displayed.

But the ultimate in train classification was the development of the 4-character headcode. It became a standard feature on all diesels and electrics from 1962 and some older types had the headcode facility fitted retrospectively, to the detriment of their appearance. While the last two numbers distinguished one train from another as the WR system had, it was the first two characters that had the most significance. The first of the two, numeric, nought to nine, indicated the class of the train; the second was alphabetic, A to Z, but without I, Q, R, U, W and Y. At the end of each sequence was a dot and then blank until one could wind no further. A letter indicated destination; E for the Eastern Region, M for the LMR, O the Southern, S for Scotland, and V the Western. X and Z were reserved for specials and each of the regions used other letters to its own advantage. On the WR the letter A denoted a service running within, or terminating in, the London Division. B indicated Bristol and C, Plymouth. Suburban services, however, did not have the luxury of an individual reporting number; for them a generic code sufficed. The Paddington-Reading 'all stations', for example, had the headcode 2A64, whereas 'semi-fasts' were 2A14.

Although the Henley line was basically a 'shuttle' service, a couple of 'through' trains ran directly to Paddington each morning, eliminating the customary change at Twyford. These trains were locomotive-hauled, with two D7000 'Hymeks', coupled, coming off Reading shed specifically for the purpose, providing a more prestigious service than the average DMU. For the same discerning passengers the direct service returned in the evening.

Although Twyford would never be as busy or as complex as Reading, a variety of traffic could be observed, and its open-access platforms meant the station was a regular haunt in the school holidays for locospotters.

Of interest was the Motorail service, 08.05 Kensington-St Austell, which allowed travellers, at a price, a journey by train, yet have their car with them on arrival in Cornwall. The vehicles were conveyed on car-flats attached to the rear of the coaches. Although the inclusion of freight stock restricted the train to 75mph, it nevertheless saved the holidaymaker some 250 miles of motoring.

Bobbie wondered what it was like to travel on the night Paddington-Penzance sleeper. Although not a train she expected to ever see, she nevertheless saw sleeping car movements as Empty Coaching Stock (ECS). Other empty movements were the various dairies' milk tanks which returned to Cardiff and Plymouth for evening milking. Diesel traction only could be observed, of course; the gas turbine duo, 18000 and 18100, had not run on Western metals for a nearly a decade and what steam still existed in 1968 was confined to in and around Lancashire and scheduled for elimination completely when the current timetable expired on May 5th.

As the weeks passed, Bobbie became a regular passenger going to and from work, and over the Maidenhead line—such a familiar figure that she sometimes rode with the guard in his compartment if the train was crowded. One guard, Mr D. Clarke, a young Hank Marvin of the 'Shadows' lookalike would always invite her to join him, and she would assist him with his duties by giving the 'right away' to the driver (buzzing twice on the traincrew communication system) and closing doors after passengers had alighted.

Despite finding the role of a guard interesting, Bobbie had no wish to be one herself as, with emphasis on productivity, guards rostered on services that called at stations where staff were no longer employed would be obliged to issue tickets—like a bus conductor—in addition to their usual duties. Many guards were unhappy with such a monetary burden laid at their door, Guard Clarke included.

It took some time for Bobbie to ascertain Guard Clarke's first name. It was, he told her eventually, Dave, and no, he did not play the drums in a pop group. However, Clarke himself welcomed the new productivity deal for goods guards, because for all fully-fitted freight services the brake van was no longer necessary, and the guard's position was to be in the back cab of the locomotive. Moreover, if the particular turn was a single-manned duty, the guard was to perform the duties of the secondman.

Of course, the locomen's union, ASLEF, were not happy about mere NUR guards invading their hallowed space, but after some 'industrial action' in protest the situation was accepted. Indeed, as time went on, drivers became amenable to the more sensible arrangement of the guard riding with them rather than in the back cab where, unable to read signals, he would see little except the end of the first wagon. A number of railwaymen saw this particular productivity deal as a first step towards eliminating goods guards completely. But the keen and youthful David Clarke saw a transfer from Slough to Banbury Yard as an opportunity to be on engines as part of his work and a boyhood dream coming true as, owing to a slight eye defect, a career on the footplate was denied him.

The Henley-on-Thames branch was not worked by Slough traincrew but by Reading men. Nevertheless, Clarke knew the branch well as he lived in Henley himself. Bobbie had yet to travel over it herself, but as she was in a way responsible for passenger information over the line she felt it was something she should do. So to amend the situation she agreed to Clarke's suggestion that, together, they patronise the 2A86 service and pay the Regatta town a visit.

On a pleasant Friday afternoon in May after both had finished their respective early turns, Dave Clarke, still in his uniform, and Bobbie, wearing a white blouse and brown Edwardian length skirt she thought suitable for the occasion, boarded the 13.15 departure from Twyford to Henley, which ambled along the picturesque 4 ½ miles of single line calling at Wargrave and Shiplake en route.

Upon arrival at Henley-on-Thames, their intention was to buy a snack from the station buffet, but Bobbie was surprised to see her former employer Peter Vere manning the establishment. Although pleased that he was continuing to serve the public, she could not think of what to say to him so to save embarrassment hurried on by with her face averted. The couple ate in a cafè in the town centre instead.

Later they strolled along the banks of the Thames, upstream, and Bobbie felt a little ashamed that, with the exception of the mallard and its famous connection to the Gresley engine, she could identify no other waterfowl at all. Dave Clarke on the other hand was quite knowledgeable. After about a mile they turned to retrace their steps and it was then that Bobbie asked Dave whereabouts in Henley he lived. "If you like, I'll show you," he replied, "and you can come in for a cup of tea."

Walking in the opposite direction to their earlier ramble Dave kept to the same side of the river, but turned down a quiet road and stopped outside what could only be described as nothing less than a mansion. "You live here?" Bobbie asked incredulously, as Dave led the way up a wide gravel drive bisecting a lawn resembling a school playing field.

"Well, not exactly," came the reply. "I live down the garden."

"Down the garden? What, in a shed?"

"No, no, you'll see. Keep walking."

They passed around the building and came to the rear where another expanse of grass led down to the river.

"*Juno*!" Dave announced.

"Hmm?" Bobbie murmured. "Do I know what?"

"I live on the boat *Juno*", Dave explained, and pointed to a red and black narrowboat gently tugging at her ropes at the end of the lawn.

"My goodness!" exclaimed Bobbie.

There were other craft tied up nearby but Bobbie fell in love with the boat straightaway. Dave helped her to get on board.

"Ooh," she said, teasing him, "that's our first hug!"

Dave let go somewhat nervously, swung the tiller out of the way, and told Bobbie to mind her head when going below into the galley—the first compartment encountered of Dave's floating home.

"Welcome aboard the Roman Goddess *Juno*," he said.

"It's... it's... "—Bobbie searched for an appropriate word—"it's enchanting! Do you go far in it?"

"No, no, it's only possible to use it on navigable rivers and the few canals still open. In fact it won't go anywhere without being towed. Years ago it would've been horse-drawn. It was derelict when I first discovered it. I was a carpenter before I joined the railway so I've done most of the restoration myself. A firm in Banbury, Tooley's, would put a diesel engine in it for me—and do the electrics—but I don't really want to convert it. It's only half finished anyway."

Bobbie saw this for herself as Dave gave her a guided tour. Apart from the galley, a parlour and one bedroom, the rest of the vessel towards the prow was little more than a shell and used for storage. "I must stop collecting junk before she lists," Dave commented.

Bobbie laughed and glanced at the many boxes of train magazines among a number of items of railway memorabilia. She picked up what she thought was a smokebox numberplate from a Prairie tank.

"Actually," Dave said, taking it from her hands and turning it up the other way, "it's from 6919 *Tylney Hall*. I was with the fireman at the time—but that's another story!"

Bobbie laughed again, but was so enthralled with Dave's unusual home she did not want to leave it, nor did Dave want her to go. Suffice to say that, when Bobbie suggested going out for dinner later, he went to the house straightaway to use the telephone and book a table for two in the 'Catherine Wheel' in Hart Street.

Charmed by his busty companion, Dave was willing to make excuses on her behalf for being a fussy eater or boring company, but Bobbie was neither of these and the conversation was quite animated. The railways of Britain had been nationalised for just twenty years but, Bobbie pointed out to Dave, the Italian network, the Ferrovie dello Stato (FS) was nationalised as long ago as 1905. Dave for his part enlightened Bobbie on just how important the Henley-on-Thames branch line had been during its 111-year history.

The current safety device, the Automatic Warning System (AWS) in the engine cab, had its origins on the line when (as Automatic Train Control) the experiment was first introduced in 1906. An adverse aspect of a distant signal could be detected on the footplate and an alarm given which, if ignored, would result in the brakes being automatically applied. So confident was the GWR of the effectiveness of the system that when ATC was installed on the Fairford branch line in Oxfordshire all the distant signals were actually removed and not replaced. The signal box at Henley was also a pioneer of modern Panel signalling technology.

A 'Berni Inn' could always be relied upon for a reasonable meal at a reasonable price, and so it was; and once the bill was paid the couple returned to the *Juno*. Back on board Bobbie made herself at home by turning on the radio while Dave made coffee. Although the craft was blessed with a cast-iron oven range it was never used; instead Dave relied on a Calor gas cylinder for both cooking and heating. Illumination was by means of paraffin lamps which provided not only a romantic glow with the old familiar aroma, but also gave out a certain amount of heat so in a few minutes the cabin was quite cosy.

Sitting beside each other on a 'settee' (once a back seat of a Ford Zodiac belonging to Dave's father) they heard the new release from the Rolling Stones, 'Jumping Jack Flash'.

"Sounds more like a song for Guy Fawkes night," Bobbie remarked.

"Well," Dave replied. "I don't think they'll ever have a better hit than 'The Last Time'. The guitar backing riff on that was terrific."

They listened to more music then Bobbie confessed that she had missed her last train home. As a matter of fact Dave was aware of the timetable, but had failed to remind his friend of its limitations late in the evening, or of the possibility of travelling on the empty DMU that ran after the public timetable had finished. Dave's heart skipped a beat when Bobbie asked if she could stay the night. Flustered, he stood up and mumbled something about calling a taxi, but the disappointment in her eyes was plain to see.

"Don't you want me to stay?" she asked as she rose too.

"Of course I do, but I've only got a single bunk, and, it's just that, um, well, you'd would be the first, if you know what I mean."

Bobbie smiled and put her arms around his neck. "Oh, Dave, don't worry," she lied. "It'll be the first time for me too."

Dave held her close and they kissed, with increasing passion and intensity until Bobbie almost fainted for lack of oxygen. Then they began to touch one other in hitherto private places before, inevitably, clothing became a barrier to greater intimacy. Dave was pleased the way Bobbie was the first to begin to strip off. He'd thought she had been wearing black socks but as she stepped out of her long skirt he discovered they were stockings, the kind that needed no suspender to support them, the black contrasting sharply with the white of her underwear; and with Dave too almost naked, there was no mistaking the extraordinarily large bulge in his Y-fronts. Bobbie eagerly anticipated the pleasure she could expect from it and took his hand as he led her into his sleeping quarters. The door of the inner cabin swung slowly shut and, judging from the movement of the craft, later threatening to sever the moorings from stern to bow, Dave did not disappoint her.

Chapter Twenty Three

O ne of the duties for the early-turn train announcer was collecting the weekly notices from the station. Details of special trains and amendments to the timetable were listed in addition to job vacancies. Molly Davies disliked the task, but Bobbie always enjoyed pinning up the various notices in the signal box.

At times there were vacancies for signalmen in some obscure places, and great was the debate over the whereabouts of some of them. A particularly taxing example was Holesmouth Junction which, it was later discovered, was on the way to Severn Beach from Bristol, and destined for imminent closure under the Bristol resignalling scheme. Of course, of special interest were vacancies at places which Bobbie knew, and she would surmise what man had left or retired. It came as a surprise one day to see Loudwater advertised. Bobbie didn't know whether to be excited or disappointed. Suffice to say she thought about it, but at such lengths that it ceased to be advertised and was replaced by Flax Bourton (again in the Bristol area) and both Hinksey North and South in Oxfordshire.

These vacancies got Bobbie thinking about her father's involvement there during the war, and one day she told Henry Collinson about it and how once she had considered a signalling career herself. The signalman endeavoured to put the issue beyond doubt. "Look," he said, "deep down, it's obviously something you're still hankering after. Do it now before it's too late and there's not a job to go to. I mean, even this place won't last for ever. If you ask me there'll only be two jobs on the whole of the Western in years to come, Old Oak Common and Bristol."

Encouraged by Mr Collinson's philosophical approach Bobbie looked out eagerly for the Loudwater vacancy, but it did not reappear and, after a further two weeks had passed, he suggested that she rang up Western Tower and make some enquiries. Not surprisingly, Bobbie felt this was something she was unable to do, so one morning Henry 'phoned on her behalf. Bobbie listened to the one-sided conversation. "Well, if you can't help, will you put me on to someone who can? Yes, I'll hold." There was a pause so long the signalman dealt with the 'South Wales Pullman' going down and a D800 running light for Old Oak Common before he spoke again. "Yes, I'm still here. That's right, Loudwater, no, not in Hertfordshire—Buckinghamshire! Near Bourne End—that's the one. Right... I see... 2.30... OK, I'll let her know." Once he'd put the telephone down he turned to Bobbie and smiled. "If you get yourself down to Reading tomorrow afternoon at half two, someone'll see you about taking over at Loudwater." Bobbie punched the air in delight and gave Mr Collinson a hug. "Put me down," he laughed. "I'm old enough to be your Grandad! You just make sure you're there on time."

Bobbie did exactly that, and the next time she was on duty with Henry she was able to tell him in words of mixed emotions that, subject to being successful on rules and regulations etc. etc., Loudwater Signal Box was hers for the taking.

"I'm really pleased for you, love," Henry beamed. "You might find it a bit quiet at first but who's to say it won't be your only box."

Bobbie's final week as train announcer at Twyford passed

all too quickly. Having been brought up, as it were, on a rural line, she realised the significance of Signalman Collinson's words about the volume of traffic when, in a rare moment late one afternoon, trains were passing the box on all five tracks. The 17.24 to Henley was squealing its way round the curve on to the branch line; the 16.36 Paddington-Reading was leaving the platform on the down relief line while being overtaken on the down main by a Brush 2750 on the 1F38 17.00 Paddington-Fishguard. Racing each other in the opposite direction on the up main and up relief respectively was a maroon 'Western' on 1A66, the 14.20 ex-Swansea, and 1A67, the 16.15 from Bristol hauled by D0280 *Falcon*.

Bobbie's last day at her desk was June 21st, the summer solstice, and on that Friday afternoon she and Henry Collinson went for a farewell drink once their shifts had finished. Molly joined them too as the late-turn signalman had offered to man the microphone in her absence. The trio's venue was the 'Golden Cross', almost opposite Twyford Station, and the only hostelry nearby since the closure of the Royal Station Hotel. Bobbie bought the drinks but, as she'd secretly hoped they would be, both colleagues were laden with gifts.

Mr Collinson presented her with a book, a paperback edition of L.T.C. Rolt's *Red for Danger*, a classic in the annals of transport literature on the safety of railways.

"It's a book," Henry commented, "that every railwayman—and woman—should read," as he put his signature to the title page.

Molly's present resembled another framed picture, Bobbie thought, but on removing the wrapping paper discovered it was a large letter 'M', white on black, that once would have been part of a train reporting number.

"I was having a clear out of my ex-husband's stuff," Molly

said, and I know how interested you are in train headcodes. I hadn't realised 'til now, though, that there's an 'H' on the back!"

"Well," broke in Henry," you can't forget us now. As I remember, all the plates were double-sided, on the back of a '1' was a '5'. Letters were used quite late on as a development of the Western's 3-number system before all this 4-character stuff came in. Back then, the engine lamps indicated the class of train while the letter and two numbers were on the smokebox."

It was a very pleasant hour or so in the 'Golden Cross' but Molly had to return to her work, and after promising to keep in touch, was the first to leave, followed by Henry Collinson whom Bobbie watched pedal off home to Sonning, waving frequently, until he was out of sight.

Before she caught her train home, Bobbie took a final look at Twyford Station. She hoped she'd made the right decision to leave as another chapter in her life came to an end.

The guard on Bobbie's train from Maidenhead was Dave Clarke, and he reassured her considerably, especially when he invited her aboard the *Juno* again. It would be, he told her, the last night at the present mooring as, with his imminent move to Banbury the boat would soon be tied up at Aynho on the Oxford Canal. The only practical solution to the transport problem was to have a tow into Hobbs' boatyard and thence by lowloader to Aynho. The move would be expensive but, whilst out of the water, Dave planned to take full advantage of the situation and do some essential maintenance and paint the underside of the hull.

Dave had booked some holiday for this and Bobbie would have liked to have helped, but she was going away on holiday herself with her parents and it wasn't possible. Nevertheless, she and Dave enjoyed another night aboard the *Juno*, and Bobbie was gone before the tug boat from Hobbs arrived at 9 a.m.

Although Bobbie had ridden in the cab of the Wycombe diesel shunter and also up front in a DMU to Wooburn Green, she had had but little experience of the locomotive footplate. However, Dave Clarke was confident that, with holidays over and himself settled at Banbury, she would be able to join him when he was route-learning over the 'new line' to Acton.

Mr and Mrs Gherardini, accompanied by their daughter, went north to Ingleton on the Lancashire and Yorkshire border to explore the latter county's 'Three Peaks'—Whernside, Ingleborough and Penyghent. Ingleton had once been on the railway map, but although trains no longer ran, the impressive viaduct across the Greta Gorge still stood. Moreover, the significance of the names of the hills they were to climb (they could not be called mountains) was not lost on Bobbie as she recognised the names of the 1Co-Co1 Type 4 diesels D6, 7 and 8.

The Gherardinis were initially blessed with good weather, but having little to do with their Saturday evening except relax in the bar of their guesthouse and anticipate a hard day's hill climbing on the morrow, Bobbie became absorbed with her book *Red for Danger*. With a forthcoming career in a signal box it was natural that a chapter on train accidents caused by signalmen interested her most. One she found particularly fascinating and happened not so very far away.

But the next day the weather was more typically Pennine, and instead of climbing, the Gherardinis drove out to Hawes. On the way, Bobbie persuaded her father to stop at Garsdale, a former Midland Railway station on the Settle-Carlisle line, and the story of its gale-protected turntable caught his attention. The large number of upended sleepers that prevented an engine being turned uncontrollably by the wind had gone, but one could still see where the 'table once was. Garsdale had formerly been a junction, and the track bed off to Northallerton could also be defined. Garsdale (as Hawes Junction) was the scene of a disaster at daybreak on Christmas Eve 1910.

The Midland had nothing larger than four-coupled locomotives for its premier passenger trains, and therefore double-heading assistance up to Ais Gill, in both directions, was frequently necessary. One might have thought that building larger engines would have been a more practical exercise, saving numerous crews and light-engine movements, as well as coal and water and pathing difficulties, but the Midland pursued its small-engine policy; indeed, it had continued building 4-2-2 'single wheelers' long after other companies had abandoned the design. Hawes Junction was a relatively minor station yet a very busy place on account of the pilot engines congregating there before returning to their home shed.

On that fateful morning of December 24th 1910, around 5.30, Signalman Alfred Sutton had no fewer than nine engines cluttering up his layout, using the turntable, taking water or merely waiting for a 'path' through all the other trains that were running. One driver was even up in the box pestering him about organizing his relief. Consequently, when two engines coupled were allowed out onto the down main to await a path back to Carlisle, it was inevitable that they could be forgotten. And they were.

When Sutton pulled 'off' all his down line signals for a St Pancras-Glasgow express, the drivers of the engines took the signals as their own and puffed gently away only to be viciously caught by the 65mph express minutes later some 1½ miles further on. Twelve passengers lost their lives.

Garsdale was as wet and windswept on that Sunday afternoon in 1968 as it had been in 1910. The deserted signal box appeared to be 'switched out' as all signals were 'off' in both directions; and, indeed, when D53 *Royal Tank Regiment* roared through on a northbound express, the down line signals did not return to danger behind it, just as they had not done behind the two engines setting off for Carlisle. The still-raised signal arms seemed both incongruous and poignant.

The following day the weather was once again fair for hill walking, and they set out for Whernside, at 2419ft the highest of the Yorkshire trio. It was also the most interesting as their journey to the top of it began beneath the awesome 24-arch Ribblehead viaduct, and during their climb several trains were observed. English Electric Type 4s seemed to dominate the freight they saw, while the BR/Sulzer version appeared confined to passenger work. Although no steam locomotive was seen, from the summit of Whernside the brick air shafts protruding above Blea Moor Tunnel could just be discerned.

Back in the guesthouse bar later that evening, it was agreed that, owing to losing a day because of inclement weather, the climb up to Penyghent would have to be postponed for another time. However, Bobbie got the idea into her head of climbing all the peaks associated with that class of diesel. Of the ten, four were situated in the Lake District, including the highest in England, Scafell Pike. Cross Fell was at the northern end of the Pennine chain, while the remaining two were in North Wales, namely Snowdon and Tryfan. Scotland was not represented but there was jovial speculation that had the original 'Peaks' been allocated north of the border, say to 66A Polmadie or 64B Haymarket, then Ben Nevis would have been included and perhaps the class referred to as 'Bens'!

Back home, and Bobbie looked forward to starting work at Loudwater Box, but she knew too that she had been in a similar situation once before, so tried not get too enthusiastic about it, and first there was a footplate trip from Banbury to enjoy.

Chapter Twenty Four

It was on Thursday 27th June that Bobbie Gherardini stood waiting in the sunshine on the up side of Banbury Station anticipating the 09.40 off the yard to appear. First through was the 08.40 from New Street, which left on time for Paddington at 09.38. and, sure enough, shortly afterwards a coal train, hauled by a grubby Brush Type 4, nosed its way around the back of the station and drew to a halt in the up loop. There was plainly a malfunction with the reporting number mechanism as the headcode showed 'blank' M 'dot' O. It should have read 7V34. The consist was mainly sixteen tonners but with a number of '21's and a couple of '24½s' loaded with dinosaur-age black diamonds.

Bobbie looked across to the locomotive D1740 and, as expected, her friend David Clarke appeared in the cab doorway and beckoned her over to join the enginemen on the footplate. Just slightly disappointed with the choice of motive power that day (Bobbie knew that the Banbury could be hauled by anything from an LM D52xx Bo-Bo to a WR 'Warship',) there was no denying the sound investment by BR in the standard Type 4 design. With considerably fewer locomotives required to replace steam, the Brush Type 4 was as ubiquitous, relatively if not numerically, as the Stanier 'Black 5'.

Using an uprated version of the same 12 (cyl) LDA28 (cm.bore) Sulzer engine as found in the 1Co-Co1 'Peaks', it was less weighty ancillary equipment that enabled the power plant to be contained on a pair of 6-wheel bogies only. The Sulzer engines, of Swiss origin, but actually built in Barrow-in-Furness, were delivered to BR Workshops at Crewe, or to Brush at Loughborough, who shared the construction of the 512 locomotives. Numbered D1500-1999 and 1100-11, with the exception of the Southern Region, the locomotives were widely distributed. However, to help alleviate an acute short-age of electro-diesels on the Southern, D1921-6 were currently shedded at 70D Eastleigh.

In the cab of D1740 that sunny morning Bobbie introduced herself to the loco-men on duty. The driver was the younger of the two, and it seemed a case of the secondman getting driver experience while his senior mate took it easy—yet Bobbie was wrong. The older man was indeed the secondman but, as he made his point very firmly, he was not a really a secondman, but a 'put-back' driver and, somewhat morosely, went on to explain his unfortunate situation.

Owing to rationalisation of services and losses to road transport, the quantity of trains run was much less than before, and consequently a number of drivers faced redundancy. One way to avoid this was to offer the engineman concerned the chance to remain at his depot, but to be 'put back' to second-man status; hence the term. The arrangement suited BR very well as it eliminated a redundancy payout and also saved them recruiting secondmen who, with the continuing trend for less double-manning, would also be surplus before very long.

By now they had passed Banbury South Box, and the site of the locoshed, and were heading out into the country on what was virtually level track. The driver opened the controller wider, and speed rose to 40mph before conversation became difficult on account of the noise from the engine; but at King's Sutton the crew were at pains to point out not just the former junction for the old railway through Chipping Norton to Cheltenham, but also the River Cherwell and Oxford Canal, whose courses ran so close in places that it was possible, with a rod in each hand, to fish in both at the same time. The river, after days of heavy rain, was also prone to flooding, and the low-lying meadows to both left and right of the railway were frequently underwater.

A further mile, and the signals at Aynho Junction routed them left up the 'new line' while the old road to Oxford continued straight on. With the controller wide open, the climb out of the Cherwell valley began in earnest as they crossed the two Souldern viaducts and attacked the 1 in 200 bank up to Ardley. With a shout, Dave Clarke pointed out his boat, the *Juno*, just visible on the Oxford Canal towpath below them. Dave's position in the cab was immediately behind the second-man, whereas Bobbie stood beside the driver, enabling her to observe not only him, the controls, and his actions, but also the road ahead.

Halfway up the bank, despite full power and 2500 amps flowing to the traction motors, speed fell noticeably. Ardley Tunnel loomed ahead and the driver invited Bobbie to sound the hooter before they roared into the black mouth of the 1147-yard feat of engineering under the the southern extremity of the Northamptonshire hills. Conversation became impossible as the noise of the engine reverberated off the tunnel roof, and speed was down to 27mph before they emerged once more into the sunshine. But then the gradient fell, and once the whole of the train was 'over the top', the driver shut the controller completely and let the momentum of the loaded wagons assist him down the bank; but, bearing in mind the maximum speed limit of 45 mph for 4-wheeled stock, such was the weight of the train that the driver had to let the engine brake rub on a little to avoid excessive speed.

Two miles on and power was applied again as the station of Ardley was passed. Like the majority of stations on the route, Ardley closed in 1964 and lay sadly derelict. The signal box survived, but it too faced closure when later in the year the line would be reduced to a single track. Of all the intermediate stations between Aynho Junction and Princes Risborough, only Bicester North remained open.

It was only from the vantage point of the locomotive foot-plate that one could appreciate the quality of the engineering of the 'new line'; much of it ran dead straight or almost so for mile after mile and no-one made any comment when speed rose to 55mph before the brake was applied approaching Bicester North. Back in September 1960, Bicester had witnessed the very last 'slip coach' working on BR. 'Slipping' was an inno-vative method of passenger train working where a coach at the tail end of a train was automatically decoupled by its own individual guard and braked to a stand in the platform while the express sped through non-stop. Once clear of Bicester, and having crossed the ex-LNWR Bletchley to Oxford line serving Bicester London Road, speed again passed the 45mph mark, the driver again taking advantage of the falling gradient and a maximum of 57mph was achieved passing Blackthorn, a station closed in 1953.

But all good things are finite, and following the 1 in 450 down beyond Blackthorn, the stiff climb up to Brill & Ludgershall, at 1 in 200, commenced. Yet such was the lively approach to this bank that at no point during the ascent did speed drop below 35mph, and through the short 191-yard tunnel Bobbie again made herself useful with the hooter. Clear of the tunnel, one could see the remains of the bridge where once the Metropolitan Railway crossed to its incredibly distant outpost of the London 'Underground' system.

It was Guard Clarke who was puzzled about the mileage posts. Back in Banbury he had seen milepost 86, but remembered seeing 13 at Ardley, and now, beyond Brill Tunnel, was post 2¼. It was the 'put back' driver who offered the explanation. Banbury mileage was that from Paddington via Oxford. Distance markers for the 'new line' went only as far as Aynho; and the point at which they started, milepost nought, was Ashendon Junction, which lay immediately ahead.

The approach to Ashendon, a 'flying junction' layout similar to that at Aynho, was unmistakeable as the up line deviated away and rose above the down metals. But as D1740 rumbled over the girder bridge, no tracks ran beneath them where once the old Great Central turned off towards its northern origins by running beneath the bridge they were crossing. Apparently, sections of the GC route were still intact and that former gas turbine locomotive, No. 18100, could be observed on resistance tests for pantographs, but quite how the locomotive, renumbered E2001 on conversion to 25kv electric, was used or moved was a mystery as there was no overhead catenary!

With both sets of rails back in alignment by milepost 33 (as measured from Northolt) there was a level stretch before D1740 faced the long climb up the Chiltern Hills, the gradients roughly increasing in severity the nearer one got to the summit.

It was unimportant how unkempt D1740 looked—mechanically it was sound and more than master of the task set as it powered on past disused Haddenham and the remote traces of Ilmer Halt. Approaching Princes Risborough, they experienced their first signal check of the trip. The colour light distant signal for the North box was at caution and the AWS siren duly sounded. It was, as the driver cursed, probably the worst place to be stopped, but happily the home signal dropped 'off' before speed had reduced too much. Full power was applied immediately and with a plume of exhaust D1740 manfully recovered the lost momentum.

As the line swung righthanded, on the hillside opposite one could plainly see Whyteleaf Cross cut in the chalk. Clearly some importance was given to Princes Risborough in the past and this was reflected still to this day. The station mimicked Crewe as no fewer than three separate branch lines encroached upon the main line simultaneously. One came in on the left and was from Aylesbury, which terminated in a bay platform. To the right, and with all the appearances of a double-track main line, were the 'freight-only' truncated branches from Thame and Chinnor, the former being part of the early route to Oxford.

Princes Risborough could still boast two signal boxes but for the signalman at the South box a problem seemed imminent. Resplendent in blue, with full yellow ends, was a NBL Type 2 diesel-hydraulic standing on the main to platform line points and, judging by the number of men surrounding it, gesticulating, pointing and shrugging their shoulders, surely a failure despite its immaculate appearance. The Banbury men looked away pretending not to notice—they knew the score. Almost immediately, they passed 1M12, the 10.35 Paddington-Birmingham, stopped at signals outside the station, the second-man already getting down off sister engine D1749 to carry out Rule 55. The Banbury men speculated how the dead diesel would be shunted out of the way, but all agreed they were fortunate not to have been commandeered do it.

Beyond Princes Risborough the main lines parted company to follow separate ways over the Chiltern Hills summit. The down main was the original route, the up line was 'new', and not only a marginally shorter deviation, it also provided a more favourable gradient. Nevertheless, the bank was no easier than

1 in 167, and in an exceptionally deep cutting culminating in yet another tunnel, but one of only 88yds.

The ammeter was 'in the yellow' on 2600 amps and the speed was barely 20mph as Bobbie did her duty with the hooter. As Saunderton Tunnel was little more than a bridge it seemed unnecessary to 'blow up', but the driver insisted and Bobbie was happy to oblige. It was when she resumed her stance at the driver's side that she became aware of him grinning and winking at his mate, nor was it the first time she'd observed the exchanges. It dawned on her then that the driver was enjoying her leaning across him to operate the hooter lever as body contact was unavoidable, and even though she wore overalls, her missing top buttons ensured he had an eyeful of cleavage each time!

But now they were over the Chiltern summit. The power controller was at last moved back, easing the demands on the generator as speed rapidly increased, and they romped away down the other side of the bank with the driver saying how pleased he was to be several minutes ahead of schedule. Today there would be no danger of being held at High Wycombe for a local passenger to precede them.

It was strangely pleasant to be reunited with the 'old' line just before Saunderton, and passing through the quiet station inevitably evoked comments as to why suffragette arsonists in March 1913 should have chosen Saunderton at all.

In contrast to the GW/GC 'new line', the old Wycombe Railway route was far from straight and the driver had to resort to the brake in order to check his descent from the Chilterns through West Wycombe and on to the approaches of High Wycombe—notorious for its sharp curves. More historical comments were forthcoming concerning the golden ball above the church on West Wycombe Hill and the riotous 'Hell Fire

Club' caves cut deep below it.

Wycombe's outer distant signal was green, and this one aspect told the crew they were right away through the whole of the Wycombe layout, and for Bobbie it was especially thrilling to observe all her old familiar signals from the locomotive cab.

As expected, all Wycombe North's signals were 'off' and there was a ribald exchange of tooting as the men on D1740 encountered their depot colleagues boarding D1928 to take the 11.19 a.m. freight out of the yard to Banbury. On the up side of the line, opposite the sidings, was one of the many furniture factories for which High Wycombe was renowned, the establishment they were passing being 'Parker-Knoll'.

All the Middle box signals were 'off' up the main, and passing under the Amersham Hill bridge the driver had the severest of the curves behind him, and could open up D1740 again with confidence and accelerate away through the station, making the newspapers flutter on the bookstall where Bobbie used to work.

In the up platform a 4-car DMU stood, engines idling, and due to depart imminently as a stopping service to Marylebone at 11.42; but the Banbury, still accelerating and running beneath the unique gantry of five signals, was in no danger of delaying it whatsoever. If passing through High Wycombe on the footplate was exciting, it was doubly so on the approach to White House Farm crossing and the tunnel, the old trainspotting haunts of years before.

It had been agreed that Bobbie would be dropped off at Seer Green where she could safely alight onto a platform; and, moreover, it was an ideal spot to pull up, being just over the top of an incline before the driver let 'wagons roll' again down the other side.

Clear of Beaconsfield at milepost 11¼, the driver told

Bobbie to get herself ready to leave the train, and added that Seer Green was at milepost 10. Bobbie began counting down her last moments with the crew using the quarter-mile markers, and taking the opportunity to express her sincere thanks to one and all. They'd had, the driver said, an unusually good run, and he would be apologising to the poor guard when they arrived in Acton later!

Seer Green Station lay on a sweeping righthand bend in a very rural location, yet its naming seemed to be of some debate as the suffix 'and Jordans' was periodically added, but just as regularly taken away. On opening in 1915, it was known as Beaconsfield Golf Links, which was not surprising as the eighteenth hole of the course was opposite the station entrance on the down side.

As Bobbie waited for her train home she realised how weary she was. She had not sat down once the whole of her journey. The driver, of course, had to be in his seat but his 'put back' colleague had not offered his. It was also quite tiring mentally. If there was no particular scenery to admire, and one merely watched sleepers coming and disappearing under the loco, it was almost soporific—like counting sheep. Yet she envied the team she'd just bade farewell to. They would later travel 'on the cushions' to Reading, then relieve an Eastleigh crew on a Fratton-Oldham freight as far as Banbury where they in turn would be relieved by Bescot men

Chapter Twenty Five

T he morning of Monday 8th July was pleasantly sunny, yet as Bobbie walked onto the platform at Loudwater she was struck by a pervading air of despondency and decay. No one was about, and surveying the deserted station she could not help but wonder how it must have looked when her father worked there. The fact that a stationmaster had once been present seemed incredible. It still wanted some minutes before 6 a.m. as Bobbie waited for her mentor to arrive. Naturally she hoped it would be someone with whom she was acquainted—but alas! A Morris Traveller drew up, the sort with the ash wood trim, and a short elderly man with a semi-circle of white hair around a bald head, got out and accosted Bobbie. "I was expecting a real signalman," he said, but as he looked Bobbie up and down he remarked, "Yes. I remember you from that little teashop in Wooburn Green. A good cuppa too. I would've thought that that job would've been enough for you 'til you got yourself a husband. But seeing as you've arrived you may as well get the kettle on here. This week you just watch what I do, and maybe next week, if you're still interested, you can have a go with the levers—but I can't imagine you being able to pull one."

Bobbie smiled politely at the termination of his speech, but her heart sank as she did as she was told. She could have mentioned working Wycombe South Box, and that it might have been she on the other end of the bell allowing him to withdraw a token, but she said nothing.

The signalman had not introduced himself, and rather than ask his name Bobbie stole a peep in the train register book where he had signed his name, but she was unable to decipher it. While he enjoyed the tea Bobbie had made he spoke of the problems currently besetting BR. His words seemed to imply that Bobbie was somehow responsible. He had obviously worked on the railway many years as he talked of trains hauled by 'Twenty-Niners' and the last of that class (*Saint David*) had been withdrawn from Hereford in 1953. There was only the one armchair so commonly found in signal boxes, and naturally the signalman commandeered it for himself. Bobbie made herself comfortable on the wide window sill in the front corner of the box from where she could watch the road traffic pass below her, and also the trains on the 'new line' on the far side of the valley—just as she done years before from the school playground. Wiser now, she knew that destinations were no more romantic than Birmingham!

It was not long before their first train was rung from Wooburn Green. The bell tolled the 3–1 for the 06.52 departure for High Wycombe, a train which Bobbie had used herself many times. She watched the signalman closely, and although she understood what he was doing he made no attempt to explain his actions. Indeed, his only comment was when he wound the gates across the road to stop the traffic. "I can't imagine you doing this."

While for off-peak services invariably a single unit coupled to a driving trailer would turn up, the 06.52 originated from Paddington (departure 05.17) and was formed of two 3-car units. The same six cars worked back to Paddington as the 07.22 from Wycombe (Loudwater 07.27). One detail Bobbie observed was that only drivers in the Wycombe section used the token secured within a large steel hoop. Between Loudwater and Wooburn they took the token just as it was.

"I can't imagine you doing this," the signalman commented shaking his head. He was referring to the imminent token exchange as he and Bobbie waited on the platform with a number of passengers for the 07.27 service. To save a lengthy walk along the platform the token switch was accomplished as the train ran in, the signalman passing the Loudwater-Wooburn token to the driver while simultaneously collecting the hooped example from him. Once again Bobbie heard the same derisory words, "I can't imagine you doing this."

Barely thirty minutes later, the procedures were repeated exactly for another well-patronised service to London. The units for this, again totalling six cars, had run ECS from Southall to Wycombe, not through Loudwater but via the 'new line'.

A couple of other trains were dealt with, but then, by mid-morning, the level of service became meagre, a situation that would continue until late afternoon. After providing the signalman with more refreshment, Bobbie took the opportunity to study the Working Timetable. It was the same volume that covered the West of England main line, which she had used at Twyford, but she had to thumb through over 200 pages to find the Loudwater service. Bobbie counted the number of trains she could expect. On the 6 'til 2 shift there were five up trains and four down, and by as early as 8.30 in the morning, five of the nine had been dealt with already. It seemed to Bobbie that Henry Collinson's comment about finding things a 'bit quiet' was a complete understatement, and she was beginning to regret her decision to walk away from Twyford.

After providing the Signalman with further refreshment still, Bobbie, to alleviate the boredom, announced she should acquaint herself with the rest of the layout over which she would have control. It also gave her opportunity to have a smoke, which her colleague had very strongly disproved of. He was also against religion, as when he'd caught the tail end of a whispered 'Hail Mary', he told Bobbie he wanted no Catholic mumbo-jumbo in his signal box, it was causing enough ill-feeling in Northern Ireland as it was, thank you very much.

As she explored the station, Bobbie made a mental note to ask her dad the purpose of the many derelict buildings. She recalled that once there had been six sidings but now only one remained, and the goods yard was as depressing as the rest of the place. Bobbie leaned on the buffer stop as she smoked, and as she relaxed she imagined herself going back in time, easily conjuring up visions of the 8.15 p.m. Slough-Bescot storming through with a Hall or Grange, barely slowing for the token change, and how, in just three or four years, it had all gone; the yard, through freight, steam, everything practically. Finishing her cigarette, Bobbie noted that the lamp on the buffer stop was out, but considered it pointless to fill and relight it. The odds of anything going down that overgrown stretch of track were greater than those of Bob Gillespie's Grand National winner.

Retracing her steps to the signal box she arrived on cue, as it were, to hear the Newbury-Aylesbury parcels offered from Wooburn Green, belled as a 1-3-1. This produced W55992, one of the Gloucester-built single-unit diesels dedicated to the carriage of parcels and mail. With so much time on her hands Bobbie mentioned that she might run a broom over the platform. Her mentor was aghast at the suggestion, and said that if BR wanted the platform swept then they must employ a porter to do it.

A little later, thinking of something safe to say, Bobbie ventured to ask who was expected to relieve them at 2 p.m.

"Terry Meehan," was the reply, "but he's only been on the railway five minutes; you won't learn anything from him."

During the course of the morning, Bobbie, from her window seat, had observed an unusual number of American cars pass. She guessed it was on account of the USAF base nearby as well as the golf course up the hill at Flackwell Heath. The level crossing at Loudwater was exactly that, and resulted in a short flat section of road against the gradient of the hill the railway crossed. The long low cars, the Buicks and Pontiacs, inevitably scraped their fenders on the tarmac as they went over the crossing. Following the noisy passage of a particularly large finned sedan, the signalman came over to the window too. He chuckled something derogatory about Yanks, then opened his locker to reveal a collection of licence plates that had been wrenched off cars negotiating the crossing in the past.

"Serve 'em right," he laughed. "Ha, ha, ha!"

Bobbie shook her head in disbelief, but nothing more was said as footsteps were heard, and in another moment Signalman Meehan appeared in the box, cheerily greeting them both. To Bobbie his manner seemed quite engaging yet with barely a word the older signalman had put on his jacket and left. Bobbie watched him go, curiously, but Terry appeared quite unconcerned.

"I'm a Class 1 reliefman and I'm still only twenty-six. That was unheard of in his day. I started out as a Class 4 man, here actually, then went to Bourne End as a '3', Beaconsfield a '2', and finally got my Class 1 at Oxford. Now I'm back here on the relief. Anyway, enough about me; what brings you to this godforsaken dump?"

In a few words Bobbie told him of her lamping days and her time at Twyford and how disillusioned she was with her new career.

"Has he been tough on you with rules and regulations?" Terry asked.

"No, he hasn't told me a thing. He hasn't let me touch a single lever."

At this Bobbie was struggling to hold back the tears. Terry wanted to comfort her but, unsure of what to do and sensing her reluctance to depart, resorted to a proven source of succour.

"Get the kettle on!"

Bobbie laughed away her tears. "That's all I've been doing all day!"

But as she performed the familiar task Terry made a suggestion. "Why don't you switch to late turn?"

One glance at Bobbie was enough to know that the proposition was well received, and Bobbie looked very happy as Terry continued. "I'll leave the old boy a note so he's not wondering where you are and reporting you as AWOL."

"But he'll have to make his own tea!"

"Tough! But if he's ever difficult about anything just mention 4091."

"4091," Bobbie repeated. "The Castle class?"

"Yeah, it's a long story—I'll tell you sometime over a pint."

The next day Bobbie found herself looking forward to working with Terry very much; furthermore, her father was on late turn too. It seemed she had hardly set foot in the box than she was put to work as the Wooburn Green bell rang one beat for the 'call attention'.

"Answer that, will you?" said Terry.

Bobbie stepped over to the instrument and pressed the bell plunger once to ring the bell in the box at Wooburn by way of reply. Her bell then tolled out the 3-1 code for a local passenger.

"OK to accept it?" she asked.

Terry nodded. "Yes, the Pullman's not due yet."

"And—don't tell me—the freightliner's late!" Bobbie added.

They both laughed, and Terry only had to remind Bobbie to hold in the plunger on the '1' to allow the Wooburn man to extract a token. She wondered if the former booking boy from Wycombe South was also on duty that afternoon.

Soon, 'train entering section' was received, and Bobbie was prompt to acknowledge the two beats on the bell.

"Get the road now from Wycombe," Terry advised.

Bobbie was delighted to be doing some real railway work at last.

"Right," Terry continued, "we must now open the gates. For obvious reasons you can't just open them. You must always check first that no one is passing. Some old boy would be very upset if you knocked him off his bike."

Waiting for a number of cars to pass, Terry then wound over the large wheel opening the gates to the railway. Explanations had taken longer than the actual performance, and the 14.01 Maidenhead was braying sarcastically for signals.

"Pull 1 and 2, Bobbs!" Terry called, once he had the gates in position. Bobbie did as he asked and lowered the home and starting signals, the latter a very easy lever to pull as the signal was opposite the box with a wire run of a few yards only.

Both Terry and Bobbie went to meet the arrival of the 2-car set, a single unit, W55026, with a driving trailer W56289 in tow, the driver and signalman exchanging not only single-line tokens but friendly banter over the signal check—but the train still departed on time. Back in the box, Bobbie returned the token the driver had surrendered to the Wooburn Green instrument and sent the 2-1 'train out of section'. Terry threw the signal levers back in the frame, belled 'on line' to Wycombe South and reclosed the gates. Motorists resumed their journeys, and peace and tranquillity prevailed once more. Later, when the same 2-car set returned, Bobbie performed all the procedures herself and, knowing it would be the same driver, got the signals 'off' in good time even if it did mean holding up the traffic a little longer than necessary.

Signalling trains from Wycombe Bobbie found more interesting, as it involved pulling the up advanced starter. This signal was necessary as the points from the yard were situated beyond the platform starter.

Of interest too was the 'track occupied'/'clear' miniature banner repeater that provided a visual aid to enable signalmen to know when the train had passed the signal before returning it to danger.

Under Terry's guidance Bobbie's confidence soared, and she began to warm to the prospect of being a signalwoman. Where previously the lack of a serviette at the teashop might have been an issue, the art of signalling trains was one of few careers she could think of where one's presence was so vital. Hundreds of lives—well, a dozen at least—depended on her lowering a signal and sending their train safely on.

Needless to say, in Terry's company, the interludes between trains passed very quickly with intelligent conversation. He was able to recall the purpose of the disused levers in the frame, those now crudely painted white and bolted 'out of use', and also explain why the up home signal (No.23) was on a bracket. Formerly, a subsidiary arm for 'backing up down main' had been present (No. 20) to allow for greater flexibility in shunting.

The shift passed very pleasantly, and all too soon the last train of the day, the 21.10 from High Wycombe, was pausing at the platform as dusk fell. Bobbie alone dealt with the token exchange, and, with cheery goodnights from driver and guard, sent them on their way. Back in the box Terry had done every-thing that was necessary so there was nothing to do but sit and wait and mentally follow the train's progress. Eventually from Wooburn Green came the '2-1' and Bobbie acknowledged it.

"When the train clears Bourne End," Terry said, "the Wooburn man will send the 7-5-5 'closing signal box' bell code. If you stay here to answer it I'll lock up the station."

Bobbie waited patiently, and when the bell finally rung, felt important to be alone in the box to answer it. She knew too that her father at Spicer's Crossing would also have been listening out for the peal of bells telling him that he too could go off duty. Bobbie sent the 7-5-5 to Wycombe South when Terry returned, and after he'd written up the train register book he said emphatically, "Right, that's it! Let's get out of here!"

He offered Bobbie a lift home, but instead she said she would walk up the track, knowing for certain that no train would come along. On parting, both agreed that the shift pattern should continue for the rest of the week.

Chapter Twenty Six

By the end of that week Bobbie had gained sufficient confidence to believe that a signalling career was well within her grasp. She had learned a great deal from Terry, and the very least she felt she should do was to buy the man a drink in the Happy Union pub when they came off duty that Saturday evening.

Terry was pleasantly surprised therefore that afternoon to find Bobbie wearing a skirt rather than her uniform trousers.

"Are you out on a date later?" he asked.

"Well, yes, I am. You can take me down the pub and I'll buy you a well-deserved pint!"

Each day, during the quiet spells on the late shift, the conversation got around inevitably to rules and regulations pertaining to signalling but that Saturday was too pleasant a summer's day for such academic talk. Nevertheless, one rule (No.70) got a mention, and this turned the conversation to the tale of *Dudley Castle*.

"It was one night in 1941," Terry began, "at Dolphin Junction near Slough. 4091's coming up on the 6.20 from Plymouth and gaining on a government stores train on the up main. So the Dolphin man turns the Plymouth onto the up relief to overtake it. But in making that manoeuvre it has to pass right across the down relief on which he's already accepted a freight. Your old mate swears it wasn't him, but he had the same name and he was working there at the time. What it is thought happened is that he put his signals back for the approaching freight, taking the chance that the driver hadn't seen them off already. But there's little doubt he had, and either didn't look at them again or was unable to pull up in time, and collides head-on with the Plymouth.

"The important point is, once you've pulled off for something, if you change your mind and want to put back, think about Rule 70 and wait 'til the train has come to a stand before you make any conflicting movement. The Dolphin man acted in the best interests of those on the Plymouth express in not wanting to delay them, but five of them died because of it."

As the evening wore on, the couple looked forward to going down the pub, and 'ere long the last train was sent on its way and the locking up and closing procedures followed.

With the rituals completed, the pair made haste to their local hostelry and managed no less than four drinks apiece before 'chucking out' time. Again the gallant Terry offered to see Bobbie home and being a little unsteady on her feet she accepted his arm gratefully.

Bobbie had always known that her parents had had their wedding reception in the Happy Union, but was unaware, as she and Terry walked off the platform at Loudwater and continued up the line to Spicer's Crossing, that it was the route the newlyweds themselves had taken.

Arriving at the gates, Bobbie found the key to the cabin and invited Terry in for a coffee. He himself switched on Bobbie's transistor radio and got Radio One, confessing that in the past he used to tune in to Caroline, the 'pirate' radio ship anchored off Frinton-on-Sea, Essex, just to listen to the atmospherics!

The caffeine sobered up the couple to an extent, but Bobbie couldn't resist playing with the block bell above Spicer's tiny lever frame. "The Queen and the Duke are on their way back from a night out in Wycombe," she announced and manually rang the 4-4-4 bell code. Then misfortune appeared to strike their Majesties as 'train running away' (2-5-5) and 'train divided' (5-5) were rung. As the night was balmy, the cabin door had been left open, and the sound of the bell soon brought Mr Gherardini down from the house to investigate. But when he reached the cabin door it was closed, and on opening it discovered his daughter dancing rather too slowly and closely with a young man to the strains of P.P. Arnold's *Angel Of The Morning*.

Mr Gherardini was not the sort of father to chastise his daughter in the presence of another, so merely suggested that Spicer's Crossing cabin was not the place to party, especially in the early hours of a Sunday morning. Terry agreed, and took the opportunity to say goodnight, leaving a disappointed Bobbie to apologise to her father, then tidy and secure the cabin.

Bobbie had started at Loudwater when the Ministry of Transport had sanctioned a new motorway (M40), and its course would affect Loudwater considerably. The M40 would bridge the hill above the station, run roughly parallel to the railway, then cross it diagonally only some 100 yards from the end of the platform. In effect, it would be a short tunnel beneath the six lanes of carriageway.

Back at work after the weekend and now on early turn, Terry was so pleased with Bobbie's progress as a signalwoman that he telephoned the Slough District Inspector's Office (under whose aegis Loudwater came) to arrange examination for rules and regulations. Someone, Terry informed Bobbie, would be down to see her soon.

For the remainder of that shift, Terry subjected Bobbie to such an intense grilling on rules and regulations that she went home feeling unhappy and inadequate. It seemed every time he spoke it was to ask what would she do if so-and-so happened and what steps would she take if... if... if... . She knew deep down he was only doing his best to help, but she came to dread the sound of his voice.

On Tuesday there was more of the same, and the next day. But on Thursday, a benign elderly gentleman alighted from the 10.01 from Maidenhead, and Terry introduced him to Bobbie as Mr Wheatley, the D.I. (District Inspector) from Slough, and after showing them to a platform seat, left them to discuss rules and regulations while he continued with his signalling duties.

The Inspector spoke first. "I haven't got long, you know."

"You poor thing... " Bobbie began.

"I have to catch that same diesel when it returns from Wycombe."

"Oh! Oh, I see!"

"Which means we've got about twenty minutes, so let's get on."

Despite all the questions Terry had envisaged might be asked, the Inspector's first question took Bobbie completely by surprise.

"Which way do the gradients run from here?"

Frankly, Bobbie didn't know, but rather than admit her ignorance she considered how the trains were driven away and concluded that, "It's a rising gradient towards Wycombe, but downhill to Wooburn—I think." However, the two last words were inaudible.

"The reason I ask is... well, why do you think it's important?"

Poor Bobbie. This was a nightmare. Why anyone apart from a driver or fireman would need to know whether the line rose or fell she could not imagine. Then she remembered the dangers of runaway wagons and where they might end up, and the answer became obvious.

"How might you know a train has become divided?" Wheatley asked.

"If the train passed me without a tail lamp."

"And what bell code would you send?"

"9 to the box ahead, 4-5 to the box in rear."

"But supposing you had a runaway crash through your gates?"

"I would send 'Obstruction Danger'—six bells."

"And how about if your gates are open, what then?"

"Send the 'Train Running Away' '2-5-5' to Wooburn Green."

"Who else would you keep informed?"

"Er, you? Control?"

"Yes, but isn't there someone more important? How about your Dad?"

"Well, I would probably tell him when I got home." It was as Bobbie finished what she knew was a banal statement that she realised the implications of the question and exclaimed, "Oh, of course! Spicer's Crossing!"

Mr Wheatley smiled and nodded. His train was signalled and there were no more questions. Once on the train he remained standing at the door with the window down to continue to speak to Bobbie. "I think you'll do very well. You still have to go before the Chief and have a medical at Paddington. Nothing wrong with you, is there?" He had seen Bobbie's face change at the mention of a medical.

"No, no," she replied. "But must I go to Paddington?"

"Well, there's always Swindon. But you would have to pay for your ticket as it's out of your division."

The Guard had buzzed his driver 'right away', and anxious to avoid delay, the Inspector ended the conversation with a wave of his hand. "I suppose it'll be a day out for you. Leave the arrangements to me."

The train moved off leaving an excited Bobbie behind on the platform. Terry could plainly see that Mr Wheatley had been satisfied with her and mentioned celebrating in the pub that evening—a suggestion to which Bobbie readily agreed.

* * *

Over drinks in the Happy Union the conversation got around to the imminent and total demise of BR steam. "I'd have thought you would've gone up to see the last of the steam engines," Bobbie commented.

No," Terry replied. "I steer clear of the hordes of enthusiasts now. I toured the north-west last May when things were more sensible, and paid my respects then."

"Which sheds did you do?" asked Bobbie.

"Mainly those around Manchester, like Heaton Mersey, Trafford Park and Patricroft. I did Reddish too, which sparked my interest—literally, ha-ha—in the fifteen hundred-volt electrics."

"I was at Patricroft myself last year," Bobbie remarked. "I was, er, passing through that way and the shedmaster tried to give me an old shedcode plate, but as it wasn't 9H Patricroft I didn't take it."

"What was it he offered you?" Terry asked.

"26F."

"Oh, darling Bobbie, 26F was Patricroft at one time!"

The conversation then moved on from steam to the future of the railways, and they both agreed it lay with electric traction. Yet, as Terry informed Bobbie, over twenty electric locomotives, both old and new, were stored out of use at Bury, and that he intended to go and see them for himself, and knowing that Bobbie had the Hornby-Dublo E3002 model, suggested that she might like to come too. With the mention of Patricroft, Bobbie had already been reminded of the weekend she had spent assuming the role of Mrs Gillespie, but as Terry began to quote train times and connecting services it soon became clear that it was to be merely a day out. Bobbie was at first relieved that there would be no charade of being husband and wife, but then disappointed that the trip would lack excitement.

On leaving the pub they walked up into the woods above the station to look on the construction progress of the motorway although there was not a great deal to see. To their right a great swathe of chalk subsoil indicated the route the future M40 was taking through Fennels Wood. To the left the workings were interrupted by the road up to Flackwell Heath before reappearing again on the far side to run more closely to the railway. It was also easy to discern the watercourse taken when rains washed the spoil down the hill to pool at the first available level surface. This, of course, was the railway line, and BR made several complaints to the motorway construction companies in respect of the need to dig out the alluvial mass on a regular basis from the inspection pockets of the crossing gate mechanism and the interlocking room below the signal box itself. When the maintenance work was carried out it provided lucrative Sunday overtime for the signalman.

On that warm July evening the air was pleasantly cooler under the trees that had escaped felling, and the couple could have stayed for longer and done more than just survey the extent of the workings.

That a certain 'chemistry' existed between them was plain to see, but other people about thwarted any romantic thoughts just as Mr Gherardini had done when catching them smooching to the radio on Saturday night last. Even their positions in the trainer and learner relationship tended to keep emotional feelings under control but, as Bobbie knew, success in Swindon would make her and Terry equals.

* * *

Indeed, it was only the next day that Bobbie received the summons to attend Swindon for a medical examination and an interview with a chief inspector. With a free pass being granted after all, the check-up was in complete contrast to the doctor she had seen at Paddington, and later, when being shown into the chief inspector's office, she was surprised to be greeted by Mr Rees-Black!

"Yes, it's me," he said. "I've been here almost a year now."

Again ill at ease in the man's company, Bobbie felt that she should make some sort of polite conversation so enquired after his uncle.

"Oh, still going strong, thanks," came the reply. "Now he's retired he lives with me and my wife. But we're not here to discuss my domestic arrangements. Let's talk RULES!"

This Bobbie was quite happy to do. Normally the opposite situation was preferred, but she was anxious to avoid allusion to any previous encounter. She remembered very little of the evening they had spent together and wanted it kept that way. She feared she would be too embarrassed by even the smallest clarification. The session with Rees-Black lasted some forty-five minutes, and at its conclusion he congratulated Bobbie and was pleased to inform her that on and from Sunday 28th July 1968, Loudwater signal box was hers; and not once did he ask why she had travelled all the way to Swindon for the pleasure.

Back in Loudwater there was some serious drinking to be done in the Happy Union, and the barmaid, sensing celebrations, began pouring their 'usuals' before she and Terry had got to the bar. During the very convivial evening, glasses were raised several times for good luck in the future with no derailments or collisions. Bobbie promised to do her best to avoid both.

They did not leave the pub until ejected by the landlord, and then took advantage of the mobile fish and chip van doing a brisk trade in the pub carpark. Knowing that their supper would be cold if they walked far, they decided to picnic up at the station on the platform seat. The late turn signalman, 'dolphin man' as Bobbie called him, had sent the 7-5-5 long ago and gone home. The whole place was in darkness and deserted.

It was quite a warm night, but Bobbie still snuggled up to Terry on the pretext of feeling cold. It seemed that with one appetite satiated, another demanded satisfaction; and this time no Mr Gherardini would intervene.

Bobbie spoke softly in Terry's ear, and he straightened up in surprise and asked her to repeat what she had said as he'd never heard her use obscene words before.

"I want you," she said, "to—" and again she put her lips to his ear and whispered softly, and as if to add emphasis to her words hitched up her skirt, positioned herself astride him and began unzipping his jeans.

Terry had fancied Bobbie from the day he'd set eyes on her, and as Nelson expected every man at the Battle of Trafalgar, Terry willingly did his duty.

Chapter Twenty Seven

No longer frustrated by lack of authority now that she was the only regular officer at Loudwater, Bobbie felt she had every right to assert her position, and one thing which had sustained her during her days as the learner was that she could take charge of the box and give it the thorough clean it so desperately needed. Rather than wait until her first shift, Bobbie opened Loudwater box on the Sunday morning. It seemed surreal to be the only person around. But it did not take long for Bobbie to realise that getting Loudwater up to the same gleaming standard as Saunderton (considered to be the best-kept signal box in the London Division) was going to be a very long process.

The condition of the linoleum on the floor was such that it was only that which she worked on during the morning. By the time she'd scrubbed away the layers of grime it was time to go home for Sunday lunch. In the afternoon she returned, having enlisted the help of her mother, and the two worked together to restore some dignity to the place, just as Doris Day and her friend had done to a hovel of a cabin in Deadwood from the film *Calamity Jane*.

By the time Mrs Gherardini had cleaned the inside of every pane of glass (there were over 100), and Bobbie had polished the floor to a respectable shine and cleaned the lever handles with emery cloth, concentrating for the moment only on those in use, it was time to call it a day.

While the majority of railway employees preferred early turns to late, for Bobbie (never a good riser) the reverse was the case; therefore she was pleased to start her signalling days on 2 'til 10. Her mother complained that this meant opposite shifts to her father, but Bobbie was secretly happy to leave the duties as they stood, as it avoided working alongside the young signalman at Wooburn Green. It was 'dolphin man' that Bobbie relieved for her first turn of duty, and he was just as reticent as he had been with Terry Meehan, saying not a word about her success. All he did say, or rather demand, was that the kettle was filled ready for the morning; perhaps, Bobbie thought, he was still mindful of the old days when a churn of drinking water was delivered off an engine of a local train.

Bobbie watched him go, heard him drive away and then dismissed him from mind. She looked around knowing that whatever happened during the next eight hours the responsibility was hers alone. When she stepped over to the desk to sign the train register she became aware of a small package addressed to her. Upon opening it she discovered a present from Terry to wish her good luck as signal-woman. With the gift came an explanatory note, which was fortunate as what Bobbie originally thought was something from a lavatory cistern was in fact the whistle chain from a 4-6-0 Grange class. The provision of a tiny hook and eye indicated that it was intended for wearing as a necklace! More railway memorabilia—never chocolates or flowers.

* * *

Bobbie took over at Loudwater at a time of considerable change as the 'new railway' began to establish itself firmly. A significant feature of the 1968 Transport Act was social consideration of unremunerative lines that under Beeching would likely have closed. Financial support for the maintenance of such services would be in the form of a 'grant aid' from regional Passenger Transport Executives. As expected, the first week of August saw the complete elimination of steam locomotives from their last hideouts in the north-west. When Driver Ernest Heyes of Lostock Hall closed the regulator for the last time on 45318 before arriving in Liverpool's Exchange Station, the final curtain came down on steam traction on BR, and judging by the news of enthusiasts literally besieging crucial vantage points, Terry's wisdom of giving it all a miss seemed well placed.

Ironically, it was not only steam locomotives that were being scrapped. Large numbers of diesel shunters, particularly those with a mechanical transmission, had been withdrawn. Some main line classes too were eking out their last days in service, examples being the expensively refurbished 'half-Deltic' D5900 class, the NBL D8400s and many of Swindon's 0-6-0 D9500 series, which were barely three years old. In many respects the Western Region were allowing history to repeat itself after the questionable building of 0-6-0 pannier tanks as late as 1956, when freight was in serious decline and diesel locomotives in production in quantity. However, it must be said that many redundant locomotives were sold to other industries, the National Coal Board and British Steel in particular.

With the rationalisation of the diesel fleet, opportunity was taken to make individual class descriptions less wordy. A BR/Sulzer 1Co-Co1 2500hp Type 4 class, for example, became simply a '45'. Furthermore, with the elimination of steam, the D prefix to loco numbers could be dispensed with, although E continued to be used for WCML Electrics, as they had cast numbers on the cabside.

Terry still wished to see the electric locomotives in store up at Bury, and on the last day of August (a Sunday) he and Bobbie made the trip up from Euston. The journey was rather tedious owing to much engineering work, but it did give them time to chat without recourse to rules and regulations. It transpired that both had gone to Loudwater school, and had even been there at the same time, Bobbie's first year coinciding with Terry's last. He was also able to explain how he came to possess the whistle chain from *Resolven Grange*. On secondment to Banbury South, not far from the steam shed, a local steel merchant, James Friswell, whose premises were opposite, was cutting up number 6869 where she finally rested, and Terry had witnessed her demise. He could have wept, he said, as over the course of the week just two men reduced the 4-6-0 to lumps of scrap metal, sorted for non-ferrous and ferrous into a rake of a dozen open wagons. The engine was devoid of name and numberplates, but Terry had managed to secure not only the whistle chain but the regulator handle too.

Up in Bury, it was disappointing to see so many modern loco-motives silent and idle. With the exception of E3043 which had been moved to Rugby, all the North British-built AL4s, E3036–45 (now Class 84), were present alongside E3024/32–34/98 of Class 83. The LNER-built prototype for the 1500-volt system over the Pennines, EM1 Bo-Bo E26000, was also there together with all seven of the larger Co-Co EM2s now pointlessly designated Class 77. These, still numbered E27000–6, were destined to be sold to the Netherlands, where E26000 had run earlier trials and been named *Tommy* out of respect for British soldiers. A further twelve of the EM1 class, and all of the EM2s, were given names from classical mythology. Of special interest to Bobbie was the EM2 named *Juno* (E27004).

The return journey from Bury was more straightforward as much of the engineering work had been completed, but Terry confided to his friend that although she was now competent at Loudwater, he might have the pleasure of working with her again in the near future. To the east of Loudwater station, the six-lane carriageway bridge under construction to enable the motorway to cross the railway was reminiscent of the 'cut and cover' technique developed by London Underground. To avoid danger to passengers during working hours special arrangements to allow trains to pass the site safely were to be introduced, Terry said.

His predictions proved correct as, later, the person in Loudwater box was instructed not to operate signals in the immediate vicinity of the bridge, but to transfer this responsibility to a handsignalman on the spot, who could ensure that the line was not fouled by cranes or any materials and that workmen were aware of the approaching train. Although the construction site was referred to as 'the flyover' or 'the bridge', at ninety-three yards it was actually five yards longer than Saunderton Tunnel!

The relief signalmen recruited for flagging the trains came from far and wide, but one memorable week the individual reporting for duty was indeed Terry Meehan. Bobbie was on early turn, and after 2 p.m. joined him at the workings and saw for herself just what happened when a train arrived; and taking over Terry's role, got quite a thrill blowing a whistle to warn the men and showing the driver a green flag to send him past a signal at danger.

After the 14.23 train (which went through to Aylesbury) there was not another until it came back at 16.15. During the lull the couple took advantage of the privacy of the stationmaster's office and locked themselves in, and once young Terry had chased the girl around the room, caught her and undressed her. He gave her an even greater thrill flat on her back on the old GWR-monogrammed carpet. It was an energetic week as the stationmaster's armchair and even his desk were put to good use.

For Bobbie's twentieth birthday, to Terry's surprise, she wanted only a torch! As the days got shorter and the nights longer, it was an item she badly needed to open up or close the station facilities. At night, to lock up, it meant switching off all the lights from within the booking hall and walking through that office and the waiting room—all in complete darkness—to secure the outer door. A paraffin lamp was inadequate in such a situation, and Bobbie did not wholly disbelieve in ghosts.

Later in the year Bobbie found herself in demand for some overtime. The task offered her was to look after the signal lamps for both Loudwater and Wooburn Green—a duty which she readily accepted. The role lasted for most of November while the regular man was away. To her delight, the only criterion was that the lamps were done. As to when—do both areas together or singly, before a late turn or after an early—was entirely up to her. It was nice to call in on her father at Spicer's Crossing, but she had nothing to say to the signalman at Wooburn Green, the former booking boy; and no one was ever the wiser that she used to do her own lamps for the signals at Loudwater in the quiet spells between trains.

Unfortunately, her distant signals were too far out to leave the box unattended. Nevertheless, she was paid four hours' overtime for her trouble with barely an hour of work left to do. With no trains through Loudwater on the Sabbath it was a guaranteed day off, therefore Bobbie could make herself available for lucrative Sunday work. Almost every weekend there was some engineering work going on somewhere in the London Division, and probably in the Bristol, Cardiff and Plymouth Divisions as well. In many cases the work involved disconnecting points and signals, and qualified signallers were in demand to work 'on the ground' and guide trains through by handsignals and flags. Bobbie had Terry Meehan to thank for getting her involved in Sunday engineering work.

Chapter Twenty Eight

Bobbie's first duty as a competent officer on the ground
fell short of the exciting role she had initially imagined
one to be. It was a typically sunless November day
and single line working was in force between High Wycombe
and Beaconsfield with all trains running over the up line. The
reason for the work was the removal of a set of points and some
overgrown sidings in the vicinity of High Wycombe that had
once faithfully served Gomm's furniture factory. The connection had been out of use since 1962, but was only now being
replaced with plain track. The district inspector was one of the
officers in charge of the engineer's occupation, and was the
same man who had passed Bobbie on her rules and regulations
a few months before.

Out in the dank countryside, seemingly miles from civilisation but near the ominously named Cut-Throat Wood, lay a
set of catch points in the up main line. The line rose towards
Beaconsfield at 1 in 225, and these trailing points, pushed shut
by wheels of a train but springing open again once the train
had passed, were designed to derail and deflect to safety a raft
of 'breakaway' wagons running back. It was Bobbie's task to
secure these points using a massive G-clamp and exhibit to the
driver of each down train a green flag handsignal held steady.
She had been told that the clamp could stay in position until
double line working resumed later in the day, and as all up
trains ran normally there was little for her to do. Two schools

of contention occupied her thoughts: one that a minor role was a sensible way to be initiated into the world of Sunday occupation work; the second, which she considered the more probable, was that she would not yet be trusted with anything more demanding.

At first Bobbie felt quite important displaying her green flag to drivers of approaching trains, but by late morning the novelty had worn off. Luckily it wasn't raining for there was nowhere to shelter, nor could she leave her post, because, as the inspector pointed out, the hammering vibration of a passing train might cause the G-clamp to fail and the points open.

Bobbie wondered what her friend Terry was doing. As it happened he was at Dolphin Junction (of all places). There was no longer a signal box there, but the crossovers (worked from Slough Panel) were the same as the day when Stanier '8F' 8293 collided with *Dudley Castle* head on. She wondered, had Terry been with her and the month May not November, what they might have got up to in the tall grasses in such a secluded spot.

Bobbie found the Sunday engineering work interesting, but was not over keen to repeat the experience despite the financial rewards. She told Terry as much, when he rang her at home later. Were there not better ways of spending a Sunday than being out in the sticks near only to old haunts of footpads and highwaymen? Nevertheless, when Terry asked about another session of single line working booked for the following Sunday, Bobbie opened her mouth to refuse but heard herself saying yes; but at least she asked pertinent questions, and was cheered to learn that she would be one of the 'groundmen' at Wycombe Middle Box, and friend Terry would be another. However, the original reason for his call was to invite Bobbie along to Hinksey, Oxfordshire.

Bobbie had long expressed a wish to see the wartime-built

yard and the signal boxes that her father had helped to construct. Apparently Oxford district were so short of signalmen that they needed the return of Mr Meehan to help them out. Terry was booked for a week on twelve-hour days (6 a.m.–6 p.m.), and the only practical way to join him was for Bobbie to get a day off, which she was able to do.

Hinksey North was rather unprepossessing as a signal box. Bobbie saw it first from her carriage window, and was struck by its austerity. The solidly built brick and concrete structure with a flat roof was, Terry explained, intended to be resistant to bomb blast damage. A conventional wooden, frivolously ornate, cabin would have been flattened in those circumstances. Another unusual feature was the internal staircase. However, from within, the signal box was like any other. Hinksey South and Oxford North Junction were of a similar design. Hinksey North was the busiest box Bobbie had visited, more so even than Twyford, and certainly appeared worthy of its Class 1 status. What put it into a category above others was the involvement with shunting rather than merely passing a train onwards.

The North's neighbours were Hinksey South going up and Oxford Station South in the down direction, and in between lay Hinksey Yard itself and Oxford South End Yard, all of which was controlled by the North box at Hinksey, situated more or less centrally to both.

Hinksey Yard was slowly becoming redundant, but the South End Yard saw continual use, and its resident '08' shunter D3971 buzzed around constantly; disappearing into the yard shed then reappearing again like a bee in and out of a flower.

Like the majority of signal boxes Hinksey used the conventional 'absolute block' for main lines—one train in a section at any one time, but over its goods loops (of which there were three) 'permissive block' working was also used. This system allowed several freight trains to cautiously buffer up within the same section if they could not be signalled away immediately. A correctly maintained train register book was necessary to keep a tally of the number and description of each train in the queue. It was all too easy for one to be overlooked in darkness or in fog. Terry laughed when he recalled some of the pleas by delayed locomen keen to be on their way, 'I'm getting married this afternoon' or 'my wife's in labour' being particular favourites.

Given the volume of freight that went via Oxford, the additional goods-running lines were an essential part of the layout. Much of the traffic was inter-regional, originating in southern yards, Eastleigh or Fratton for example, with destinations in the Birmingham area such as Washwood Heath or Bescot. A considerable number also put off or attached more wagons at Oxford. All that freight produced a variety of motive power, more than Bobbie had seen at Twyford. Class 33s unique to Southern Region worked through, while the London Midland produced a 'Peak' and even a struggling Class 25 deputizing for a failed '47'.

Working timetables supplied to railwaymen (as opposed to those available to the public) gave details, amongst other things, of crew changes. A cursory glance only at the Oxford tome revealed that for many of the inter-regional freights Oxford men relieved their Southern Region peers at Didcot, and went only as far as Banbury (a distance of forty miles) where they in turn were relieved by LMR men. Terry remarked that the volume of freight was going to increase further still when the coal-fired Didcot Power Station became operational. Oxford's local passenger service consisted to a great extent of trains to Paddington. Many of these, provided for the morning season-ticket commuter, were locomotive-hauled with a Class

1 headcode and considerably more prestigious than a mere DMU. A similar express service was provided for their return in the evening. A number of cross-country services linked Oxford with both the Midlands and the South West, while Oxford was also a stop for the erstwhile 'Cathedrals Express'; Hereford and Worcester to Paddington and return. Bobbie could not help but comment on the plethora of 'light engine' movements. Barely half an hour passed without the 2-3 on the bell being heard.

Terry explained that Oxford still had a loco shed (81F), and sent out engines to shunt various yards such as Cowley and Abingdon. These would return and be sent out again later after being remanned or refuelled. Special freights seldom had a booked return working so engines off these would work back 'light' whence they had come. And if this were not enough, an engine might need attention at Swindon, running under its own power to the works or being towed by yet another.

Terry explained that 81F still existed on the same site as it had in the days of steam, situated between the Oxford Canal and the River Thames.

"Lovely place for a picnic—in summer time of course! I could show you the old swing-bridge over the cut that trains used to cross to get into Rewley Road." Terry Meehan was referring to the former LMR (ex-LNWR) station, which closed in 1951.

Bobbie spent several hours at Hinksey and on her way home realised that, by comparison to Oxford, her own eight trains in as many hours would never be sufficiently challenging again. Despite some of her father's genes discouraging her, Bobbie knew she would have to seek promotion from Loudwater.

The next Sunday engineering project effectively turned back the clock a hundred years, as one line between High Wycombe and Princes Risborough was closed to allow the bridge over the lane that formed part of the ancient Icknield Way to be rebuilt with new steelwork, necessitating single line working over the up (new) line.

Bobbie was posted with Terry Meehan at Wycombe Middle Box. The pilotman was again the district inspector, and the signalman on duty was the gay young man Bobbie had known previously. Few trains on a Sunday ran north from High Wycombe so the only trains the officers were expecting to signal 'wrong line' were two expresses from Paddington and three local DMUs. Only five, but each would involve a considerable amount of effort. Trains would leave the down platform at Wycombe as far as the Middle box then shunt back through the crossovers onto the up main. Such a move was a regular occurrence for DMUs which had discharged their passengers in the down platform, and were shunting across the layout to form another service back to London.

However, for any train conveying passengers, it was necessary that all facing points were securely locked in position. Normally this was achieved from the signal box by a lever-operated mechanism, but in unusual circumstances, such as when trailing points in a crossover became facing for 'wrong line' working, then an individual had to clamp the points manually in order to comply with transport regulations. This was Bobbie's role for the day. But rather than just secure the points and leave them thus, as had been possible near Beaconsfield, she had a busy day in front of her.

Her first northbound train was the 09.00 Paddington, and once this had come out from the platform and drawn to a stand beyond the points at Wycombe Middle, the signalman switched them over and then it was up to Bobbie to go out and clip them safely. She had two sets of points to secure and she was conscious of the fact she was delaying the train by being slow and clumsy and wished she had the role Terry had. He was positioned some way down the line to where he could be alongside the locomotive and able to liaise with the crew. Once Bobbie handsignalled to Terry that the points were reversed and clamped, he could then produce his green flag and tell the driver he was OK to set back.

It took some minutes for D1928 to propel its eight coaches back through the pointwork, whereupon Bobbie then had to unclamp the points, shout up to the signalman that they were free, wait while he pulled the levers to change them, then reclamp them again in the reversed position. It was somewhat nerve-racking having D1928 towering above her while she bent to her task on the track. It was so close she could've counted the dead flies on the headcode panel. Glancing up at the crew, she knew they were watching her struggle, but the second-man encouragingly gave her a thumbs up sign and cheekily applauded her as, her task done, she stepped away from the secured points. Bobbie could then exhibit her own green flag, but just as she did so the district inspector intervened.

The rules for single line working over double lines stated that it was not essential for a pilotman to accompany each and every train; the officer could send a train through on verbal instructions only if it was necessary. This avoided the situation, in a sparse service, of the man being stranded at the wrong end of the system when required at the other. The inspector decided he would send the Paddington train through and ride with the driver of the next down train (a DMU for Princes Risborough) and later accompany the 09.40 Birmingham, due 11.18, back to High Wycombe.

The inspector had already spoken to the crew whilst in the station, but nevertheless repeated his instructions to the driver looking down from his cab.

"Just to reiterate, driver, we're single line working between here and Risborough, and as pilotman,"—pointing to his red cloth armband with white sewn-on letters—"I authorise you to proceed cautiously in the down direction over the up line."

The driver nodded in agreement as he pushed his cab window up, and maybe piqued at all the delay, moved his power handle round almost to its full extent and roared away towards Princes Risborough under a veritable plume of black exhaust smoke. The inspector turned to Bobbie as they made their way to the Middle Box for warmth and refreshment.

"I suppose it's how you interpret the word 'cautiously'!"

As they crossed the tracks, two young lads who had been enjoying the fun from the footbridge called down to ask if they could visit the signal box. The inspector waved them away dismissively, but remarked to Bobbie that all 'ground-men'—and women—were in fact guests of the signalman and had no God-given right to make themselves at home with him. He knew of some individuals, he said, who really did keep their signal box strictly private as the cast-iron notice on the door stated.

However, with the regular signalman, Terry, and the inspector it was a convivial atmosphere in the box, and on a cold November morning, Bobbie thought, so much better than being out in the countryside. For the quartet of signallers past and present (the inspector himself had been a signalman before promotion to management) the chatter turned inevitably to signalling matters, the routine, the bizarre, and the frankly unbelievable. Bobbie, lacking the experience of the others, could contribute little to the conversation, but did suggest that if High Wycombe came under the aegis of the LMR, as was expected in the future, would Middle Box become High Wycombe Number Two? "At Crewe, Gresty Lane", she said,

"I've seen one numbered as high as Number Six."

The inspector trumped her statement easily by saying that 300 miles north from where they were sitting was Carlisle Number Thirteen! His next comment was "Come on, everybody. Action stations!"

The 10.13 departure, a 4-car DMU only, was observed coming out from the down platform and this was dealt with in the same way as the previous 'fast' train except for the fact the inspector met the driver and joined him in the cab to travel through to Princes Risborough.

Back in the box, the trio's conversation remarked on the idiosyncrasies of the Sunday timetable: two trains to Risborough within forty minutes while a little later there would be a gap of no less than five hours. With the absence of railway management, the signalman took his radio from his locker and tuned it to Radio One, primarily as a source of entertainment for Bobbie and Terry. For her part Bobbie was not interested in the pop scene, being unimpressed with such recent acts as the Crazy World of Arthur Brown, Scaffold and the shouting Joe Cocker; but a hauntingly beautiful instrumental piece was played as the new release from Fleetwood Mac entitled 'Albatross'. However, later, when 'A Whiter Shade of Pale' was aired, to both men's surprise Bobbie insisted the radio be turned off. "The D.I. wouldn't be happy," she said.

The good man duly returned on the 09.40 ex-New Street (due 11.32). As the Birmingham train snaked into view, the locomotive looked very unusual causing Terry to remark, "Hello, what have we here?" Bobbie, too, stared at the oncoming train then exclaimed, "It's a 'Peak'!" And 'Peak', or Class 45, it was. The driver of D59 *The Royal Warwickshire Fusilier* was braking hard to save the man with the familiar armband a walk from the station. Bobbie witnessed the usual firework display as cast iron brake blocks bit on steel wheels. The sparks were a common cause of fires when the accumulation of dirt and oil on the bogies ignited. Once the inspector had alighted the driver opened up again and accelerating away the massive 8-wheel bogies, protruded alarmingly left then right as it negotiated the tight curves of the pointwork at High Wycombe. It was the inspector who later explained the unusual motive power.

"The booked '47' failed coming off Saltley Loco. The 'Peak' was the only thing available with a train heating boiler."

The signalman remarked that the headcode (1Z54) was incorrect and obviously not altered from an earlier special working. The code should have been 1V08 which then prompted discussion on the usefulness and reliability of train headcodes generally. Terry remarked on how he'd heard that a number of Class 47s were to have their headcode blinds reversed to show black figures on a white background as an aid to greater visibility.

"Well, I don't know why they're bothering," the inspector replied. "The new Class 87s for the electrification north of Crewe are going to have plain fronts like the old Woodhead electrics—no headcode box at all."

The inspector then announced that he would accompany the next down service, then stay at Princes Risborough for 'a bit of dinner'. This suited the rest of those at the Middle box for, as nice as the officer was, they were more relaxed without him; and once he had left they made their own arrangements for lunch.

The signalman decided that it didn't require three people to look after the box, especially when no train was expected, so that he, living quite near, would have his lunch in the comfort of his own home. Bobbie and Terry had their meal break quietly together. Meanwhile, the inspector had had but a brief snack, having accepted a lift back to High Wycombe with a senior permanent way man calling at the site of the bridge repairs on the way. Returning to Wycombe Middle much earlier than expected, the Inspector was astonished to find the signal box door locked. His repeated knocks were eventually answered by Terry Meehan, somewhat red-faced and breathless; while Bobbie kept her back turned, which the inspector thought impolite; but when she did turn to face him she was fully buttoned up with all her uniform in place. The regular signalman then reappeared, having apparently just emerged from the toilet.

"Boy, did I need a crap," he lied.

The inspector looked at each person suspiciously in turn, but three faces smiled back at him innocently. He guessed they had been up to mischief in his absence, but to the relief of all, he did not interrogate them.

Later, when the signalman brewed up, Terry joined him.

"I was obeying signal box rule number seventy-six," he said quietly so none could overhear. "You know, the one that says 'Upon entering, every signalman must satisfy himself'!"

Chapter Twenty Nine

Back at Loudwater on the Monday, Bobbie was interested to learn of the vacancy at High Wycombe North, and on further enquiry learned that the man there was retiring. She reckoned that few, if any, would apply for the single-shift weekday-only job. The principle role of the North box was to control the one remaining goods yard in the area.

It was no Hinksey, but it would be more interesting than Loudwater. Furthermore, Wycombe North was a Class 3 box, so a grade up the promotion ladder from the lowly '4' position Bobbie currently held. She was happy at Loudwater, but it was becoming increasingly difficult to operate the gates, particularly when a maintenance session was overdue.

The most troublesome part of the gate mechanism was that from lever 25, which activated in the roadway outside cast-iron pegs which rose out of the tarmac and effectively secured the gates in position across the road. The lever had to be over in order to release the interlocking on the signals. The real trouble began when this lever was put back; one or both pegs seldom retracted completely, so prior to operating the gate wheel, one had to leave the box and physically prise the heavy gates over the still proud pegs, using what looked like a huge poker but actually was a steam engine firebox pricker.

It was embarrassing to have to perform such a task in front of waiting motorists, and one could only hope that automatic lifting gates might be installed one day as they had at Bourne

End in November of the previous year. There, one only had to press a button to raise or lower the barriers.

Nor was Bobbie plagued at all by Jon Rice. She had heard gossip to the effect that he had fully recovered from his run-in with the bass guitarist and had been back at work for some months. But his work took him to various locations north of Princes Risborough where the 'new line' was about to be reduced to a humble single track.

Meanwhile, at Loudwater, as the motorway flyover neared completion, it was deemed no longer necessary to appoint a handsignalman but to allow all signals to be used normally once again. However, it was thought that a railwayman should still be present and someone from the permanent way gang would be allocated to Loudwater instead. Bobbie heard this piece of information with considerable dismay.

The first day of the new programme Bobbie was on early turn, and the gang member duly arrived on Monday morning saying that he would be on that particular 'lookout' duty throughout the week. But Bobbie was relieved to learn that the most elderly or infirm of men were being sent to Loudwater. The individuals themselves did not trouble Bobbie at all as, invariably, after seeing a train safely through, each man would return to the warmth of the box, have some tea from a flask, say a few words, then nod off behind his newspaper until the next train was belled. Bobbie fervently hoped that the criteria for allocating lookout men would never change.

The expense of the flyover construction seemed to indicate that the line still had a future, and this was further reinforced by the announcement that an entirely new freight service was to be introduced. A Marlow-based merchant had decided that his twice-weekly supply of timber from Finland should be transported by rail. From the Baltic Sea, the shipment would arrive in the Thames estuary, then be transferred to rail and thence across London to join the GW/GC line to High Wycombe, where the engine would run round before taking the train over the branch to Marlow. Crews would be changed at Acton where Old Oak Common men would relieve their Stratford colleagues, but Eastern Region Class 31s would work the service throughout. Normally only Slough men worked over the Marlow branch line so for Old Oak men it meant learning a new route as well as being trained up on 'foreign' motive power.

The special light engine movements were planned for December, and January too if necessary, and booked for Tuesdays and Thursdays only, the trips easily being accommodated within the regular service. The diagram allowed for an engine off Old Oak Loco to run to High Wycombe, then shunt to the bay siding and make two return trips to Marlow before working back to shed.

The first run followed the 11.00 out of High Wycombe by leaving at 11.10 and was due back at 12.09. The second trip departed at 12.40 and also returned just under an hour later in the wake of the 13.01 ex-Maidenhead. Questions were asked why the 'trainees' could not simply have accompanied the driver of a booked train, but the official reply was that a DMU cab would be too crowded and the service over the Marlow section too sparse to be useful.

Bobbie was on early turn the first day of the crew training runs. She expected to see the unusual A1A-A1A type Class 31 but was surprised to find a '47' on duty, all the more so because '31' D5535 had recently been reallocated from Norwich to Old Oak Common, the first of a number to be transferred to replace the increasingly degenerate NBL D6300s.

Unusual too was the fact that the '47' was invariably Cardiff-based, judging by the 86A shed-code stencilled on the cabside and the head-codes left showing in the 4-character boxes. Most likely the engine had come up from the valleys overnight and been commandeered for the crew training trips before working back. D1924 was the first Brush to be seen (back from loan to the SR), but others noted were D1589/94, and 1605. It was remarkable that each out and back run had as many as seven enginemen in the cab—the booked driver and his regular mate, two sets of men learning the road, and a traction inspector trying to keep order.

A thirty-odd minute layover between the first and second runs was no doubt to provide a meal break, but after the first run on the Thursday once the '2-1' had been received, the signalman at Wycombe South promptly offered back (2-3 on the bell) the same light engine. For freight and light loco movements it was not unusual for the timetable to be ignored. If the men could get away sooner than schedule they invariably did. Bobbie accepted the engine, of course, and no sooner had she done so than the 'train entering section' was also received. The enginemen were certainly in some haste, however; on arrival at Loudwater the driver pulled down his cab window and gave up the Wycombe-Loudwater token, but wouldn't accept the one for Wooburn Green.

"What's your name bobby?" he asked.

"I'm Bobbie."

"Yeah, I know, but what's your name?"

"It's Bobbie."

"Oh—oh, I see." The driver did not seem entirely convinced but let the matter drop. "What we want to do, love, if it's OK with you, is tuck this inside the yard while we nip down to the boozer for half hour. Back in Wycombe there was a DMU stuck where we normally park up."

Bobbie agreed but, giving the request more consideration,

frowned. "I don't know as I'll be able to get the road over. I mean, it's not been used for years."

There was laughter as the driver turned to the inspector.

"'Ere, George, she knows all about your sex life!"

Bobbie smiled too, but suggested that they stayed where they were.

"There's nothing else about, and I can always run down and fetch you if I need to."

The mass exodus of enginemen from D1924 indicated that Bobbie's idea was a sound one, and within a minute the station was deserted.

It was a pity to have given up so easily an opportunity of performing a rare shunt at Loudwater, but Bobbie doubted her own ability to get the points over, and the mechanical ability of the disused rodding was also open to question. Another consideration was the possibility of not being able to reset the points to 'main line' afterwards. Bobbie realised she still had both tokens in her hands so she hurried back to the box, sent the 2-1 to Wycombe South, and put the relevant token back in the machine; then, rather than send the cancelling code (3-5) to Wooburn Green and replace that token, she telephoned her colleague instead to expect some delay before he received 'on line' for the engine.

Wanting a cigarette, Bobbie thought it would be audacious to smoke it in the cab of the '47' and returned to the locomotive to do so while the lookout man hurried off to the pub in the wake of the locomen in the hope of being bought a pint.

Puffing away in the secondman's seat, Bobbie considered again how successful the Class 47 design had been. Although derated a few percent from the original 2750 horsepower, one had to raise a hat to the American Charles Brush and the Swiss brothers Salaman and Jacob Sulzer. The Brush/Sulzer combination featured strongly in BR's current national traction plan as of course did English Electric. The latest locomotives from that manufacturer were the '50's (D400–449), the last of which had just been completed for the LMR.

With the exception of the 'Peaks', in particular those with headcode boxes either side of gangway doors, a '47' was Bobbie's favourite diesel. She wondered if the appeal would have been there had they been numbered from D1200 ('Deltics' were originally allocated the D15XX series) as it was interesting to have engine numbers that matched the year and those of the near future and recent past.

BR's overdue traction plan identified where economies could be made in servicing and operating costs by rationalising the locomotive fleet and eliminating the chronically unreliable and the non-standard types. It was adieu to the Metro-Vic Class 28 Co-Bo, a machine as prone to failure as it was ugly. The writing was on the wall, too, for the Clayton D8500 Class 17, equally disastrous, and unbelievably once intended to be BR's standard Type 1 and, sadly, much of what was produced by the once great North British Locomotive Company in Scotland.

Bobbie was comfortable in the secondman's seat in the rear cab; that is to say, from her position she could see both signal box and gates. The driver's seat would have been more exciting, but she was afraid she might knock something and find herself moving off. She recalled Terry telling her of an old Great Western loco running away early one Sunday morning and destroying seventeen sets of crossing gates. Bobbie wasn't to know that although the engine was still running, it was not in gear and the handbrake was fully wound on.

Having finished her cigarette she stood looking at the controls which she had first studied when a guest on the Banbury goods. Although permitted to run at 95mph, it still puzzled her why the speedometer on a '47' only went up to 100. 'Main reservoir' and 'brake cylinders' gauges were also mysterious, but the vacuum gauge obviously registered the amount of vacuum created (and maintained) to keep the train's brakes off (air braking was, then, confined to the loco wheels only). The ammeter was marked in green up to 4000 amps; thereafter it was shaded yellow ('use power cautiously') up to a maximum of 10,000; and Bobbie wondered what situation would require 10,000 amperes to the traction motors and the risk of burning them out. Perhaps going up the Lickey with a heavy train unaided by a banker.

She was tempted to blow the hooter and hear the rather melodious sound, but thought better of it. It would put the flyover construction men on the alert and might summons the locomen back from the pub. All she did do was to change the headcode to 0Z00 (in both cabs), the winder and selector handle being down in front of the secondman's seat. Would anyone notice if the Royal Train headcode (1X01) was displayed? But once again Bobbie resisted temptation.

The enginemen returned from the pub in time for a departure from Loudwater as scheduled. The lookout man had obviously been included in the driver's 'round' as he was unusually happy and chatty, the alcohol having loosened his tongue. He had without doubt been in the p-way gang many years and he spoke of his colleagues now doing all the heavy work while he had a easy time of it. Poignantly, he had worked with Nigel Frost on the day he was killed and spoke very highly of him; but he also thought well of Jon Rice. Another comment he made, actually both to Bobbie and her late turn relief (still 'dolphin man'), was that having travelled extensively in Europe, he reckoned that in the future an engine class number would be incorporated with the running number as it was on the Continent and therefore

D1500 (first of the '47's) would become 47000.

The following week when Bobbie was on late turn herself, she missed the additions to the normal service, and one day was mortified to learn that a maroon liveried 'Western' (D1041 from Laira) had been used owing to the failure of the Brush Type 4.

The third week of December was bitterly cold, and while no snow was forecast there were hard frosts that weak rays of sunshine did little to disperse. It was on such mornings that Bobbie was glad of the box stove, and not out and about tending signal lamps and climbing up treacherous ladders.

Probably, Bobbie considered, on account of the accumulative chill in the ground, the gate mechanism was becoming even more difficult to use. The clay quagmire beneath the gates and in the flooded interlocking room was beginning to solidify. Winding the big wheel in the box was insufficient even to open the gates properly. One had to turn the wheel its maximum distance, then leave the box and physically push the gates fully home to enable them to 'catch up' with the retarded mechanism. Fortunately, when reopening the gates to road traffic the 'travel' was not affected, but one still had to go out and use the old firebox pricker.

As it happened, difficulties with the gates became the least of Bobbie's worries. She knew that her lookout man was chosen from the most elderly of permanent way staff, but the position was also available to anyone on what might be termed 'light duties'. She learned that a young member of the gang had been struck by a length of old rail as it was being raised by a crane, and it had swung round and caught him across the shoulders, aggravating an injury sustained during a fight earlier in the year.

To Bobbie's dismay, the third week of December brought Jon Rice to Loudwater as lookout man.

Chapter Thirty

It was not until the Thursday, December 19th, and a bitterly cold day with freezing fog that Bobbie saw Jon Rice alight from the 07.55 from Wycombe and go straight up into the signal box. It annoyed her that he had entered her domain without a single word of invitation, and she joined him once she had despatched her train; but in fairness to the man, he had merely come to tell her of his role for that day, and the next—something that he was obliged to do. He must have read the anxious look on her face with some enjoyment. "I've got my own flask of tea," he said. "I won't bother you—much!" He looked out of the window up the line to the flyover and shivered, and Bobbie even felt a little sorry for him and his lonely vigil.

"I hope you won't be too cold," she said. But her concern was short-lived as Rice remarked with a grin that she might like to warm him up if the need arose. Bobbie watched him go, but despite her doubts he kept his word, and did not bother her until much later when he came up to refill his flask.

The first of the special engine trips had already gone up to Marlow and the return trip was belled as Rice entered the box. He should, of course, have hurried off to the flyover, but warming himself by the stove he muttered something about there being no one working near the line. Every time he opened his mouth Bobbie worried over what he might say. Yet, to his credit, he never mentioned old pennies or night clubs. But despite his outwardly pleasant demeanour that day, Bobbie knew she could never trust the man and, mindful that he might snoop around while she was attending a train, took the 1933 penny from her purse and moved it to a safer place. Their conversation was mainly on the weather, but he did add that his sister Donna wanted to get in touch with her again.

As the '47', D1912, ran in, Bobbie realised that still no effort had been made to carry the proper headcode. 1F50 was displayed instead of 0Z00, and the rear of the locomotive was no better, showing 1A71. But there was one man less in the cab; the loco inspector had given up trying to maintain any discipline and retired to the back cab where he could be seen reading a *Railway Modeller*. As tokens were exchanged, and Bobbie gave the driver the token for the Wycombe section, there was more of the suggestive banter to which she had now grown accustomed.

"Come and have a ride with us, love," one of the crew offered.

"What about that lot?" asked Bobbie, pointing at the waiting traffic.

"Let 'em wait. We'll be back here in ten minutes!"

"But there's no room—"

"We'll squeeze you in; you can sit on Drive's lap. Drive won't mind!"

"He won't be able to see where he's going."

"He never can anyway! Ha ha ha!"

Jon Rice, making his way back to his post, then added his twopennyworth by offering to look after things while she was gone. But the inspector, irritated by the delay, stuck his head out of the rear cab, and Bobbie felt that the conversation had gone on for long enough.

"I'll see you on your way back. Right away, now!"

A little later Bobbie received the '2-1' for the engine, and in due course the signalman at Wycombe South offered her the same engine back, 2-3 on the bell. She accepted it of course, and within the next few minutes received the 'on line'.

Pleased that the morning she had dreaded was passing quickly and uneventfully, Bobbie's own thoughts turned to Christmas and whether hints she'd dropped to Terry Meehan had been strong enough for him to buy her the Trix EM1 or Triang 'Electra'. Since their visit to Bury she too had become interested in the Woodhead dc route, and either model she thought would look good on her bedroom mantelpiece creating a balance with the Hornby Dublo E3002. Little did she know that Terry planned to give her something much more expensive and intended for the third finger of her left hand.

Having decided that motorists had had priority long enough, Bobbie closed the gates to the road and 'pulled off' for the engine. With the signal levers over Bobbie leaned on them and considered the Class 47's number and what events had occurred in 1912, a year that witnessed much tragedy. Captain Scott's expedition party to the South Pole had been beaten by the Norwegian Roald Amundsen, and frostbitten, short of food, and bitterly disappointed, all had perished on their way back. But the year would be most remembered for the loss of the RMS *Titanic*. In both sad events circumstances of folly and ill luck combined to make tragedy inevitable, and where a single amendment might have averted disaster and changed the course of history. It was as Bobbie waited for the engine to appear that her own fateful situation arose.

Down the hill towards the station came a police car with its blue light flashing and two-tone siren blaring, Bobbie's dilemma only becoming worse when she saw an ambulance was following closely behind. In a moment both were waiting impatiently at her gates. The sirens went off but the lights continued to flash.

As the police patrol car driver looked up at her. Bobbie knew what she had to do. She had not heard D1912 hooting for the crossing by her old school so took it that the engine was still some distance away. Against Rule 70 (and Terry's advice) Bobbie returned her signals to danger and opened her gates to let the emergency vehicles continue on their errand of mercy. As they sped away, the ambulance men gave Bobbie the thumbs-up to show their appreciation, but she was more concerned to 'pull off' again for the expected engine.

As Bobbie hurriedly wound over the gate wheel for the second time, the rodding in the frozen clay protested spitefully at the haste, and Bobbie had to double her efforts to make any impression. Having left the box to complete the operation manually, she saw, to her horror, the light engine suddenly appear through the mist and overrun her home signal at danger. As the driver frantically braked, one gate was still foul of the line, and Bobbie had to leave it to its fate once she realised a collision was inevitable. But her overcoat snagged on some broken wire mesh that had come away from the gate wood-work, and, caught like a rabbit in a snare, she was unable to jump clear.

She screamed as the engine bore down upon her. Still moving at 20mph, the 114-ton diesel struck the gate, took it clean off its massive hinges and destroyed it. Bobbie, trapped between the remains of the gate and the buffers of the engine, disappeared beneath it.

Horrified by what had happened, everyone jumped down from the cab, fearful of what they would see. The driver, particularly distressed, paced about aimlessly holding his head in his hands and shouting obscenities. It was the loco inspector, getting down from the back cab alarmed by the sudden stop and commotion, who took control. He addressed the second-man first.

"Go to the station house and dial 999. If there's no one in, run across to the vicarage."

"Who shall I ask to come? Fire, police or—"?

"Christ, lad—use your loaf—get the whole bloody lot if you have to!" He then turned to the driver. "Pull yourself together and back this thing up. I'm going to the box to ring Control."

The driver got back in the cab and did as he was told; and as the diesel reversed several yards, all eyes present looked to the body lying among the remains of the gate. Bobbie had been crushed between the six-inch beams of the gate and the buffers of the locomotive. She was dead.

The secondman returned from telephoning and rejoined his mates, and he too stared down at the lifeless body. He could barely speak. "The board was 'off'. We all saw it. We said we'd tease her about being quick to get 'em off. What the hell was...?" But his question remained unfinished as he turned away to hide his tears. Within seconds, sirens could again be heard hurrying through Loudwater. It was not the same ambulance as before, but it was the same officers in their patrol car; a constable and his sergeant. Followed closely by the police, the ambulancemen were first at the scene, but there was little for them to do except extract Bobbie gently from the debris; transfer her to a stretcher; place her in the back of the ambulance; and, without need for blue light or siren, drive slowly and reverently away.

The police officers, in contrast, had much to do. First they assisted the enginemen to clear the track and let the waiting traffic that had built up pass; then they wanted statements from each of the men to rule out, they said, foul play and suicide.

The police report would assist BR officials when they held their own enquiry at a later date.

Jon Rice should have been interviewed at this stage too. He had heard Bobbie's terrible scream and witnessed much of what had happened, but instead he slunk around at the flyover and did not get involved. Not, that is, until a malicious thought entered his head and he made his way stealthily along the platform.

While the police were concluding their work, two senior railwaymen arrived, the district inspector from Slough, and area manager from Maidenhead. They decided that Loudwater Box would remain closed until the late turn signalman came on duty. In any case there would be no train for some considerable time as the 13.01 ex-Maidenhead (due 13.23) would be terminated at Wooburn Green and depart from there in the path of the 14.00 from High Wycombe. A taxi would be offered to any inconvenienced passenger. A handsignalman was also to report for duty as, until the damage to the gate mechanism and interlocking was repaired, no signals could be operated.

Locomotive D1912 was relatively unscathed. The cab windows were broken but intact, and the headcode box was destroyed—the front plating had received a knock, but it was still able to move under its own power. There would be no more road-learning trips that day, and once each engineman had given his statement to the police, subdued to a man they rejoined their footplate, and it was the inspector himself who drove D1912 back to High Wycombe and thence to Old Oak Common.

The four men at Loudwater felt that some sort of refreshment was called for. The district inspector told the policemen that they should find what they wanted to make a brew in the box. Meanwhile, he and the area manager were going for something considerably stronger in the 'Happy Union'.

When the policemen went up into the signal box they were surprised to find Jon Rice rifling through Bobbie's satchel.

"Oi, what do you think you're doing, chum?" the Sergeant demanded.

"She had something that belonged to me. I—I was just looking for it."

"Well, you just clear off—this is a police investigation scene now."

Rice knew he had no choice, and left, slamming the door behind him so hard that a coin lodged in the rafters above fell to the floor at the Sergeant's feet. He picked it up and scrutinised it. "Someone's lucky penny, I'll be bound," he said. "1933, the year I was born. We'll toss the coin to decide which of us goes to inform the girl's parents. Heads you do it, tails I do."

He spun the penny in the air but, failing to catch it, the coin clattered between the levers and fell into the quagmire below and disappeared.

"I think you'll find that was heads, Constable."

"Yes, Sarge. Heads it was, Sarge."

THE END